WATERLOO MAP

Also by Stephanie Barron

Being the Jane Austen Mysteries

Jane and the Unpleasantness at Scargrave Manor
Jane and the Man of the Cloth
Jane and the Wandering Eye
Jane and the Genius of the Place
Jane and the Stillroom Maid
Jane and the Prisoner of Wool House
Jane and the Ghosts of Netley
Jane and His Lordship's Legacy
Jane and the Barque of Frailty
Jane and the Madness of Lord Byron
Jane and the Canterbury Tale
Jane and the Twelve Days of Christmas

OTHER NOVELS

A Flaw in the Blood
The White Garden

WATERLOO MAP

BEING A JANE AUSTEN MYSTERY

Stephanie Barron

Published by
Soho Press, Inc.
853 Broadway
New York, NY 10003

Library of Congress Cataloging-in-Publication Data

Barron, Stephanie.
Jane and the Waterloo map:
being a Jane Austen mystery / Stephanie Barron.

ISBN 978-1-61695-425-3
eISBN 978-1-61695-426-0

1. Austen, Jane, 1775–1817—Fiction. I. Title.
PS3563.A8357J39 2016
813'.54—dc23 2015028756

Interior design by Janine Agro, Soho Press, Inc.

Printed in the United States of America

10 9 8 7 6 5 4 3 2 1

To my fellow Regency buffs,
Dana Stabenow and Barbara Peters, in case they never do
get all the way through *An Infamous Army.*

1
A COMMAND PERFORMANCE

Monday, 13 November 1815
23 Hans Place, London

There can be few things more lowering to the female sensibility than to be caught in a shower of rain at exactly the moment one most desires to appear to advantage. It is not that I care two straws for His Royal Highness the Prince Regent's good opinion; indeed, I should regard the admiration of such a roué as bordering upon insult; but there is an undeniable duty to answer a summons to Carlton House that demands the donning of one's best carriage gown, the coiffing of one's hair, and the hiring of a suitable chaise.

To be thoroughly drenched, therefore, in the simple act of gaining that chaise, is a rebuke to misplaced vanity and expence. As I shivered on the threshold of the palace, my elegant boots damp at the toes and my curls lank upon my brow, I could not bear to look at Manon hovering two steps behind me. My brother's French housekeeper had deplored this visit from the outset. She had no opinion of the Royal House, and appeared certain that all I should achieve by accepting the Prince's invitation was ravishment at his hands. She had insisted, therefore, upon accompanying me—my brother Henry being as yet too ill to leave his bed.

It was because of Henry—who else but Henry?—that I was known to Carlton House at all.

I arrived in London a month ago, expressly to negotiate the terms of publication of my latest novel, *Emma*—an eventuality by no means assured. It has not been enough that my earlier works were generally admired, and briskly sold, nor that the third of these—*Mansfield Park*—has exhausted its first edition. My publisher, Mr. Thomas Egerton, refused a second edition of the latter, and spurned my fourth book entirely. I am inclined to attribute his disaffection to the dislike felt by some readers—and perhaps Egerton himself—for my saintly *Mansfield* heroine, Fanny Price. Where the arch and impertinent Lizzy Bennet found favour among the abandoned inhabitants of the Metropolis, Fanny was simply too *good* to be entertaining. Egerton must have feared that my spoilt and headstrong Emma should be similarly received; but in this he showed the limitations of a journeyman publisher. I suspect that Emma will prove the darling of the frivolous *ton*.

Another lady might have read in Egerton's rebuff the instruction of Providence, and left off writing such dubious stuff as *novels*; my brother James, in his role as Divine Intermediary, counseled as much. He regards the indulgence of novel-reading as a dangerous diversion from Duty, particularly among women. To embrace the scandalous project of actually *writing* such books—and profiting by them!—is to tempt Satan. I would not have had James learn of Egerton's defection for the world, but my mother let slip some part of the intelligence, when relating the news of my journey to Hans Place.

My beloved Henry, far from scolding my arrogant proclivities, actually encourages them. In the face of Egerton's stupidity, he proposed that we approach none other than the illustrious Mr. John Murray, of Albemarle Street, founder of the *Quarterly Review.* As Murray is well known to publish Lord Byron and Sir Walter Scott, the hubris of this notion was staggering. Only Henry could assume that a tale dismissed by an Egerton might be coveted by a Murray; our Henry has been tilting at windmills all his life. But in the event, his wager answered: Murray deigned to glance at my *Emma*. It seems he was a little acquainted with Lizzy Bennet, and found her charming.

All matters of cost and gain being uncertain in these straitened months after Wellington's great victory, however, Murray proved cautious.* He required a second opinion—none other than that of the *Quarterly Review's* editor, Mr. William Gifford, who found "nothing but good" in my manuscript, and offered to edit it for publication. *Emma* having survived the scrutiny of so critical a reader, Murray offered me his price: £450 for the copyright.

For *Emma* alone, this should have proved acceptable. But being a rogue as well as a man of letters, Murray demanded the rights to *Mansfield Park* and *Sense and Sensibility* as well. Such terms being likely to beggar me, I refused them. Miss Marianne Dashwood and Miss Mary Crawford cost me too much effort in their fashioning, to be cast upon the world for a pittance.

---

* England's economy was severely disrupted by the conclusive fall of Napoleon Bonaparte in June 1815, as markets spurred by warfare contracted and soldiers returned home in search of employment. —*Editor's note.*

The delicate business was complicated by my brother's falling ill, of a trifling cold. He attempted to dictate from his bed an indignant letter to Mr. Murray, protesting the publisher's terms, but was unequal to completing it. Henry's indisposition turned to something far more dangerous by the third week in October—a low fever that worsened every hour. I had little time or thought for business. Days passed with no improvement in my brother's condition. He was delirious and wandering, his pulse depressed.

The excellent Mr. Haden, our surgeon, bled Henry copiously, but urged me to inform my family of the gravity of his illness. I was so alarmed by Haden's sombre looks as to send Express to James at Steventon and Edward in Kent, that Henry's last hours might not go unwitnessed by those he loved. Indeed, so wrapped in misery was I, and so deprived of sleep, that I required the presence of others to support me.

James collected Cassandra on his way to London, which suggested he was not so entirely bereft of sense as I usually judge him. They were all three arrived in Hans Place by the twenty-fourth of October, so that Manon and her mother had their hands full of Austens. Edward immediately urging the services of a more experienced man than Mr. Haden, Dr. Matthew Baillie, the Court Physician, was summoned—and so answered his patient's need, that by the thirtieth October, Henry was on the mend.

I cannot describe the exquisite relief of being spared my particularly beloved brother. Suffice it to say that when the crisis was observed to have passed—a little before dawn on the twenty-ninth October—that Cassandra and I, who had been sitting up together at the bedside, neither being willing to fail in the final moments of Henry's life, fell into each other's arms and wept.

It was some days before the patient could stand, or consume more than a little thick gruel. By the first week of November, however, Edward was gone back into Kent and James into Hampshire, taking my sister with him. I remained here in London to nurse Henry—and see what could be done with my difficult *Emma*.

I wrote directly to John Murray and desired him to wait upon me in Hans Place. He was so good as to appear the following morning, and the briefest of conversations secured our mutual satisfaction. I am to retain the copyright of *Emma,* publishing the work at my own expence; and Mr. Murray is to take ten percent of the profits, for his trouble in putting out the volumes. As I followed a similar course with all my dearest children but *Pride and Prejudice*—which copyright Egerton purchased outright for the sum of £110—I am untroubled by fear of risk. Murray has agreed to publish a second edition of *Mansfield Park,* on similar terms.

James shall be appalled to learn that I have become a woman of Business, as well as Letters. My fallen nature is confirmed.

I HAD SCARCELY CLOSED the door on one visitor, than another appeared in Hans Place—entirely unknown to me, and unsettling in the extreme.

Mr. James Stanier Clarke is a clergyman notable for his reliance upon Royal patronage. He is Historiographer to the King (tho' what a madman may want with learning, is open to question), a Canon of Windsor, and author of the yearly *Naval Chronicle,* which must endear him to everyone in the Austen family. He also wrote a fulsome biography of Admiral Lord Nelson, that praised all the hero's better qualities and ignored whatever was lamentable in his character—an office Clarke undertook with the aid of the Duke of Clarence and the Prince Regent.

When he sent in his card, I instructed Manon to convey Mr. Austen's compliments and the intelligence that he was as yet confined to his rooms. But Manon looked darkly and said that Mr. Clarke wished to interview *me*. I bade her show him up to the parlour, therefore, and prepared for a tedious quarter-hour.

"Miss Austen!" he cried, as tho' we met again after many years parted. "What pleasure is this, to trace in your gentle looks and modest attire the Genius that lends such animation to your works—and, I need not add, provides amusement to so many!"

He bounded forward from the threshold, a round little man with fair hair and innocent blue eyes, very finely turned out in a dark green coat. I stepped backwards, a trifle disconcerted, but managed a feeble curtsey. The fact of my authorship is but lately known, my first novel having been published as "by a Lady." Henry chose to explode my anonymity, entirely against instruction, and deposit the books at my feet for the World to criticise. I should have preferred to write in all the freedom of obscurity, without the weight of either censure or praise.

"Mr. Clarke," I acknowledged. "I am grateful for your good opinion, sir. But I confess I cannot account for the honour of your presence in Hans Place. My brother is only lately delivered from his sickbed, and is quite unequal to the strain of visitors. How may I serve you?"

"By accepting my sincere congratulations on Mr. Henry Austen's deliverance, madam, and the good wishes of His Royal Highness the Prince Regent, who was informed of your brother's illness in recent days—and of your own angelic office, in nursing him back to health—by our esteemed mutual acquaintance, Dr. Matthew Baillie."

The Court Physician. He had impressed me as a quiet and efficient fellow, spare of figure and ugly of countenance, with a monkey's shrewd eyes. Why should he canvass the difficulties of a common banker and his sister around the card tables at Carlton House? Henry's pockets had been thoroughly emptied by the Regent's circle in the past—he was forever lending money on generous terms to friends of Eliza's, and my late sister had been acquainted with far too many of the Great; but—

"The Regent, I may say, was instantly electrified to learn of *Miss Jane Austen's* residence in the Metropolis," Clarke persisted, bowing low, "and despatched me to your door with all possible haste."

I groped behind me for a chair.

That the presence in London of a woman unremarkable for birth, beauty, blowsy corpulence, or loose morals should be immediately electrifying to the Prince Regent!

"You must know," Clarke added, "that His Royal Highness keeps a complete set of your works, handsomely bound, in each of his residences. The young Princess Charlotte has also found them vastly entertaining."

"Pray sit down, sir," I said faintly.

The cherub beamed, and did so.

"I am instructed to convey all that is proper of His Royal Highness's esteem and commendation, Miss Austen, and to offer the considerable resources and ample solitude of the Library at Carlton House, for your use and pleasure, should you require it, during your stay in London. I may add that His Royal Highness has further instructed Dr. Baillie to call here in Hans Place each day and carry a report of your brother's progress to Carlton House—the Regent being most anxious for Mr. Austen's return to robust health."

I am afraid I openly frowned at the little man, so incomprehensible did this speech seem. Had Henry been in his usual high spirits and stout form, I should have suspected him of hiring the fellow to trick me.

"The Library at Carlton House? The Regent intends for me to *write* there?"

"Not if you should dislike it," Mr. Clarke said hurriedly. "But I cannot conceive why you should. It is in every way an admirable chamber, lined with a varied and thorough selection of works on every subject; handsomely appointed, the lighting good, the warmth without question (His Royal Highness is highly particular about the heating of his rooms)—and as nobody at Carlton House is excessively devoted to literature, generally empty."

This last, I could well believe; and as the final note rang true, I must credit the whole.

"You are very good, sir," I said, rising with an air that must be read as dismissal—"and the Regent's generosity is nothing short of remarkable. Please say everything proper to His Royal

Highness, of my gratitude for his notice and his esteem. It must be impossible for me to accept his kind invitation, however. The demands of my brother's precarious health make any interests of my own immaterial at present."

The expression of dismay on poor Mr. Clarke's face was so sudden and ill-disguised that I very nearly disgraced myself with laughter. His disappointment was vast, and his discomfiture palpable. He stood to his full height of five feet and turned agitatedly before the hearth, his hands clasped upon his stomach. It was evident I had committed some solecism, and by my refusal presented Mr. Clarke with a problem.

"My *dear* Miss Austen," he managed at length, "be assured I have every sympathy with the family difficulties you entertain. I am sensible of the burdens that rest so heavily upon the shoulders of a writer, too, being not unacquainted with the demands of that celestial endeavour myself. —You *are* in the midst of some noble creation of the pen, I assume? An understanding as fertile as your own, cannot long be occupied solely with the sickbed."

"I am," I conceded. *Emma* being complete, I had begun to trifle with a tale I thought suited to November—the story of a slighted young woman despairing of her present, whose heart is buried with her past.

Clarke came to a standstill and studied me with his earnest child's eyes. "I am afraid you do not entirely apprehend the situation," he said. "An invitation of this sort, from a personage such as His Royal Highness, to a lady of your station and accomplishments . . . is by way of being impossible to refuse. It is as much a Royal *summons,* as an extension of gracious notice. Forgive me, madam—but do I make myself intelligible?"

I hesitated for a moment. There are few people of whom I think less than the Prince Regent. His entire history is either foolish or despicable, and his injured wife—tho' little better than he—ought to be the object of every woman's pity. But poor Mr. Clarke was denied the luxury of my sentiments. He had arrived in Hans Place as the bearer of joyous gifts, of Royal favour and attention; his position must be miserable, did he return to Carlton House unrequited. As ridiculous as I might find his manners and appearance, he had taken the trouble to call upon me and fulfill his Prince's errand. I could not be so cruel as to deny him success.

"Perfectly intelligible." I sighed. "Pray let us name the day, Mr. Clarke, when I am to visit the Regent's Library."

2
THE BODY IN THE LIBRARY

Monday, 13 November 1815
23 Hans Place, London, cont'd.

Carlton House sits at the southern end of Pall Mall, behind an imposing set of gates and a broad sweep. Having stated one's business to an imperious porter, one jogs forward into the semi-darkness of a massive porte cochere, fronted with Ionic columns and all the bustle of lackeys at the carriage door. As one descends (quite damply) from the conveyance and endeavours to ascend the short flight of steps with insouciance and composure, the regal doors are swept wide as if by invisible hands. And there, in the foyer, stands Mr. James Stanier Clarke—rendered even shorter and more absurdly round by the loftiness of his setting.

"My dear Miss Austen!" he cried. "What a pleasure—what an *honour,* indeed, to welcome you to Carlton House!"

I advanced a little and curtseyed. The pheasant plume secured to my bonnet, sodden with rain, bobbed unhappily by my left cheek.

"Come straight in to the fire," he commanded, "and recover

yourself. His Royal Highness should be most distressed if you were to take a chill, given your brother's late indisposition. Indeed, I wonder if I ought to summon Dr. Baillie to you now, with a paregoric draught—"

I assured him that such a precaution was unnecessary.

He led me anxiously from the foyer into the vast space of the hall beyond, where fires burned in twin stoves to the left and right.

Behind me, Manon drew a swift breath and muttered a faint *mon dieu* at our surroundings.

Severely classical, the rectangular hall rose a full two storeys to a domed ceiling, constructed much as the Pantheon appears in old prints. An oculus pierced the dome, throwing light on the black and white marble floor at our feet. Columns of orange marble flanked the sides of the room and simple chairs were disposed before the duelling hearths. I may say that I was pleasantly surprized at the restraint of the decoration—I had once had occasion to visit the Regent's folly in Brighton, where every flight of exotic phantasie is indulged.* Tho' equally costly, this place had more real elegance.

And unlike the usual run of London houses, it was remarkably warm. The Prince was notorious for his fear of draughts; and as my boots began to steam before the excellent stove I recalled that more than one lady had *preferred* to dampen her skirts before entering the Pavilion at Brighton. It must be the same at Carlton House.

"Does this suffice? Are you throwing off your chill?" Mr. Clarke enquired.

---

* See *Jane and the Madness of Lord Byron* (Bantam, 2010)—*Editor's note.*

I assured him that the warmth was delightful and that I was in a fair way to being recovered; and stole a glance around the hall as I did so. It is a curious sensation to enter a private home—albeit a Royal one—and to find oneself in a publick thoroughfare. Half a dozen footmen, as like one another as possible from their excessive height to their powdered wigs, were stationed impassively along the walls. They appeared lost in contemplation, indifferent to the trivial nothings of a Mr. Clarke or a Miss Austen. I was aware of various persons crossing the marble floor and disappearing into the vastness beyond, some of them in groups of two or three; a faint murmur of conversation travelled around the walls, as though one were at an exhibition in a picture gallery.

"Then let us not waste another moment, my dear lady," Mr. Clarke said. "We shall proceed to all the delights of the Library, where I flatter myself a modest refreshment has been provided, not unsuited to the hour of the day and the inclemency of the weather. If your maid prefers, she may of course await your return here by the fire."

Manon, however, made no sign of having heard Mr. Clarke and looked determined to dog my footsteps. I gave her a quelling glance from under my brows, and with a muttered oath she seated herself in one of the chairs. I shall be forty next month, and must be allowed to pay a call upon a gentleman without a chaperon. But the tedious interval Manon contemplated in the hall, surrounded by inhuman footmen, should remind me of my duty. I would not remain with Mr. Clarke above half an hour.

We proceeded through the hall to an octagonal vestibule, where the Regent's more flamboyant taste was evident—the walls were a vibrant green picked out in Adamesque mouldings of white. Heavy crimson draperies, fringed in gold, lined four archways. One let out onto a courtyard, drearily soaked with November rain. Another led to a magnificent oval staircase. Here Mr. Clarke hesitated.

"Before we descend—for I must tell you that the Library, along with many of the publick rooms, is below ground at Carlton House—should you like to *just peek* at the Rose Satin Room?"

"If you think it advisable," I said.

"Oh, Miss Austen—I do! I do! In my experience it is the one of His Royal Highness's rooms most generally commended by ladies." He bustled through the octagonal chamber to the anteroom beyond. This was decidedly French, done up in white and gilt boiseries with hangings of Prussian blue, and an early portrait of the Regent in ermine and ostrich feathers.

I followed Mr. Clarke discreetly, aware that a pair of strangers was disposed on a settee before the fire. One of them was a very fair-haired lady who had eyes only for her companion. *He* possessed a profile that must be instantly recognisable from a hundred print-shop windows and notices of publick thanksgiving: a broad brow, a hawk's prominent nose, an air of impatience about the curling lips. I averted my gaze and hurried after my clergyman, who had merely inclined his head to the couple.

Mr. Clarke had drawn up before a set of doors guarded by another pair of footmen. These silently admitted us to the Rose Satin Room and waited until we had satisfied our interest.

"I am anxious to learn your opinion," Mr. Clarke whispered.

It appeared to be the fashion at Carlton House to mark every chamber by a different colour scheme. This one was hung entirely in pink damask, gathered with gold medallions and fringe. The ceiling was painted with classical subjects picked out by gilt lozenges. In candlelight, the atmosphere of old rose must be vastly forgiving of aging complexions. Paintings of the finest quality and subject were arrayed on each side; it wanted only a pianoforte and a harp to be utterly delightful.

"Charming," I said.

"It *is* a sweet room," Mr. Clarke agreed, "tho' only rarely frequented. I have known the whist tables to be set up here, of an evening."

When we returned through the French anteroom, it was empty of its interesting couple. I profited from the moment and enquired, "Was that not the Duke of Wellington I saw?"

"Indeed," Mr. Clarke replied, his breast swelling visibly. "He is often to be found at Carlton House. It is not only the Regent's intimates who frequent these halls, I assure you."

An embarrassing admission, to be sure—that the Duke was not to be confused with—nay, was to be *distinguished* from—the Prince's usual friends. Mr. Clarke must be well aware of the reputation of the Carlton House Set—as disreputable a covey of well-born gamblers and rakes as ever convened under a Royal roof. I speak not simply from rumour, but from certain knowledge: my late lamented Gentleman Rogue, Lord Harold Trowbridge, was one of the Set's founding members. That he had put his intimacy at Carlton House to good use, in the prosecution of the Crown's enemies, was a subtler truth few could know.

We had returned once more to the residence's octagonal heart, and passed through a different arch this time—towards the sweeping oval staircase. This was a work of art in its own right, the steps broad and wide, the railings intricately fashioned of iron and gilt. Far above in the reaches of the house, an oculus shed light on its turnings. But Mr. Clarke was waiting by the lower flight of stairs, and gesturing that I must go before him. Card tables might hold pride of place in the sumptuous publick rooms of Carlton House—but books, it seemed, were relegated to the cellars.

"I am sure you are thinking that it is out of the common way for so much of the residence to be below-stairs," Mr. Clarke confided. "Indeed, it is considered extraordinary that even the principal reception chambers are at ground level! For you know that is not the usual manner of houses in Town. But the Regent requires so much *room*—" He paused on the lowest step in a sudden agony of embarrassment, no doubt fearful that I had misconstrued his words—for the Regent is an immense figure of a man, barely able to mount a horse at present, and dependent upon corsets for his clothing's accommodation. But I fancy my countenance betrayed no hint of a mischievous construction; the trembling only of a lifted brow, may have hinted at the mirth within.

"Undoubtedly," I agreed. "He is everywhere regarded as an inveterate collector, and such passions require an infinite succession of lumber-rooms. Is His Royal Highness in residence at present?" We had achieved the lower vestibule: a dramatic space divided along its middle by a colonnade of dark green marble columns. Here, where windows must be difficult to construct and natural light fugitive, the interiors were a tapestry of scarlet and gilt, with mirrored lustres intended to throw back the glow of countless candles. Pier glasses lined the walls, in a fashion that recalled all my late, lamented sister Eliza had told me of her youth at Versailles—I found myself repeated a hundred-fold in their reflections.* Being accustomed to only a small looking-glass at home, I must be fascinated by the image of myself: appearing taller than I suspected, more angular, with suggestive shadows beneath my eyes and hollows in my cheeks. I had chosen my carriage dress well, however—one of the delights of being a dissipated novelist being the unwomanly management of my own purse. Before Henry's illness demanded all my hours, I had profited from this trip to Town to order some neat but elegant gowns. This, a Prussian blue French wool, was trimmed with dull bronze braid at the bodice and wrists; my hussar bonnet was dull bronze, as were my boots. Prussian blue and hussar bonnets are all the rage this autumn, owing to the general enthusiasm for things military following the victory at Waterloo; but I was no mere slave to Fashion. In practical deference to the inclement weather, I carried a sable muff that had once been Eliza's. Tho' I should hardly pass for a member of the *haut ton*, I was no dowd; and my colours looked very well against Carlton House's canvas.

"His Royal Highness is indeed in residence," Mr. Clarke

---

* Henry Austen's late wife, Eliza, who styled herself Comtesse de Feuillide after the title of her guillotined first husband, was born in India and raised primarily in France. She was commonly believed to be the illegitimate daughter of Warren Hastings, former governor-general of India. A first cousin to the Austen siblings, she fled to England after the French Revolution and although ten years older than Henry Austen, accepted his offer of marriage. She was therefore both Jane's cousin and her sister-in-law, although the latter was not a term employed in Austen's day. Jane referred to Eliza variously as "my cousin" and "my sister" throughout her life. Eliza died of breast cancer in 1813.—*Editor's note.*

returned eagerly, "tho' deprived of his freedom by the demands of an artist this morning. There is to be a series of paintings in commemoration of Waterloo, you know. That is why His Grace the Duke of Wellington will have been waiting in the Blue Anteroom."

"His Royal Highness was hardly present at the battle in Belgium," I observed, a trifle bemused. "He cannot be necessary to any tableau of victory."

"No-o," Mr. Clarke conceded. "But that is not the point, my dear Miss Austen. He shall appear in any picture as the presiding genius by whom our beloved Duke was *guided.*"

What little I knew, by reputation, of the Duke's character, was in violent opposition to every syllable of this facile sentiment; but I preserved an interesting silence, and followed Mr. Clarke through the open doors at the far end of the vestibule.

The Carlton House Library is a feast for the eyes of anyone abandoned from birth to the seductions of literature as I must confess myself to be. It is not so imposing as the Long Library at Blenheim, nor the remarkable galleried room at Chatsworth, which are soaring in height and overlook pastoral scenes.* The five windows marching down one side of this room looked out onto an area formed only of Portland stone. But Blenheim and Chatsworth are the county seats of dukes; for a collection of books in a London home, the Carlton House Library will do

---

*Austen scholars have long debated whether Jane ever travelled farther north than Hamstall Ridware, Staffordshire, where she visited her cousin Edward Cooper in August 1806. As readers of these edited journals have discovered, however, she stayed at Bakewell in Derbyshire (and visited neighboring Chatsworth) during the period recounted in *Jane and the Stillroom Maid* (Bantam Books, 2008).—*Editor's note.*

very well. I should judge some thousands of books, beautifully bound in buff-and-blue leather (the Prince's household colours), were shelved from waist-height to ceiling on every side, and in perpendicular bays that reached towards the centre of the room. A spacious aisle ran from our entry to the exit at the far end, furnished with three long tables placed at intervals. These were set with oil lamps ideal for reading, and supplies of ink, pens, and paper in handsome tooled-leather boxes. A roaring fire in a massive marble hearth punctuated the shelves on my left; before this was an arrangement of easy chairs.

How I should have loved to while away my hours, writing in the warmth and solitude of this room, had the acceptance of the Prince's invitation been remotely possible! But it could not be. Henry was too close to danger, still, to spare me; and even if he were not, I must be made uncomfortable by the generosity of a prince I held in contempt.

I set my muff and reticule on the nearest table and began to scan the shelves. "What an admirable collection, Mr. Clarke. You must be happy in your hours of reading, with such volumes to hand."

"Indeed." He inclined his head. "And given that the exquisite peace of this room is seldom disturbed—"

As tho' in mockery, his speech was interrupted by a heart-rending groan, deep in timbre and suffering. It seemed to emanate from the far end of the room.

I gazed enquiringly at Mr. Clarke.

"Forgive me, dear lady." The clergyman frowned at finding our literary idyll overlistened by a stranger, and bustled towards one of the perpendicular bays.

I followed.

"Colonel MacFarland!"

I came round the end of the shelves and stopped short. A soldier in the redcoated uniform of a Scots Greys cavalry officer, his grey pantaloons distinguished by a scarlet stripe down their length, was sprawled at the clergyman's feet. I could not fail to recognise the dress; it was everywhere represented in shop vitrines, after the Greys' heroic charge at Waterloo. The officer's eyes were startled and wide. Tho' clearly conscious of his indecorous position, he made no attempt to rise. As I watched, however, his right hand trembled spasmodically and his lips worked.

Mr. Clarke bent with effort—he was neither young nor nimble—and said distinctly, "Are you ill, sir?"

A second groan issued from the Colonel's depths, as tho' his very soul twisted in his bowels.

"He is going to be sick," I said urgently.

Mr. Clarke stepped back in haste.

Without so much as turning his head, the unfortunate man expelled the contents of his stomach with a dreadful choking sound.

"Get help." I gathered my skirts in one hand and crouched low. Mr. Clarke scurried to the Library door.

Colonel MacFarland was retching horribly, his gaze imploring. I tore off my gloves, drew a clean handkerchief from the sleeve of my gown, and wiped his mouth. Then I forced his head to one side. He drew a stifled breath, vomit dripping to the Prince's parquet. He could no more summon command of his limbs than he could of his neck. One foot jerked and was still.

"Wah," he forced out. The syllable was strange and distorted, as tho' his tongue had thickened. "*Waher*—"

I pressed one hand to my nose. The stench was dreadful, and for an instant I feared I might be sick myself. Then I suppressed my weaker impulses and forced myself to my feet. I glanced round. There must be a ewer of water *somewhere* in this gilded room.

"Waher . . . Loo."

"*Waterloo*?"

His eyelids flickered as if in assent. His fingers clenched. The choking sound again. His breathing, more stertorous.

I dropped once more to my knees and leaned close to the struggling fellow, regardless of the foulness of his breath.

"Mah-h-p," he whispered. His pupils were enormous and dark.

"Waterloo map?"

His lips worked, but no sound came. I lowered my ear to his mouth, straining for a syllable.

The clatter of rapidly approaching feet drowned anything the Colonel might have attempted to say. I glanced round, and caught the spare figure of Dr. Baillie.

"MacFarland," he said calmly. "Are you unwell?"

I got to my feet and stepped back as the physician knelt by the sick man's side. Mr. Clarke hovered in the doorway, wringing his hands.

The Colonel lay immobile as before; but at the doctor's words, he expelled a gurgling breath.

Baillie listened to his heart, then grasped his wrist. "The pulse is weak and the flesh cold. We must get you to bed, Colonel! Come, man, let me help you to your feet."

There was an instant of tension, when it appeared the sick man exerted all his force of will to lift himself, without the slightest result or sound.

"Is it apoplexy?" Mr. Clarke asked in a lowered tone.

"Some sort of fit," the doctor replied. "Be so good, Clarke, as to summon a footman."

Mr. Clarke hurried through the doorway. I heard him cry out, "James! James!"

All footmen in each of the Prince's homes are called James. It saves the Royal the trouble of distinguishing one from another.

"Has he moved whilst you observed him, Miss Austen?" Dr. Baillie enquired.

"His limbs jerked some once or twice. But a few moments ago he lacked the power even to turn his head. It was I who placed it thus to the side, when he became ill."

The doctor frowned, and rose from Colonel MacFarland's inert form. "Nervous collapse. Most strange. He was well enough when I saw him this morning."

Further speech was forestalled by the appearance of three strapping footmen arrayed in buff-and-blue livery. They bore Colonel MacFarland away on their shoulders without comment or fuss. I wondered if they were often pressed into a similar service, when the Regent's cronies had sampled too much of His Royal Highness's claret.

Dr. Baillie made as if to follow the cortège. Then his monkey gaze met mine. "Did the Colonel say anything whilst you attended him, Miss Austen?"

"He did. Waterloo Map."

"I beg your pardon?"

"That is what the Colonel said. *Waterloo Map.*"

"Was his speech slurred?"

"Yes. But he went to great effort to utter the phrase, and I am sure I heard him distinctly. I believe his tongue grew too swollen for speech shortly thereafter."

The doctor hesitated a moment, but our tête-à-tête was broken by Mr. Clarke—who stood panting on the threshold as tho' he, and not the footmen, had suffered all the exertion of MacFarland's transport.

"It is decided," he declared. "We shall take our refreshment in the Bow Room, Miss Austen, as it would not do to lay the table *here*. You will find that the stove in that room is excellent and the view from the window delightful. One would not credit the arrangement of boxed shrubs in the Area with being *subterranean*."

Dr. Baillie bowed. "Do not be in a hurry to run away, Miss Austen. Mr. Clarke—you are not to quit Carlton House either. I may have need of you, by-and-by."

"Dr. Baillie," I said impulsively, "did Colonel MacFarland take part in the battle at Waterloo?"

"He did," the physician replied. "Indeed, there are many who call him a hero for it."

3
THE SOILED HANDKERCHIEF

Monday, 13 November 1815
23 Hans Place, London, cont'd.

"Dear me." Mr. Clarke sighed as one of the Jameses offered glasses of ratafia and macaroons from a silver tray. "How terribly upsetting to see one's friends unwell. First your admirable brother, and now the poor Colonel! The Regent will be most distressed."

"His Royal Highness has a particular regard for Colonel MacFarland?"

"Not at all," Mr. Clarke returned. "But he *does* have a horror of infection, and you know the Colonel partook of the Regent's nuncheon this morning. I wonder if I ought to warn him immediately?"

I choked a little on my wine.

"It is unfortunate that the Colonel has been allowed to remain under His Royal Highness's roof in such a dangerous condition." Mr. Clarke offered me the platter of macaroons. They appeared delectable, and I was fainting from hunger. I selected one. "But it could not be avoided, I conclude. Dr.

Baillie took a good deal upon himself, to be sure—and will answer for it to the Regent."

"His Royal Highness must value Dr. Baillie's medical opinion," I suggested. "Else he would not have named him Court Physician."

"As to that—" Mr. Clarke lifted his shoulders. "The Regent, God be thanked, is his own best doctor. I should not wonder if he quits Carlton House immediately upon learning of the Colonel's illness. A Prince—with such heavy burdens of policy and government as His Royal Highness commands—cannot be too careful. The Regent would be wise to retire to Brighton until Colonel MacFarland is recovered and so I shall tell him. The sea air must always be salubrious. Indeed, I begin to think that the smokes and fogs of London carry every sort of contagion, Miss Austen. You will be wanting to fly into Hampshire as soon as your brother may spare you."

"I do not think of quitting London before December," I replied. "My business with Mr. Murray precludes it."

"John Murray, the publisher? Of Albemarle Street?" Mr. Clarke sat up a little straighter in his chair. "He has the printing of your latest work, I presume? As how should he *not*—the publisher of Byron, to link his name and fortunes with so celebrated an authoress as Miss Jane Austen! Pray, is the work very far advanced?"

"We have only just embarked on the proofs of the first volume," I replied. "My brother's illness, as you may imagine, must take precedence."

"And will it be as admirable in every way as *Mansfield Park*? I confess that is my favourite of your works—so pleasing in its treatment of Ordination and its sober picture of the clergy. Is your heroine to be as modest and humble a lady as Miss Fanny Price?"

"Not at all," I replied, without noting that such a poor-spirited heroine must be a death to sales. "Indeed, I cannot think Emma a creature many but myself will like. She is too full of spirit, self-assurance, vanity, and pride; and she is in the habit of always getting her own way."

"The very picture of the Princess Charlotte!" Mr. Clarke cried.

He rose and began to turn in some agitation before the stove, which threw out a good deal of heat. I was fortunate in having a fire screen close at hand, however, and employed it. The Bow Room was a marvel of luxury and comfort—and this, by all appearances, was the least of the Regent's chambers. The window that gave the room its name looked out on an area clad in Portland stone, the insipid color dappled with the silhouettes of perhaps a dozen yew trees in glossy black tubs. The shrubs had been clipped into fantastic shapes—a charger's head, mane blown back; a sea nymph rising from a wave. Placed in a spot where no garden could grow, an entire storey below ground, they refreshed the eye on a dark November afternoon. Again, I suppressed the desire to accept Mr. Clarke's invitation, and write in the peace and comfort of this remarkable house. I might be undisturbed for hours, treated to good coal fires, and have my pick of myriad Jameses to bring me ratafia and cakes whenever I desired them.

"I hope you will not think me impertinent." Mr. Clarke broke in upon my reverie. "—Although it must be impossible for the Notice of the Regent to be considered as anything but a Blessing. I wonder, Miss Austen—I have informed you, I know, of His Royal Highness's immense regard for your work, and indeed that of his daughter, Her Royal Highness Princess Charlotte—would it be indelicate, nay, *presumptuous* of me to offer a little hint?"

Bewildered, I stared at him, my ratafia suspended. "If you could perhaps speak more plainly, sir," I said.

"Of course. To be sure." He turned again, hands clasped behind his coat. "You are aware that on occasion the Regent grants the favour of Notice to various Luminaries of Art and Letters. It is to be your honour, Miss Austen, to receive that Notice."

I felt heat in my cheeks. What *was* the absurd little man suggesting?

"It is His Royal Highness's pleasure and happiness to command that your next published work be dedicated humbly, and gratefully, to *Himself*, as Regent of the noble land that gave you birth, Miss Austen—that inspired your Genius—that has so warmly embraced your interesting histories of Genteel Romance."

He beamed at me, confident of the joy that must even now be surging in my spinster's breast.

"You will wish, I know, to send a simple note of thanks to the Regent for this Notice—which I will be happy to convey myself. I will procure you pen and paper directly. The Dedication, when composed, may also be sent for my perusal, so that any little improvements that might strike my fancy, and that have escaped your scrupulous intellect, may be subscribed therewith."

I, commanded to dedicate my cherished *Emma* to a man I abominated? Commanded, moreover, to regard His Royal arrogance as an occasion for gratitude? Absurd.

I had endured enough of Carlton House for one day.

"You are too kind, Mr. Clarke," I said stiffly. "But now I must take my leave of you. My maid will be wondering what has become of me."

"As to that—surely it is a maid's office to wait upon her mistress? You will be wanting another glass of ratafia, I am sure."

"You are all politeness, but I am unequal to—"

A sound at the Bow Room doorway brought my head around. Dr. Baillie was silhouetted in its frame.

"You are wanted, Clarke," he said brusquely. "The Colonel ought to have Absolution, and there is no time to waste."

"Good Lord! It cannot be so bad as that!"

"It is. You will find him above, in the Green Velvet Room. Make haste, man!"

Mr. Clarke looked to me imploringly. His lips parted, but no pleasantries came. I inclined my head, dismissing him.

He bustled away. The doctor, however, lingered in the doorway, as tho' conscious of my abandonment.

I collected my reticule and muff. The precipitance of death must always be chastening; my own petty pride was instantly banished. "How dreadfully sudden. *The poor man.* Is it indeed a case of apoplexy, Doctor?"

"How else to account for the total immobility of the limbs, in a hardened soldier of three-and-thirty, who was in riotous good health only hours ago?" He spoke almost indifferently, but I detected an unquiet intelligence behind the words. Baillie was perplexed by his patient's case, and hiding it poorly. "And now, Miss Austen, if you will forgive me—"

I hastened to the doorway. "Of course."

"I shall send a footman to conduct you above-stairs. I am sure, with all this disturbance, you are desperate to get away."

I curtseyed. "You are very good, sir."

He was gone, leaving me no less puzzled by events. My late father died of an apoplectic fit a decade since. But in his case, only one side of the body was affected. The unfortunate Colonel could move neither right nor left.

Beyond the bow window, daylight was failing; but the Regent's excellent lustres supplied an adequate glow. I determined to await the footman in the vestibule at the foot of the great staircase. As I crossed the marble floor, however, I recollected my handkerchief—tossed on the floor by the Colonel's head, and forgotten in Mr. Clarke's desire for refreshment. It was my very best handkerchief, embroidered with my initials, and brought purposely to complement the grandeur of Carlton House; I did not like to leave it. Had the Colonel been felled by a fever or stomach ailment, I might have avoided the possibility of contagion and left it where it lay, but Dr. Baillie appeared certain that apoplexy was the cause of MacFarland's misery.* I glanced towards the stairs and detected no sound of servants; I should require but a moment to retrieve my property.

The Library was quite deserted, the only sound the fire in the hearth. I hastened towards the secluded bay where MacFarland

---

*In Austen's era, apoplexy referred broadly to any loss of consciousness or sudden paralysis prior to death. In the colonel's case, she implies a condition we would more likely call cerebral hemorrhage or stroke.—*Editor's note.*

had suffered his fit—but was arrested by the sight of the very handkerchief, awaiting me on a reading table.

I crossed the parquet thoughtfully, and picked up the malodorous object. It was neatly folded still, for I had drawn it thus from my sleeve, and applied it immediately to the Colonel's lips. One side of the cream-coloured linen was stained with ochre, and it stank of the Colonel's entrails. But something else was trapped in its weave—three narrow plant needles, torn from an evergreen.

Spruce? Fir? Or—

I recollected the shrubs beyond the bow window.

Yew.

There were any number of tubbed evergreens in the area of Portland stone, lately clipped by the Regent's gardeners. With trimmings left on the ground, the servants might easily have tramped yew needles throughout Carlton House. A few had adhered to my handkerchief, perhaps, when it fell to the floor.

I gathered my skirts and studied the Prince's parquet.

The wood had already been thoroughly cleaned. Whilst I drank ratafia and listened to improper proposals, a maid had restored the Regent's picture-perfect room to its frame; the wood smelled of lemon and beeswax. There was nothing to be discovered from its shining surface—and not a stray needle anywhere.

I drew forth my handkerchief and examined it again.

The needles lying there were stained yellow, like the linen itself. As tho' they had been vomited with the contents of MacFarland's stomach.

Given furiously to think, I tucked my elegant bit of cloth away in my reticule.

4

THE SNAKE IN THE GARDEN

Monday, 13 November 1815
23 Hans Place, London, cont'd.

It was nearly five o'clock when Manon and I regained Hans Place, and the rain was falling steadily. Henry was sitting up in bed, drinking beef tea from Madame Bigeon's spoon.

Madame Bigeon is Manon's aged mother. Both ladies left France long ago in the service of Henry's wife, Eliza, and when the little Comtesse died, they had no intention of deserting her husband. Henry is fed and mended and cosseted with such care that it is a wonder he ever contracted a fever at all, much less a dangerous one. I should have no qualms at leaving my brother to the Frenchwomen once the demands of Mr. Murray and my manuscript were at an end.

"How do you get on?" I asked as I took the beef tea from Madame's hands and assumed the duties of the spoon. Henry was propped among his pillows, and his eyes were no longer veiled with fever; I could not like his countenance, however. It was haggard, and deep crevices ran from nostril to mouth.

"I am as weak as a kitten," he said irritably. "As how should I not be, when all I may do is drowse? I am bored senseless, Jane! And now Madame Fusspot tells me I am not to look into the newspapers. Why, pray, should the Court Physician presume to censor my reading?"

It was not Dr. Baillie, but I, who had proscribed the major London broadsheets. Henry is Receiver-General for the Oxfordshire militia, which requires him to pay the salaries of the troops; in the aftermath of the Waterloo victory, with so many soldiers demanding to be paid off and released from service, the funds are exceedingly strained. I know my brother to be anxious over reports from the Exchange and news of the Crown's finances. I would not wish his monetary concerns to destroy his health. In the grip of delirium last week he called my name, and that of his dead wife, but also that of his banking partner, Mr. Tilson—a grouping unusual enough to betray the depth of his uneasiness. Until he is able to walk unassisted from his bed to his table, he will not be permitted a glimpse of newsprint.

"Speaking of the Court Physician," I said as I lifted the spoon to his mouth, "I was thrown in his way today."

The sally diverted Henry's mind, as I had known it would. I told him the tale of the unfortunate Colonel in as protracted a manner as possible—I am adept at the art of framing a story—and before long the beef tea was gone and my brother's cheeks were flushed.

"That is a dashed sorry history, Jane," he observed. "I am not acquainted with MacFarland myself—but by general report he is all that could be wished in a gentleman and a soldier. Too young, I should have thought, to be seized by an apoplectic fit. But perhaps that is the sad cost of a cavalryman's life."

"Dr. Baillie judged him three-and-thirty, and observed that he was in excellent health in recent days. He called the Colonel a hero."

"I do not know the particulars of his service." Henry leaned forward as I plumped his bolster. "But I believe he cheated death in some publick fashion. At Waterloo, of course."

"He mentioned it."

"Who?"

"The Colonel. He referred to Waterloo. As he was failing. Two words, only—*Waterloo Map.*"

Henry's brow furrowed. "He can't have needed one at this remove, Jane. The battle was all of five months ago."

"What exactly did the Scots Greys do there?"

"Charged the enemy, like all fools on horseback." My brother glanced at a slim volume in boards that sat near his bedside. Sir Walter Scott's poem, entitled *The Field of Waterloo.* "Our friend here writes glowingly of it, in his trifling verses."

My new publisher had only waited for the agreement of our terms, to offer any books in his establishment that might cheer Henry's convalescence. I judged this latest work of Scott's to be indifferent poetry, dashed off to seize a material moment in the Great Man's sales; but it served very well to divert a mind still weak from fever.

"*Then down went helm and lance,*" my brother intoned. "*Down were the eagle banners sent/Down reeling steeds and riders went/ Corslets were pierced, and pennons rent;/And to augment the fray/ Wheeled full against their staggering flanks/The English horsemen's foaming ranks/Forced their resistless way.*"

I groaned aloud. "Enough, Henry, I beg."

But he was no longer attending. Manon had taken bowl and spoon to the kitchen and reappeared with Henry's surgeon.

"Ah!" my brother said, his expression easing. "There you are, Haden!"

Henry being much improved, the Court Physician has resigned him to Mr. Haden's care. He is a pleasant man of modest height and looks, living nearby in Sloane Street. Although some fifteen years Henry's junior, he is almost as much an intimate of this household as Manon or Madame Bigeon—being the one who eased our poor Eliza's final suffering. I nodded to him cordially and quitted my brother's bedchamber, so that the two gentlemen might have a comfortable coze.

MANON WOULD BE LAYING the table soon for my own dinner, in the solitary state of Henry's dining room, but I intended to take the meal by the parlour fire. The effort of appearing in Carlton House had tired me; and I wished to intercept Mr. Haden on his departure.

His light tread descended the stairs just as I was sampling Madame Bigeon's pudding. He hesitated in the parlour doorway, and I bade him enter.

"Will you take a glass of Henry's port, Mr. Haden?"

"Thank you, Miss Austen—I should like that very much."

He seated himself in the chair opposite as Manon carried away my tray.

"And how did you find my brother this evening?"

"Mending apace. The fever is entirely abated, and other than a fluttering in the pulse and weakness of the limbs—hardly unusual in one confined so many weeks—your brother appears to have suffered no lasting injury from his illness. Your decision to consult Dr. Baillie proved sound. I am relieved that his greater skill could save Mr. Austen when I could not."

The humility of his words must disarm reproof. But I confess I felt no sense of injury at Mr. Haden's unhappy treatment of Henry; he had attempted all he could; we were merely fortunate to have a wealth of natural philosophers in a city so great as London. Had my brother fallen ill in Chawton village, he should have expired within the fortnight.

Manon appeared with a glass of port. As Mr. Haden took his first sip, I observed, "I am sure you possess skills that Dr. Baillie does not. We each of us complement the strengths of the other. His experience is in physical decay; yours lies, I believe, in remedies and tinctures. You spend a good deal of your time at the Brompton Dispensary, do you not?"

"That is true." A wave of eagerness swept over his countenance. "I have not the practical learning of a Baillie—he has spent years in the hospitals of Edinburgh and Town, and has mastered much—but I hope you will credit me, Miss Austen, when I say that I have done something else—I have spent hours unnumbered in a labouratory of my own devising, studying the effects of various medicines."

"Upon whom do you experiment?" I asked with a smile. "The unwitting sheep among your flock of patients?"

He shook his head. "I have used stray cats, such mice and rats I may trap near my lodgings—both in Sloane Street and at the dispensary—and occasionally, myself. I should never risk the health of a patient on an untried remedy. Every healing tincture may prove to be poison, if administered without care."

I had wagered on my notion that Haden was an adept of potions and compounds; I had guessed as much, from his beneficial dosing of poor Eliza two years ago. She had suffered as little as possible in her dreadful final throes, and her oblivion was due in great part to Charles Haden. I meant to learn as much as I could of the science of poison from the open-hearted fellow.

"Now you put me in mind of a cherished family dispute, Mr. Haden," I said archly. "My brother and I cannot agree on the nature of *yew*. Henry insists that it has no virtue under Heaven, and that he will not have it in his garden. I tell him he does not know what he is about. There is nothing so charming as clipped yew, in all its fanciful shapes. Tell me: Is there any benefit to the shrub?"

Mr. Haden frowned, and took a sip from his glass.

"It is often employed in a rheumatic liniment," he said, "that may be rubbed on joints and limbs. The aromatic nature of the plant induces a spurious warmth, and a fleeting relief of pain. But yew is also a deadly poison, Miss Austen. To ingest the needles or chew the berries is mortally dangerous."

"Only an innocent child should do such a thing, surely?"

"Perhaps," Haden conceded. "Tho' it is also deadly to drink a tea in which yew is steeped."

"Yew tea!" I declared. "That smacks of witchcraft and incantation! Why should anyone drink such a thing, pray?"

Haden looked at me strangely. "There are homely healers in villages all over England who concoct the brew."

"To despatch their neighbours?" I returned satirically.

"Their neighbours' dogs," he said, "or unborn babes."

I had admired Mr. Haden for his openness; but this was frank indeed. I wondered suddenly how many unfortunate young women in my own village might have resorted to such a remedy—and shuddered. "How does the poison act?"

"Upon the nerves," he replied. "First the tongue tingles; then a gradual numbing of the limbs occurs. There is often an intense nausea as the body attempts to dispel the noxious stuff. At last the lungs and heart cease to move. Like Medusa, yew turns the body to stone."

"In a matter of seconds?"

He shook his head. "Over the course of a few hours, perhaps."

"But . . ." I swallowed with difficulty. "In the cases you mention—of an unwanted child—how does . . ."

"The mother escape? She rarely does." Haden set down his port as tho' it no longer agreed with him. "It depends upon the strength of the yew tea. If she is fortunate, she is merely ill to the point of death for several days, and loses her child in the process. If she dies, she takes the secret of her remedy with her. Yew is rarely exposed for the poisonous quackery it is."

We were both silent in reflection; then Mr. Haden collected himself and essayed a smile. "How serious we are become, Miss Austen! I have never known port to induce a similar effect! But you and Mr. Austen have no cause for alarm—one may clip a yew tree into something charming without the slightest injury. I shall persuade your brother to plant it, solely for your enjoyment."

"I am satisfied," I said, with an attempt at lightness. "But for my part, I shall never enter the garden again without gloves, Mr. Haden."

~

I HAD MUCH TO consider once the surgeon had quitted Hans Place. I sat for another hour near the dying fire, before ascending to my bedchamber, where I took up this journal and pen in an attempt to order my thoughts.

Colonel MacFarland suffered a fit this morning, and his limbs gradually *turned to stone*. I had wiped the sickness from his mouth, and discovered yew needles trapped in the handkerchief. Was this evidence of the type of poison Charles Haden had just described? I had not an idea whether the unfortunate Colonel suffered a fatal injury from his fit—only that Absolution was to be given at the moment I left Carlton House. No subsequent intelligence had followed me to Hans Place; and by my own hand, newspapers were forbidden in my brother's establishment. My ignorance was decidedly vexing.

But if *indeed* the Colonel had been poisoned . . . I could name three possible methods. He might have taken the stuff quite willingly himself, with the intent of self-murder. He might have done so by mistake, the dose being meant for another. Or he might have been deliberately struck down by a malignant hand . . .

In the Regent's household?

I snuffed out my candle and hoped for enlightenment in the morning.

5

THE READER OF NOVELS

Tuesday, 14 November 1815
23 Hans Place, London

A short missive penned on elegant hot-pressed paper was laid by my cup at breakfast. From Manon's sniff of disapproval I concluded even before opening it that she could not admire the writer. When I lifted the seal with my butter knife, I observed it to bear the imprint of a signet ring. The entwined initials read *JSC*.

A note from James Stanier Clarke should not cause my pulse to quicken under usual circumstances; but today was singular. I hurriedly scanned the few lines.

Dear Madam:

I felt it incumbent upon me to offer my sincere apologies for the unfortunate disruption of our interesting conversation yesterday at Carlton House, and my own lamentable inattention to your welfare as you quitted the Regent's establishment. I know your delicacy and goodness will allow for the demands of a sudden illness within the Household, and the Duties required of a clergyman in such sad cases;

and your forgiveness must be secured upon learning that Colonel MacFarland departed this life not a quarter-hour after I was summoned to his bedside. He did not go unshriven to his Reward—which must be of comfort to every Christian.

If you desire at any time to take up the invitation extended to you—that of employing His Royal Highness's commodious Library in pursuit of your Art—pray dear Madam know that one word to me is sufficient.

Believe me at all times
With sincerity & respect
Your faithful & obliged Servant
J.S. Clarke
Librarian

Postscript—I look forward dear Madam to your Dedication to His Royal Highness, and indeed to the exalted work in which it is shortly to appear. —J.S.C.

No hint in this missive that the Colonel's death resulted from anything but a weakness in his vital forces. No murmur of doubt regarding the strangeness of apoplexy in one relatively young. Had Dr. Matthew Baillie satisfied himself, and all at Carlton House, that Colonel MacFarland died of a fit? Or was James Stanier Clarke merely voicing a neat resolution to an untidy business, in deference to the sensibilities of a lady?

Had the Colonel indeed expired as the result of poison—one possibly administered under the Prince Regent's roof—nobody should be likely to breathe a word of it in publick! Whether accident, suicide, or murder, the unfortunate affair would be swiftly buried with the Colonel's body, lest an air of dangerous misfortune taint the cherished rooms of Carlton House. If the idea of poison entered the mind of any of the Prince's intimates, the culprit should be pursued with utmost discretion and secrecy. I should never learn a word of the affair.

And yet—

I reread Mr. Clarke's studied prose. He did not even refer to Dr. Baillie, or describe the Colonel's dying moments! Indeed, the poor fellow was dismissed as briskly as his shriven soul. Was it possible *nobody* at Carlton House was alive to danger? If a cavalryman could be despatched without comment in the heart of the Royal household . . . could not the Regent himself?

Something ought to be done.

Mr. Clarke had renewed his invitation to employ the Carlton House Library. I felt it increasingly imperative that I accept his offer.

I WASTED AN HOUR first, however, over my needlework in Henry's parlour, in dutiful expectation of a messenger bearing typeset pages of *Emma* from Mr. Murray's establishment. None appeared. As it must be impossible to publish a novel that has not been proofed by the authoress, and as one cannot proof what is never delivered, I suffered extremes of vexation. I intend to quit London for my home in Hampshire in early December, and it seems unlikely that the printer's work—which I had hoped would be finished—will be even half done.

I set aside my needle and wools, and determined to walk out in the watery sunshine. I was desperate for intelligence of the sort only London could provide. Henry would do very well without me this morning—I had looked in on him after breakfast, and discovered him in close conversation with our excellent Mr. Haden.

I collected a cloak and my reticule, adjusted my serviceable bonnet in the looking-glass, and drew on my warmest gloves. It is no small matter to walk into London from Hans Place, and I meant to go as far as Hatchard's Book Shop in Piccadilly.

It is less than a mile from Henry's house to the little village of Knightsbridge, with its cavalry barracks and inns, its watchhouse and pens for straying livestock. Not quite the bustle of Town, but not entirely rural, either—London continues to encroach on the fields all about. A fine square is being laid out, and is to be called Cadogan Place, with a terrace of houses to rival Bath's Royal Crescent along one side.

I hurried a little as I walked up Sloane Street, anxious that I should not encounter our neighbour from Hans Place, Mrs. Tilson. She is the wife of Henry's partner, James Tilson, and the mother of a numerous family; a rather tiresome creature in her Evangelical fervour—and unlikely to approve of a gentlewoman on errands without her maid. I had torn Manon from Henry's care yesterday, however, in undertaking to visit Carlton House; and I did not wish to deprive my brother of his cosseter this morning as well. The opinions of a Mrs. Tilson must be as nothing to me. That my sister, Cassandra, should probably have shared them, I did not allow myself to acknowledge. There was little to remark, of course, in a stroll to Knightsbridge—but the evils of taverns and militiamen from thence to Hyde Park Gate could not be ignored. I trusted to my advancing age to preserve me from insult.

Knightsbridge was charming at this hour of the morning—a

little before noon—with a single forlorn cow lowing despondently in the village enclosure. The smell of warm bread drifted from a baker's oven.

I turned right along the Brompton road, my head down to avoid any impertinent or roving eyes; but none were abroad today, and a quarter-hour's brisk effort brought me safely to Hyde Park tollgate, sitting atop its rise, with a weighing house to one side and a watchhouse on the other. I nearly bounded up the gravel incline—being by then thoroughly warm and contented, flushed with exercise.

Passing through the gate, I was treated to the usual lively London scene: Gentlemen swaggering around Grosvenor Square en route to Tattersall's, where the most beautiful and spirited horseflesh is at auction; poor souls hastening into St George's Hospital to visit the sick; and all of Piccadilly, with its crush of carriages and mounted horsemen, stretching in a mud-churned expanse before one's feet.

Hatchard's Book Shop sits on the right-hand side of Piccadilly, at No. 187, just beyond the lengthy enclosure of Green Park; and it being the finest establishment of its kind in England, a veritable Heaven for any lover of books, I was frequently unequal to the temptation to browse among its wares. In truth, I visited it nearly every day that weather permitted. I was not yet so far sunk in depravity as to actually *purchase* many volumes, being a firm friend of the Circulating Library; but I dearly loved to caress the boards of fresh publications, feel the weight of their paper and the elegance of their type, and I frequently consulted the newspapers Hatchard's so obligingly made available to the publick for a trifling fee. That was my intent this morning—Mr.

Clarke's irksome note having incited more questions than it provided answers.

After a buffeting and determined journey along the paving—the crowds of London never cease to amaze—I achieved Hatchard's doorway, and observed a striking caricature displayed in the window, depicting an obese Prince Regent on his knees before the lifted skirts of a Painted Fashionable I felt sure I ought to recognise. I knew the engraver's setting, at least—it was the Rose Satin Room at Carlton House—and felt curiously self-conscious in the knowledge, as tho' I were privileged with information the better part of London could not share.

I opened the shop door and made my way through the displays—glorious scent of ink and paper!—to the pleasant room beyond, where easy chairs and tables were set about the racks holding the latest editions of London papers. I did not trifle with the weekly journals, or the Sunday *Observer. The Morning Chronicle* and *The Morning Post* were my objects, as they were every other person's in the room, save for a gentleman engrossed in a sporting journal and a pair of young ladies turning over the leaves of *La Belle Assemblée.* I observed the latter to be whispering over the plate of an impossibly tall nymph in swansdown, with rubies to her headdress. They had no notion, of course, what such a costume cost—and if the men in their lives were suitably up to snuff, should never be required to know. Ladies who ordered their clothes for themselves were wiser and thriftier, however.

A copy of the *Chronicle* slid across the polished reading table, discarded. I snatched it up. The paper was of a notably Whiggish turn. In the past this might have meant a protective tone regarding the Prince and his Set; but of late His Royal Highness had forgot his old friends in the Opposition, and had embraced the current Tory Government as preservers of Royalty, and thus more likely to pay his bills.

I searched the columns with a swift eye. It would be a brief notice, in the section reserved for departures, arrivals, births, engagements, and deaths. Not to mention *scandals*. Elopements did a brisk trade in the *Morning Chronicle,* whilst rumours of indecency of every kind were vaguely suggested with elisions and initials.

> *We are grieved to report that Lady R. V. has quitted her husband and all her friends for a dubious venture in the Barbadoes, where the Rum Trade has lately secured her Interest . . . A certain Duke's Fast Frigate made safe harbour with a precious Cargo, of which she was delivered this morning . . . Viscount W., a familiar of Watier's Club, was seen to disembark in Calais yesterday morning, having lost thousands in playing at macao . . .*

But no sly evasion was deemed necessary for Colonel MacFarland.

> *We are shocked to report the Passing of a Hero, with the death of Colonel Ewan MacFarland of the Second Dragoons, Union Brigade (Scots Greys), who suffered an apoplectic fit yesterday, and expired only a few hours later. Colonel MacFarland was everywhere known as a fine soldier and cavalry officer, whose daring enterprise at Waterloo earned him the Gratitude of the Nation.*

That was all. It seemed a brief and inglorious nod. Apparently "daring enterprise" required no further explication for the wise readers of the *Chronicle*. I cast about for *The Morning Gazette*, and found a solitary copy still warming a gentleman's abandoned chair. As I was a firm Tory in my sentiments, this was my preferred news sheet. I leafed rapidly through the political columns and discovered Colonel MacFarland buried under Court News.

> *The sudden death of celebrated cavalryman Colonel E. MacFarland, of an apoplectic fit, was greeted with dismay at Carlton House yesterday. Late of the Scots Greys, MacFarland gave signal service at the Battle of Waterloo and his passing is regretted by many, most notably His Grace the Duke of Wellington, who is at present on leave from his duties in Paris with the Army of Occupation at the request of H.R.H. the Prince Regent.*

This notice had so little to do with poor MacFarland—being taken up with the important intelligence of Wellington's presence in London—that one might suppose the Colonel's death had been required to make room for the Duke at the Regent's table.

I tossed the paper aside. Carlton House, if it suspicioned foul play at all, was determined in its silence—and not even the broadsheet hounds were baying at the scent. Absent a direct communication with Dr. Baillie, therefore, I was unlikely to learn anything further of Colonel MacFarland's death. Importuning the doctor would be indelicate; I should look like a common pry, forcing my interest where it had no justifiable place. On the other hand, there was the evidence of my handkerchief—

"Has any new work by the author of *Mansfield Park* lately appeared?"

I turned, startled, but the question was not directed to me. A gentleman stood by the clerk's counter, and as he leaned forward in expectation of his answer, I knew his profile: high forehead, blade of a nose, eyes deeply set. My heart beat erratically and I almost fled Hatchard's—but Mr. Raphael West stood between me and the safety of Piccadilly.

He was the son of a celebrated painter of our age, Mr. Benjamin West, who had quitted his native Pennsylvania some fifty years before in search of artistic instruction and fame on the Continent. Reared in a quixotic blend of democratic principle and intimacy with the Great—his father being Court Painter to George III—Raphael West was something of a puzzle: was he to be embraced as a naturalised Englishman, or suspected for republican sentiments? We had recently survived a second war with our former Colonies, and to my certain knowledge the British Crown had reason to thank the American: he had helped retrieve the stolen peace treaty that ended hostilities between our two nations. I had been so fortunate as to aid him a little in this extraordinary endeavour. We met at the great country home of the Chute family, The Vyne, in Hampshire last Christmas—and our joint pursuit of a traitor and a murderer had taught me to hold Raphael West in the highest esteem. He was not a simple person, to be sure, and not easy to know; but his character rewarded study. We had not encountered one another in the long months since parting in Hampshire, but he had often invaded my thoughts. As I observed his dark head bent towards the clerk at Hatchard's, I was forced to summon every shred of composure at my command. "I am afraid you will have to wait a few months longer, sir, for the enjoyment of that lady's wit," I said smoothly as I walked towards him. "I have it on excellent authority that the printers are sadly behindhand, and publication delayed."

"Do you know . . ." He broke off at the sight of my face. "*Jane.* Miss Austen! I had no notion you were in London. I—"

"Mr. West." I curtseyed, my pulse a trifle tumultuous.

He bowed. His countenance had flushed to the roots of his dark hair. He did not meet me with indifference, then. Or was this merely embarrassment at being discovered in the solicitation of a *novel*? He had not disguised his appreciation for my pen when we first scraped acquaintance, last Christmas at The Vyne.

"How long have you been in Town?" He stepped aside from the clerk's counter, drawing me with him. The touch of his fingers on my arm; the force of his gaze.

I dropped my own. "Four weeks, perhaps."

"How did I never come to meet you here? Do you move in Society at all?"

"I might have done—but my brother has been lately ill, and I have been attending him."

"Mr. James Austen is also in London?"

I smiled faintly; it was natural for West to think at once of James. He had known only my least favourite brother.

"I speak of Mr. Henry Austen. I am staying at his home near Knightsbridge." Recovering myself a little, I raised my eyes to his. They were dark and piercing, a challenge to inner peace. "You are well, I hope?"

Impossible to utter aught but banalities, when one yearned to know a thousand things at once. Did he suffer similar confusion? Or was my stumbling tongue a failing of my own? He certainly gazed at me most earnestly, but so had he ever done. The inscrutable look of Mr. Raphael West could penetrate the soul. He was an artist, bent on seizing the likeness of every face on the canvas of his mind.

"Very well, I thank you," he said.

"And your father? Mr. Benjamin West is as yet in health?"

"Indeed—and painting what may be perhaps his greatest work. *Buonaparte Fleeing the Field of Waterloo.* You must see it one day, in his atelier in Newman Street."

The publick are always welcome to enter Mr. Benjamin West's rooms, for a trifling fee, when he exhibits a painting. I had done so myself, on two occasions—but I had not then been acquainted with the son. Now the casual invitation brought the colour to my cheeks and confusion to my brain. Did West wish me to meet his family?

Nonsense. I refined far too much on far too little.

"I shall hope to do so. Is the work much advanced?"

"Nearly completed. He has been awaiting the return of the Duke of Wellington from France—for naturally no rout of Buonaparte is possible without the image of Old Douro."*

West often made preliminary drawings of his father's subjects,

* This was a common nickname for the Duke of Wellington, derived from his previous title—Marquis of Douro—and the valley in Portugal from which the title came.—*Editor's note.*

I knew—indeed, it was on just such an errand that we had met last year. But the Duke . . . I recalled that imperious profile from the Blue Anteroom. "Do not tell me *you* were the painter at Carlton House yesterday?"

"I was certainly there, attempting to sketch the Prince Regent." His voice fell to a more intimate level. "My father cannot bear His Royal Highness, I'm afraid, and he demands to be placed *in cameo* in the clouds above the battlefield, like an archangel presiding over victory. But how did you know?"

"I also was at Carlton House—being conducted through the rooms by the Royal Librarian. I was told His Highness was closeted with a painter. I never dreamt it might be you—and was not at liberty to have enquired after you, had I known the truth. Naturally we should not have looked into the Regent's private apartments, even if he had been at liberty."

"He should have been only too happy of the diversion," West said drily. "A more restless subject I have never encountered. The Duke, on the other hand, is the master of himself—as well as half of Europe."

"Mr. West—" I hesitated, then moved with decision to one of the reading room's chairs. He followed me. "Were you aware that a person expired in the Regent's Library yesterday?"

"I was not," he exclaimed.

"Colonel Ewan MacFarland, of the Scots Greys."

His brow cleared. "The apoplectic fit. I read of it in the papers this morning."

"I discovered him in his last illness."

"How very unfortunate." He raised his hand as tho' to comfort me, then thought better of the intimate gesture. "But I know your strength of mind too well. You will have felt all that must be natural in such a situation, and suppressed it firmly in order to aid the poor man."

"Yes." My gloved hands gripped each other. West was right—I *had* subdued my weaker feelings to a sense of duty, but the memory of the Colonel's helpless struggle haunted me. It was akin to seeing a fowl shot on the wing and plummeting headlong, unable to save itself. "That is why I mentioned it. I—"

There I came to a halt. I had no right to start the hare of rumour coursing through the Metropolis. But I felt convinced that Raphael West might advise me as few others could. In addition to sketching and painting, I knew a little of West's secret life. He sometimes served as a Government *spy*. The ugliness of murder could not shock his sensibilities.

"Does the phrase *Waterloo Map* bear any significance in your mind?"

He frowned at the sudden change of subject. "Other than the map my father consults for the design of his canvas—it does not. Are you in contemplation of a European tour, Miss Austen?"

"Not at all. MacFarland uttered those two words in his last agony." I untied the strings of my reticule and withdrew the folded handkerchief I had retrieved from the Carlton House Library. "Forgive me for offering you soiled linen. I tended to the Colonel's sickness yesterday. When I examined this later, I found—"

He was already peering acutely at the cloth. "Some sort of needles. Are they spruce?"

"I believe they are yew."

His dark eyes met mine. "Yew is a deadly poison. Are you

suggesting these came from MacFarland's stomach? And that you fear . . . that you believe it possible . . ."

"That he was poisoned. Yes."

There was a silence. I was suddenly conscious of our surroundings—the little nothings of a bookstore, the pleasantries of clerk and customer, the enormity of what we two discussed.

"Did you show this to Dr. Matthew Baillie, the Court Physician?" West asked softly.

I shook my head. "I retrieved the handkerchief only after he had left me."

"Then I am afraid it is your duty to return with me to Carlton House at once. If there is a poisoner in the Household—"

"But we cannot be certain the Colonel took poison—if he *did* take poison—under the Regent's roof."

"No. You will agree, however, that Baillie should be the nicest judge of that. The doctor attending MacFarland's death ought to be in possession of all the facts."

West was correct, of course. I had brought out the handkerchief for his examination because I wished to be persuaded by his opinion. Little as I relished inserting myself into the Prince Regent's affairs, a possible death by poisoning so near to His Royal Highness was nothing to ignore.

He was holding out his hand with a speaking glance, impossible to refuse.

"Very well," I said, rising from my chair. "If it must be done, 'twere better 'twere done quickly."

6

A CURIOUS MATHEMATICS

Tuesday, 14 November 1815
23 Hans Place, London, cont'd.

Carlton House fronts Pall Mall just off St James Square, a trifling walk from our position at Hatchard's in Piccadilly. We achieved the distance in a thrice, and I found myself once more halted before the porter at the imposing gates. Today, however, I was escorted by Raphael West, and was swiftly conveyed up the sweep to the noble entrance. The hall was much as it had been yesterday—supported by a phalanx of footmen as well as marble.

"James," West murmured to one of them, "is Dr. Baillie in his rooms?"

I have neglected to say that both the clergyman, Mr. Clarke, and the doctor, Matthew Baillie, are afforded quarters within Carlton House, along with several other professional men in attendance upon the Regent, despite the fact that they maintain lodgings of their own elsewhere in Town. It must be a great convenience on those nights of bad weather, when the importunings of the Prince cannot be overruled, and a comforting presence is commanded by His Royal Highness. The Court Physician in particular must be much in demand.

"He is, sir. Do you wish me to carry him a note?"

"I do," West replied, stepping swiftly to a writing desk in the Great Hall and seizing pen and paper. "You will oblige me by informing Dr. Baillie that Miss Jane Austen awaits him in the Library." He handed a slip of paper to the footman, who bowed and departed in the direction of the Regent's private apartments.

West placed his hand beneath my elbow and drew me swiftly through the octagonal vestibule towards the heart of the great house and its magnificent staircase. "I am required to sketch His Royal Highness once more in a quarter-hour," he murmured, "but we have just time enough for you to show me how it was."

We descended the stairs without attracting the notice of any; indeed, the Regent's halls seemed deserted. Had West not referred to his appointment with His Royal Highness, I should have guessed that the Prince had quitted Carlton House for Brighton, as James Stanier Clarke predicted. The lower level of the residence was similarly bereft of life; and I was unsurprized to discover the Library lit by only two oil lamps, with a modest fire burning in the hearth.

Raphael West allowed me to precede him into the room, and waited for my direction.

"There," I said, gesturing with my gloved hand. "We found the Colonel behind that farthest perpendicular bay, to the left of the centre aisle."

He reached for a lamp and increased the flame a trifle. I led him to the quiet set of bookshelves.

"This room is notorious, I believe, for its irrelevance. Mr.

Clarke assures me that none of the Regent's intimates come here."

West inclined his head.

"So why should MacFarland—a soldier rather than scholar—have sought the comfort of books that morning?" I asked. "Is it not more likely that he was *abandoned* in this secluded bay by his poisoner, so that he might expire undiscovered?"

"We cannot possibly surmise," West replied. "The Colonel might have been an ardent reader. We are strangers to his life and character, as we are to the truth of his end. How did he lie, Jane?"

"On his back. His eyes were fixed on the ceiling and his limbs extended."

"He never moved in the time you observed him?"

"He appeared incapable of it. His arms and legs were extended. They twitched some once or twice. I only understood the degree of his paralysis when he vomited. He was unable to turn his head aside to avoid choking. I knelt down and performed the service for him."

"Which is when your handkerchief was pressed into use."

"Yes. I forgot it in all the bustle of the doctor's examination and the Colonel's removal. I retrieved it later from the reading table, where no doubt a servant placed it. The floor had already been cleaned."

West bent down with his lamp and studied the parquet. "Not a needle to be found."

"Because the Carlton House maids are precise to a pin—or because the yew came from the Colonel's stomach?"

"We cannot say." He rose to his feet and looked at me. "We

require more *facts*, Jane. The simplest truths are obscure to us. At what hour did you visit Carlton House yesterday?"

"Three o'clock. I should judge that Mr. Clarke and I stumbled upon the Colonel at perhaps half-past. There was a tour of the upper floor to be got through before we entered the Library."

"No doubt Clarke conveyed you to the Rose Satin Room. I trust your praise was fulsome."

I smiled faintly.

"It is Mr. Clarke's borrowed plumage," West said carelessly, "spread before the ladies, as my father might exhibit his latest masterpiece."

"Recollect that Clarke was the instrument of Providence," I chided, "in the Colonel's discovery. Had he not invited me to visit this Library, poor MacFarland might not have been found for days."

"But what *did* you find, Jane?" West set the lamp on the nearest reading table. "Was the man poisoned? And if so, how long before you stumbled over him at half-past three? Did MacFarland take his poison at Carlton House—or was he dosed before he arrived here? Finally, and most important—who are the Colonel's intimates, who are his enemies, and which one wished him dead?"

"I beg your pardon," said a voice from the nearest doorway.

I turned and curtseyed. "Doctor Baillie. How good of you to spare me a few moments."

How much had the Court Physician overheard? His looks were austere; there was more of censure than welcome in his countenance.

"Miss Austen. And Mr. Raphael West." The Court Physician

gazed at us severally. "I did not think to find you returned to Carlton House so soon, Miss Austen, much less to this particular spot in the Library. I should have thought the recollections too painful. How may I serve you?"

For an instant, I felt all the absurdity of my interference. Matthew Baillie was everywhere known for a member of the Royal College of Physicians, a skilled and learned healer trained at Edinburgh, a Genius of Medicine. Who was I to question his judgement?

"We require your professional opinion, sir," Raphael West said.

I stepped forward and placed my soiled handkerchief in the doctor's hand. "I tended Colonel MacFarland with this bit of linen during his last illness. I would be grateful if you would examine it."

Baillie unfolded the handkerchief. Then he walked over to the reading table and held the cloth near the lamplight. Perhaps half a minute passed in silence—which may seem an eternity when the seconds are reckoned one by one.

"Yew." The doctor raised the linen to his nostrils and sniffed. When he turned to face us again, his brows were knit and his expression stormy. "That explains a good deal that has made me uneasy. But God in Heaven! The scandal you would raise, Miss Austen! Poison in the Regent's household!"

"He might have taken it elsewhere," West suggested.

"Yew does not require above a few hours to act," Baillie countered. "I enjoyed a nuncheon with MacFarland myself, at two o'clock, in the Blue Velvet Room—a light repast in honour of the Duke of Wellington's visit. The Colonel was then entirely well."

"Was it a large party?" West enquired.

The doctor shook his head. "Some dozen gentlemen were present, and Lady Frances Wedderburn Webster."

This was the famous blond beauty I had glimpsed in conversation with Wellington; she was rumoured to be the Duke's latest flirt. The fact that both parties were married made the liaison excusable, in the eyes of the Fashionable World.

"I next saw MacFarland on this floor," Baillie concluded.

He had refrained from naming the nuncheon guests; I could not blame him. It was a delicate matter to expose the Regent's intimates. But it would have to be done, if poison were at issue.

"I will be forced to anatomise MacFarland now," the doctor mused, as tho' his thoughts ran with mine. "The contents of the stomach will be decisive. If there is indeed a madman in Carlton House—if it is a matter of *murder* . . ."

There. He had uttered the word aloud.

"Suicide is not to be thought of?" Raphael West asked.

"I should have said the Colonel had everything to live for," Baillie replied simply. "He was a Hero, recollect."

I met West's eyes. *How had he earned that honour?* And might one man's reputation be another man's shame?

The doctor sighed heavily and tucked my handkerchief into his coat. "MacFarland's body lies in Keppel Street, where he held lodgings. He was to be buried tomorrow."

"Has he any family?" I asked.

"A sister, I believe. She served as his housekeeper. She will be most distressed to learn of the anatomisation—as she must. I will be required to take the body from her rooms to St George's Hospital."

"There is no other way?" I asked impulsively.

Baillie shook his head. "I should be thankful MacFarland is not already in his grave."

RAPHAEL WEST MADE HIS *adieux* and departed for his appointment with His Royal Highness, but not before he had thought of my comfort.

"I may not stay," he said hurriedly. "Indeed, I have tarried already too long, and the Regent will be exclaiming at my lateness. May I summon a footman to contrive a hackney, for your return to Hans Place?"

"There is no need," Matthew Baillie interjected. "I shall be happy to escort Miss Austen above-stairs. I wish to enquire after her brother. He has recently been my patient."

"Very well." With one serious, speaking look and a bow over my hand, Mr. West was away—and left me wondering when I should see him again.

I adjusted my gloves and reticule, and turned to Dr. Baillie. Far from being eager to carry me to the door, however, he appeared lost in the most sombre reflections. Having placed the handkerchief in the proper hands, I had relieved myself of a burdensome care—but had increased the doctor's immeasurably. As Court Physician, his reputation, career, and honour depended upon the safeguarding of the Prince's health; and if a poisoner were at work in Carlton House, Baillie's whole future might turn upon the outcome.

"Colonel MacFarland spoke to you in his last moments, Miss Austen," he said.

"To the extent that he was able."

"*Waterloo map.*" So Baillie had not forgot the odd phrase. "I find it extraordinary that *in extremis* he failed to mention he was poisoned—if indeed he was so?"

"Perhaps he was ignorant of his end, or its cause," I suggested. "But he was most urgent in uttering those two words. I remain convinced the communication was vital to him." My eyes strayed over the bookshelves in the secluded bay. "You were a little acquainted with the Colonel, I think? Should you have called him a bookish man?"

"One of courage and action, rather."

"Then why should he be discovered in a room rarely frequented by the Regent's intimates?"

Baillie's eyebrows rose. "That is a point, indeed. I had thought him engrossed in conversation with fellow soldiers yesterday, after our nuncheon was ended."

"It was a military grouping, then?"

Baillie hesitated. "Some two or three fellows from the Waterloo campaign were certainly present, in deference to the Duke of Wellington, and the Regent's passion for art. Mr. Benjamin West is to undertake a canvas—on the scale of his *Death of Nelson,* tho' with a less melancholy subject. But you will know this already, as a friend of Mr. Raphael West's."

This was the doctor's modest attempt to learn how well acquainted I might be with the West family; but I merely inclined my head. "You can think of no reason why Colonel MacFarland might have descended to the Library under his own power?"

"Perhaps he engaged to meet someone here for a private tête-à-tête."

"—And the poison already active in his body, he was then incapable of quitting the room," I said thoughtfully. "Why this bay, in particular? Was his helpless form deposited here by his killer? Or did he succumb to illness in this spot for a reason?"

The doctor's eyes, like mine, strayed over the Prince's volumes. Uniform in their elegant leather bindings, they betrayed a meticulous household: feather dusters had skimmed the spines with a regularity that might depress the most ardent reader. The perfect symmetry of the shelves suggested that no careless forefinger or thumb had disturbed its alignment for years.

Except—

Baillie and I leaned forward at the same instant. At the far end of the bottom shelf one spine was pulled out. The perpendicular shadows between wall and bay had nearly disguised the irregularity.

The doctor slipped the book from its place and turned it over in his hands. "*Pensées Politiques,* by Louis Philippe, Comte de Ségur. Do you read French, Miss Austen? I confess I cannot."

"A little." I took the proffered volume. "Did Colonel MacFarland, I wonder?"

To any woman who claims to have followed the unnatural course of the Monster in Paris—and with two brothers engaged in battle against Buonaparte, how could I do otherwise?—the name of Ségur must be familiar. It is a noble family, and a military one, Louis Philippe being the patriarch and a field marshal. His portrait showed a clever fellow, with deviously arched brows and a long nose. He had survived Madame Guillotine *and* Napoleon. A diplomat, therefore. But what Frenchman is not?

I rifled through the pages idly, muttering chapter headings

under my breath. I have not studied French very industriously, but my frequent visits to Henry's household—where in early years Manon was ignorant of English, and the late Eliza was constantly chattering to the maid in her native tongue—forced me to acquire a bit of the language. Eliza often employed it, moreover, in letters when she wished to communicate anything of a confidential nature; my mother and sister might safely read her missives without stumbling on our secrets. I read French better than I speak it.

One of the book's leaves came loose—and fluttered to my feet.

Dr. Baillie bent to retrieve it. "A watercolour drawing! How odd. Indeed, one might almost call it . . . a *map*. But I cannot make out that it is of Waterloo. Did Ségur have to do with Russia?"

"He may once have been ambassador there." I glanced frowningly at the paper the doctor held. It was of the sort used in artist's sketches, such as I remembered Raphael West employing, tho' soiled and much creased. The underlying charcoal was lightly drawn, with an effortlessness that argued a master; the wash of colour laid down on top was equally sure and true. A suggestion of hills; a clutch of Asiatic domes and the symbol of a cross; a trail that must signify a road. Smudges of trees in winter snow. The ancient features of an Eastern icon.

"How lovely," I said. "But what do the sketches signify?"

A few points were labelled in a copperplate hand. *Moscow. Smolensk.* And then, in the lower corner, I espied a minute series of numbers. 143. 87. 92. 1055. 36. 823. . . . They continued, seemingly at random, for several lines.

A curious mathematics.

"Observe the rents in the paper," Baillie said.

The drawing was pierced as by a knife-blade in each of four quarters. The slits were stained rusty red. I traced one with my fingertip and felt a chill rise along my spine.

"The map was folded within the bearer's coat," I observed. "—After which he was stabbed, and the paper taken from him."

"But what does it mean?" Baillie demanded. "And how did it come to be in the Regent's Library?"

"Perhaps MacFarland put it here."

"Or knew of its existence—and was on the point of retrieving it," the doctor returned.

Impossible to say. I turned over the drawing, searching for its author's signature. I found none. "There are words written on the reverse," I said. "In French."

The ink had faded and the script was so hurried as to be almost illegible. I carried the paper to the Library table and the light of the oil lamp.

La Belle Alliance
17 Juin 1815
Ma chère,

Si tu lis ceçi, alors je suis mort au service de l'empereur. Gardez cette lettre en toute sécurité; il en aura besoin un jour bientôt. Oh, mon Dieu, que je t'aurais embrassée une dernière fois—mon amour.

Charles

"Can you make it out, Miss Austen?"

I glanced at Baillie. "It is a soldier's last note to his lady. He abjures her to keep it safe, because the Emperor will need it one day." I saw no reason to translate the final cry from the dead man's heart—*oh, God, that I might have kissed you one last time, my love.* "It was written from La Belle Alliance. Is that not what the Prussians call—"

"Waterloo," Baillie said.

7

PROOF OF THE PUDDING

Tuesday, 14 November 1815
23 Hans Place, London, cont'd.

The Court Physician delivered me to the Carlton House porter, who immediately summoned a hackney from Pall Mall.

"I will not beg your silence on this matter," Baillie said in a lowered tone as he stood by the coach door. "I think too highly of your discretion and understanding, Miss Austen. You will know how damaging a rumour may be—particularly when it concerns the security of the Regent."

"You may trust my discretion," I replied, "provided you inform me of the results of your anatomisation."

The doctor looked a trifle shocked. Few ladies could wish to refer to so gruesome a matter as a man's dissection; but where my mind was engaged, I was prepared to argue terms. Baillie had kept the interesting map for further study, my claims on Carlton House were slight, and unless I were forthright, I should be reduced to tricks and stratagems to learn anything more.

"Very well," he said. "Commend me to your brother."

He shut the hackney door, and I bowled away down the sweep conscious of my dignity. There are few who call at the Regent's residence in any but private carriages; but at least, today, I was not sodden with rain.

I DESCENDED FROM MY hackney to a Hans Place given over to all the bustle of arrival. My dear brother Edward has despatched his beloved daughter Fanny from the comforts of her native Kent to the dreariness of November in London, so that she might share in my care of Henry! Imagine my delight at discovering an elegant female of two-and-twenty, in a ravishing pelisse of sable and merino wool, with an upturned poke to her cerise bonnet that perfectly framed her dusky curls. Not since the loss of our dear Eliza has Henry's home known such good *ton*.

"Aunt Jane!" she cried as we two embraced over a quantity of bandboxes. "I was taught to believe my uncle was at death's door, and it is all a hum! He is going on famously, but we shall not breathe a word to Papa—else my scheme of staying at *least* a fortnight in Town shall be blasted. Promise me we shall walk out every day to Gunter's and Hatchard's!"

I kissed her cheek, and promised her anything and everything she might wish, so happy was I at the sight of her blooming looks—for Fanny has suffered a succession of disappointments in recent months. Her early clutch of handsome and prosperous suitors—the charming sons of Kentish neighbours she has known from infancy—have nearly deserted her, for more permanent loves or the pursuits of career and intellect. The halcyon days of nineteen, when all the world seemed one long hunting-party or race-meeting, have given way to the sober quiet of a diminished household and circle. Her little brothers are gone off to school; her sisters are straining at the governess's leash. Fanny has left girlhood behind, with all its promise of romance, and fears she is now on the shelf.

On the shelf. It is a phrase I dreaded myself at twenty; now nearly forty, I have other pleasures to recompense for the loss of a love-match and children. But I would not wish Fanny a similar fate. She was reared almost as wonderfully as my spoilt Emma Woodhouse: with every desire satisfied, every whim indulged, every possible compliment bestowed. All she lacks is real happiness.

"How are all the Godmersham family?" I stripped off my gloves and loosened my bonnet strings. "Your brothers at Oxford—thriving?"

"The Michaelmas term is nearly at an end," she replied, "and my brothers will be with us at Christmas. We are all very well. My father has been busy in his preserves. He has sent an embarrassment of fowl in my post-chaise, in the conviction that Uncle Henry cannot get anything so good in London. Madame Bigeon has already taken the basket to the kitchens. We shall live on nothing but pheasant, I declare!"

As the hall was littered with Fanny's belongings—not excepting the massive and silk-shrouded shape of the harp she had insisted upon conveying from Godmersham, like a travelling-companion propped up in the seat opposite—I thought it just as well that some part of her luggage was meant for Henry. Did she remain in Hans Place longer than a fortnight, he should be forced to throw out an addition to the rear of the house to accommodate her missishness.

Still, I beamed as I helped her out of her becoming pelisse. And for the remainder of the evening, I banished all thoughts of poison, maps—and murder.

23 Hans Place, London
Wednesday, 15 November, 1815

OVER OUR TEA AND toast this morning, Fanny made a quantity of plans for her day. She looked exceedingly pretty in a walking dress of green French twill, worked in gold thread. Manon had dressed her curls with gold ribbon.

"I am sure you will like to look into the theatre whilst you are here," I said, "and Henry has a subscription to a series of concerts. As he cannot use the seats in his present condition, I know of no reason why *we* may not. It is so much more pleasant to venture out of an evening with a gentleman in attendance, however—perhaps we may prevail upon Mr. Haden to accompany us."

"Mr. Haden?" Fanny returned quickly.

"One of your Uncle Henry's doctors, a most gentleman-like man. Have you any desire to call on your little cousins in Keppel Street, whilst you are in Town?" I enquired. "I must do so—indeed, only your uncle's illness has prevented me, up to this point—but you need not."

My brother Charles's daughters are being reared by their maternal aunt here in London whilst he, a post-captain in the Royal Navy, serves on the Mediterranean Station. Having lost their mamma but a year since, Cassie and Harriet and young

Fanny are grown pale and solemn, with occasional bursts of temper or tears. I am so little acquainted with the girls that I hardly know what to say to them; and I confess that the grown-up Fanny's ease with children would prove helpful in any social call.

"My time is hardly my own, Aunt, for all the demands I must answer," she said. "You will know that Goodnestone has sent in its lists. I am required to purchase enough ells of purple silk for Eleanor's next ballgown. *Purple*, Aunt!"

The colour was all the rage last year in France. Purple was a royal colour; and violets bloomed in the spring. The shade was associated with Buonaparte's return—ladies who loved the Emperor wore it, to show their faith that Napoleon would return from exile with the violets. As was so often the case, French fashion took a year to cross the Channel—and now every English girl was wild for purple, when Napoleon would never come again.

Eleanor Bridges is Fanny's cousin on her late mother's side. The Bridgeses live within a morning's ride of Godmersham at the neighbouring estate of Goodnestone, and I hope they always shall. But for such a commission as Eleanor's, there could be only one recourse, and I could not like it.

"That will mean Grafton House," I sighed, "in all its misery. If we are not arrived there well before eleven o'clock, we will languish in the crush for a tedious interval until a clerk deigns to notice us. Although, upon further thought, nobody could help noticing *you,* my dear Fanny—and so I suppose we shall be whisked to the counter without the slightest hesitation whenever we chuse to appear. It is otherwise with spinsters of forty, I assure you."

"Pish," she retorted. "You will not be forty for another month at least. I am required to buy a dozen pairs of silk stockings as well, and spangled trim for an evening cloak, and a dozen ells of white linen suitable for gentlemen's shirts. And if I happen upon a *very* fetching bonnet, I am to write the particulars immediately, so that Eleanor may decide whether to purchase it. Good Lord! We shall not accomplish half these commissions in a fortnight!"

"Must we set out today?" I said plaintively. "I am meant to be proofing Mr. Murray's *sheets.* That is what he calls his typeset pages, you know—only none have as yet appeared from the printer. I am in great hopes they will arrive this morning."

Fanny's cheeks turned pink. "Uncle Henry tells me that you have resolved to dedicate *Emma* to the Prince Regent. That is very dashing of you, is it not? It is one thing to admit to authorship—which I heartily approve, I am a firm believer that one should own to one's Genius, if one is so fortunate as to possess any. But to claim the notice of the *Prince Regent,* Aunt! All of London will be setting you up as his latest flirt."

"Bother your Uncle Henry," I said testily. "He cannot be trusted with a word. I dare swear my life was more peaceful when he was lost in fever. But you remind me that I must enquire of Mr. James Stanier Clarke whether his invitation arose from a *personal* enthusiasm of the moment or a definite instruction on the part of His Royal Highness. I should neither wish to appear presumptuous—"

"—If HRH knows nothing at all about Mr. Clarke's admiration for Miss Austen," Fanny supplied.

"—Nor *ungrateful,* if the little man conveyed a Royal command."

"Ticklish," Fanny observed.

I told her then of my visit to Carlton House, and the oddities of Mr. Clarke's manners and conversation. My account was interrupted, however, when Manon appeared in the breakfast parlour with the morning post. There were two letters for me—one from my sister, Cassandra, and another whose fist I did not recognise. I set them aside in deference to Fanny, but she rose immediately from her place.

"Do not consider of your tiresome niece," she told me cordially. "I have quite finished my breakfast, and will regale Uncle Henry with news of his Kentish acquaintance whilst you enjoy your post."

Cassandra must always take pride of place in any clutch of correspondence, and rewarded me, as Cass usually does, with stories of my mother's nerves and the cunningness of little Herbert, my brother Frank's infant son, born only last week. Frank and his wife, Mary, are at present leasing Chawton Great House from my brother Edward—tho' with Frank at sea, how Mary contrives to manage such a large household, particularly whilst enduring her sixth lying-in, is a wonder to us all. Cassandra tells me, however, that she goes on very well, gaining in strength every day; tho' she shall never, perhaps, recover her fleeting girlhood prettiness.

The second note was brief to the point of rudeness.

Dear Madam:

I have concluded beyond doubt that Colonel Ewan MacFarland expired after ingesting a fatal dose of yew. Whether he did so by accident or design, I know not.

Every effort shall be made to identify the poison's source and its method of administration.

I trust you are satisfied. I rely upon your strict discretion.

Baillie

I must suppose that a gentleman deprived of sleep for the better part of the night, due to the exigencies of anatomisation, may be forgiven a certain brusqueness; but his dismissal was plain. I should hear nothing further from the Court Physician of MacFarland's death, nor of the Waterloo Map.

The doctor's lack of cordiality, however, could not dissuade me from pursuing the affair. *The Colonel was indeed poisoned.* I had been correct in my suspicions—and in my decision to show Baillie my soiled handkerchief. Unless MacFarland had taken the yew himself—which Baillie thought unlikely—he had almost certainly been murdered at Carlton House.

Was his body even now being returned to his unfortunate sister? Would he be buried quietly tomorrow, and with him, all hint of unpleasant scandal in the Regent's household?

"Uncle Henry has asked me to read the *Sporting News* to him, Aunt," Fanny said as she reappeared in the doorway, "if you have no objection. I apprehend that most journals are forbidden."

"It will do Henry a world of good," I said, "to be hearing of horseflesh and prizes; only I hope that you are not bored senseless."

"I often perform a similar service for my father, and I daresay I am as well-acquainted with the Derby, the Oaks, and the St

Leger as any girl now living. If you have no objection, I shall put off the call in Keppel Street until another morning."

"By all means, my dear."

Keppel Street. I was suddenly alive to the name. My brother Charles's little girls lived there, it is true—but so, once, did Ewan MacFarland. His grieving sister remained in his lodgings. Perhaps I should find *one* social duty less burdensome, did I unite it with another.

8

A CALL OF CONDOLENCE

Wednesday, 15 November 1815
23 Hans Place, London, cont'd.

Keppel Street lies in Bloomsbury just north of the British Museum. It offers a modest row of houses to left and right, running only a single block in length. These are the sort of respectable homes that once characterised all of London, before the mania for flamboyant terraces seized the populace. Not far away, Russell Square's brash new buildings sprout like mushrooms, but here there are no wrought iron gates; no tradesmen's entrances; no enclosed grounds landscaped by Repton in a picturesque stile that suggests an Italian ruin. It says much for the quiet respectability of the Palmer family that they settled in Keppel Street.

Charles's bride was reared in Bermuda—her father was formerly Governor-General of the island—and she had always the frail looks of a girl whose constitution was strained by the Tropics. That she died at the age of four-and-twenty, along with her fourth infant, is not to be wondered at. Her daughters will be raised in all the rains and fogs of London, and I hope shall be the hardier for it; tho' I could wish them the occasional respite of summer visits to Chawton.

I had brought a small present for Cassie and Harriet, the two eldest girls—a diminutive book I had made myself, of several squares of paper folded and stitched down the middle. I had decorated the pages with pictures and simple rhymes, composed in my neatest hand. I am at something of a loss when it comes to playing with nieces—a nephew may always be charmed by a cricket bat or a swift game of skittles; but girls are quieter creatures. Due to Henry's illness, I had lacked the time to fashion doll's clothes. I carried the book in my reticule, along with a coin purse, a clean handkerchief, and a spare needle of thread.

I was admitted immediately by the housekeeper, a kind old lady called Mrs. Parfitt, who informed me, to my dismay, that all the Palmers were gone out—the little girls being required to consult a dentist, and Miss Palmer's presence necessary to subdue them to the terror. I therefore left my card, to be examined upon their return, and promised that I should call again before quitting London.

"How you ladies do flit about, to be sure, ma'am," Mrs. Parfitt said. "London and Hampshire and everywhere in between! I never set foot out of Bloomsbury until I was fourteen—and that was only to go into service in Mount Street. With everything so strange, I cried myself to sleep each night; but I soon became accustomed, and I suppose it's the same with these poor mites. Nearly a year they've been here, and very little unhappiness there is now, and Miss Cassie growing into such a fine, big girl, what with no longer being seasick."

"I'm glad to hear it, Mrs. Parfitt." I paused at the door. "I suppose, being a native of these parts, you know everyone in Keppel Street?"

"Not to say as *acquainted,*" she said cautiously, "but I'm sure to know their servants."

"I learnt recently that a Hampshire friend of mine lives nearby," I assayed, "and is but lately bereaved. I should like to pay my respects, but I do not know the lady's direction. Her name is MacFarland."

Mrs. Parfitt's seamed face pursed into a tight bud. "That'll be Miss Georgiana," she said, "and her handsome soldier of a brother. Cavalry, he was, and rode straight at the French guns, they say. Didn't serve him much, did it, to brush through Waterloo only to die of a fit? And him so hearty, seemingly. His batman, Spence, works as butler now at number thirty-seven, and told me all about it. Bowled over, he was, at his master's death. Went through the Peninsula together."

"Number thirty-seven?"

"Miss MacFarland's house, as was her father's before her." Mrs. Parfitt tossed her head at the street. "The Colonel inherited back in '13, and with Boney gone I thought we'd have the two of them here right and tight. But I can't see Miss MacFarland sticking it now, without her brother."

I thanked the good woman and heard the Palmers' door close carefully behind me as I descended the three steps to the paving. There I hesitated, glancing up and down until I located No. 37 opposite. It was quite obviously a house in mourning. No hatchment was suspended over the front door, but the knocker was wrapped in black bombazine. The street-front curtains were drawn.

As I studied the façade, a low-slung sporting curricle with a showy pair of greys pulled up before the door. The driver handed the reins to his groom and, with some difficulty, descended to the flags. He was a smartly-dressed gentleman in a high-crowned beaver and a driving coat with numerous capes—but betrayed a decided limp. He employed a polished Malacca cane to mount the steps of No. 37. As he raised the muffled knocker, I hastened across Keppel Street.

"I beg your pardon, sir," I called out, "but is this the home of Miss MacFarland?"

He turned—and presented a far younger countenance than I expected. A gentleman not much above five-and-twenty, I should say, despite the lines of care and pain etched in his forehead.

"It is." His eyes swept my figure and concluded I was a gentlewoman. "But I am uncertain whether Miss MacFarland is at home to callers."

He spoke with the hard assurance of one who could *not* be barred, auguring a special relationship to the lady.

"Then perhaps I may leave my card," I suggested.

"Very well." He grasped the knocker and allowed it to fall once. "Walk them, Kelley," he ordered his groom, "if I am not returned in a quarter-hour."

Kelley touched his cap.

The front door was drawn open.

A short, bandy-legged man with the sharp eyes of a robin surveyed us. "Lieutenant," he said in acknowledgement, and then stared enquiringly at me.

"Miss Austen," I supplied. "I am come to condole with Miss MacFarland."

He took my proffered card and glared at it. "The mistress ain't equal to it. You come along inside, Lieutenant. She's upstairs in the parlour."

"Thank you, Spence." The gentleman thrust himself over the threshold with his cane. The manservant grasped his arm with familiar ease and said, "Steady as she goes."

In a moment he would shut the door.

"Pray inform Miss MacFarland," I said to the two men's backs, "that I discovered her brother in his final illness. If she should wish to speak with me, she may call at number twenty-three, Hans Place."

"*Spence.*"

A brittle voice, strained to breaking-point. The speaker was as yet unseen at the head of the stairs.

The manservant and the Lieutenant halted in their laboured advance.

"Who is there? Who has come to call, Spence?"

"A lady," the fellow returned, "as says she found the Colonel."

"Show her up at once."

"Are you quite sure, Georgiana?" the Lieutenant asked.

"What a foolish question. Have I ever failed to know my own mind? Do not coddle me, James!"

"Very well." He stepped farther into the hall so that I might enter, his gaze sharp with anxiety.

"Tho' if you *did* find the Colonel," Spence muttered, "why in damnation didn't you summon me or *her*? We might've watched with him to the end, and said our last—"

Some hint of my ignorance must have shewn on my face, for his own darkened with frustration. He turned abruptly and strode down the passage, vanishing through a green baize door.

"I must beg you to precede me up the stairs, Miss Austen," the Lieutenant said. "My right leg requires a degree of consideration that should make any passage *behind* me unconscionably tedious."

I submitted to his direction, and ascended under the stony gaze of a young woman gowned entirely in black. We two stood in silence at the stairs' head whilst the Lieutenant made his painful way upwards. When he had bullied himself over the final step, she allowed him an instant to draw breath, and then looked directly into my face.

"I am Georgiana MacFarland. You knew my brother?"

"Not at all," I admitted. "I merely happened upon him lying in the Library at Carlton House where he was taken ill, and tended him briefly before the physician arrived."

"Baillie," she said with profound contempt. "A physician! A ghoul, more like!"

"Georgie," the Lieutenant said warningly.

"What right had he to carry Ewan's body from this house, James? Even in death my dear one is taken from me. I am not even permitted to mourn. And for what? *Natural philosophy.*"

So Baillie had told Miss MacFarland nothing of poison when he removed the Colonel to St George's. He had let her believe that he anatomised her brother solely from curiosity about his death. I must tread carefully. The lady's loss was deep enough; to learn from a stranger that it might be suicide or murder should only sharpen her pain.

"Miss Austen," said the gentleman by my side, "we hardly meet you with politeness. Pray forgive our rough treatment; it arises solely from grief."

As tho' recalled to a sense of duty, Miss MacFarland led the way to a neat parlour done up in straw-coloured silk and draped in dark blue. An oil lamp burnt low by the fire; with the curtains drawn, the atmosphere was funereal.

"Allow me to introduce myself," the Lieutenant said. "I am James Dunross, late of the Scots Greys."

He bowed; I curtseyed. A cavalry officer, serving under MacFarland—but recently sold out, from his unmilitary dress. A prosperous fellow enough, to judge by appearances; the younger son of a nobleman, perhaps, with neither need nor desire to persist in a soldier's life. His game leg, too, had probably urged retirement from active service.

Had he suffered his wound at Waterloo?

"Pray sit down," Miss MacFarland said.

I took one of the straw-coloured chairs; Dunross seated himself in another. The lady held pride of place on the sopha, her bearing erect and her face unstained by tears. She was not to be trifled with.

I launched immediately into speech. "I am sure you are wondering why I am come—"

"Say rather that I am thankful for it," she interjected. "We learnt of my brother's illness only with his death. It is incomprehensible to me that neither Baillie nor anyone at Carlton House thought to send word of the fit—we might have expected that much consideration from Ewan's friends."

"They are all too accustomed to battle, Georgie," Dunross

said. "Better at writing letters of condolence, than a summons to a bedside."

"And in the Colonel's case," I added, "there was perhaps too little time."

"You say you found him in the Library?"

"I did. Are you familiar with Carlton House, Miss MacFarland?"

"I should as soon be familiar with a brothel."

This was frankness indeed.

"I had never entered it before Monday," I supplied, "but was obliged to call upon the Royal Librarian, Mr. James Stanier Clarke. He was so good as to escort me through the Regent's principal rooms. We had only entered the Library when a slight noise led us to your brother's position. He was already lying on the floor, in the throes of his illness. Mr. Clarke summoned the doctor whilst I attempted to aid your brother."

"Was he in pain?" she asked.

I shook my head. "He suffered some nausea. But I do not think he felt much. Indeed, his limbs appeared nerveless. I assisted him to turn his head, and tended him with my handkerchief."

"You are very good," she said unsteadily. "It is something to know that he did not pass from this life without a woman's comfort—without some apprehension of kindness. That must sustain me."

"Did he speak at all?" Dunross enquired. He leaned forward in his chair, his aspect intent. A feather of warning wafted along my spine; but it was for this I had ventured into Keppel Street: to learn something of Colonel MacFarland, of his life and associates, and perhaps some hint of why he had died.

"Two words only," I told Dunross. "Waterloo Map."

He frowned and sank back against his chair.

"I beg your pardon?" Miss MacFarland said.

"I cannot explain it. But, I assure you, those were his words."

Of the charcoal and watercolour sketch, I said nothing. I could not produce it for inspection; could not say whether it had ever been in the Colonel's possession; could not even state with certainty its present fate.

"You are confident that is what he said?" Dunross demanded. "Nothing else?"

"That was all. The force of the fit eventually prevented all speech. Doctor Baillie once appearing," I concluded, "your brother was carried to greater comfort, Miss MacFarland. Mr. Clarke gave him Absolution, and within a quarter-hour, he expired."

"So Baillie told us," she replied. "It was he who brought the news of Ewan's death. But I had hoped . . . that is to say, I had wondered . . . if my brother had imparted anything of *significance* in his final moments. But as he did not, I must assume his thoughts were far from his friends and family. It is all so strange!"

She rose and walked in a hunted manner towards the mantel, grasping it with one thin hand. I guessed she endeavoured to master her emotions, her back firmly to her company; not for Miss MacFarland the black-bordered handkerchief pressed to the eyes. I ought to have taken my leave; but I maintained a conscious stupidity. Thus far, all the intelligence had been mine to give, and hers to conceal.

"I *did* wonder whether the Colonel's final words had any

connexion to his valour on the field at Waterloo." I looked at the Lieutenant rather than my hostess's rigid form. "I have heard him described as a Hero. Would it trouble you to speak of him—or might I persuade you to recount his actions on that glorious day?"

There was the briefest pause.

"James?" Miss MacFarland queried in a lowered tone, her gaze fixed on the glowing coals.

"My dear," he replied.

"Will it distress you?"

"Naturally. But as I expect to be hearing of Waterloo for the rest of my life, I had as well become accustomed." The Lieutenant's aspect was light, but his voice betrayed his distaste. "I should not use the word *glory*, however, to describe it. *Carnage* is more apt."

"No," Miss MacFarland protested. She turned impulsively to face us. "It shall *always* be a day of glory to me, because you and Ewan were spared! I cannot tell you how incomprehensible it is, Miss Austen, that my brother survived that battle—only to end in the fashionable desert of Carlton House. Incomprehensible!"

"The Colonel belonged to the Scots Greys, I believe?"

"He began military life in a hussar regiment, and saw years of active service in the Peninsula; but being better suited to heavy dragoon work, exchanged two years ago into the Greys. That is how we came to be acquainted with Lieutenant Dunross—James served in the regiment under my brother's command."

The gentleman forced himself heavily to his feet, and crossed with the aid of his cane to the draped window. He pulled aside the dark blue curtain and leaned into the casement, staring expressionlessly down at Keppel Street.

"Are you at all familiar with the course of the battle?" Miss MacFarland asked.

"What little I learnt from published accounts."

"Then you will know that the cavalry was commanded by Lord Uxbridge."

As who did not? Uxbridge had cut a dash among the Great for most of his life: He was an earl as well as a general; head of the Paget family; a darling of the *ton;* and Wellington's reputed enemy. A few years since, Uxbridge ran off with the Duke's sister-in-law, and embarrassed all their acquaintance. Divorce and outrage are nothing new to people of Fashion, however; and tho' Uxbridge and Wellington might not sit down to whist together, once battle was joined with Napoleon, one was in command of the other's cavalry. Some ten brigades, in fact.

"In the early afternoon of that wearing day, Wellington's left was under serious attack from the French batteries," Miss MacFarland said. I collected from her unvaried tone that she had told this story—or heard it told by her brother—many times. "General Picton was killed, and shells were exploding with horrific effect all along the British line. Our troops were giving way under the assault of d'Erlon's columns. Uxbridge saw it as Wellington could not, being far down the right. The Earl threw Lord Edward Somerset and the Household Brigade into the thick of the fight, then galloped off to the Union Brigade. This is composed, as perhaps you may know, of three regiments:

the English, or Royals; the Scots Greys; and the Irish, or Inniskillings."

"Ah," I managed. I had never thought to consider which regiments comprised the Union Brigade.

"Sir William Ponsonby was in command."

Another man of Fashion. The Ponsonbys had spawned Lady Caroline Lamb, one of most outrageous ladies I have ever encountered.

"And above Ponsonby was Uxbridge," I said encouragingly, having got it all straight. "So Somerset and Ponsonby and Uxbridge—who might normally have met peaceably in a ballroom—charged off together on horseback to slaughter the French."

"Indeed. Or, at least, to silence the French gun batteries." Miss MacFarland glanced almost unwillingly at Lieutenant Dunross, but the silent figure by the parlour window gave no sign that he was attending to our conversation.

"The Greys were supposed to be held in reserve," she continued. "But in fact they attacked the longest—well after the Royals and the Inniskillings had given up."

"Of their own volition? —Without waiting for the command to charge?"

"No Scotsmen would be left in the rear whilst the English and Irish attack," Miss MacFarland said proudly. "And, indeed, the Union Brigade succeeded in their object so well that the French were turned."

"For a little while, perhaps," James Dunross tossed over his shoulder. "A half hour, even. But as is so often true in the smoke and confusion of battle, the hunters became the hunted."

"I am sure my brother regarded that charge as having won the day," Miss MacFarland argued.

"So he may have done! But he was wrong, Georgie. The battle was won by Blücher and his Prussians, not the Scots Greys." Dunross turned abruptly from the window and stumped back to us on his cane, his countenance alight with anger. "You must apprehend, Miss Austen, that most of our cavalrymen know nothing of military *science*. Excellent fellows, to be sure—Uxbridge was a hussar in his youth, and could not be called *green*—but we are gentlemen first and soldiers a distant second. What we know of cavalry manoeuvres was learnt on the hunting field. We are apt to get carried away by our own daring, as tho' a confrontation with the French were a day's sport with the Quorn. Which is rather what happened at Waterloo."

I looked all my bewilderment. "You were diverted by a fox?"

"In our enthusiasm to have at Buonaparte, we charged *too far*," Dunross explained, "and then could not get back again to the British lines. Most of us had never been in battle before. Ponsonby was unhorsed—he'd left his best charger in the rear because he could not bear to expose so expensive a mount to enemy fire. When the hack he rode into battle failed him, he was shot dead where he stood. The French cavalry counterattacked with Lancers. Do you know of them?"

I shook my head.

"Quite a new thing in military circles, but utterly terrifying. They carry something like a jousting stick and can stab anything on two or four legs to death. One of them stabbed me as I lay on the ground, unhorsed after that celebrated charge."

"The hunters became the hunted, as you say?"

He smiled thinly. "Our cavalry were broken up, cut off, surrounded, and destroyed."

I glanced at Miss MacFarland. Her expression was grim, as tho' it were physical pain to hear Dunross speak.

"You will admit, James, that the Greys showed the most dramatic charge of all, in the midst of a sunken lane between hedges, where they sabred the French to pieces?" she cried. "You *will admit* that they seized one of Napoleon's Eagles—the most dreadful shame a Frenchman may know?"

"Certainly," he returned. "And then the French threw themselves down and pretended to surrender to us. Being honourless rogues, however, they stood up and fired on us as we approached to disarm them."

She threw up her hands. "I wonder you regard even *my brother* as worthy of your respect!"

"I must," he returned. "I owe him my life. Such as it is."

There was an awkward silence.

"But what did Colonel MacFarland *do*?" I persisted.

"Two thirds of our regiment were killed or wounded in a matter of moments once we fell among the Lancers," Dunross said matter-of-factly. "MacFarland was one of the few who kept his mount and his wits about him. He seized the reins of any riderless horse he met and remounted such men as he saw fleeing on foot. When he came upon me with the lance wound in my hip—when another might have left me for dead—he dismounted and lifted *me* onto his own horse."

I stared at him. "I had understood it was the height of folly to dismount in the midst of a cavalry charge."

"It is," Miss MacFarland broke in, with bitter satisfaction.

"James could not even stand to help himself. Ewan heaved him into the saddle, got his own foot into a stirrup, and clung to his horse's back as they made for the British lines."

"—Until the shuddering blow that struck him to the ground," Dunross murmured. "A French hussar, Miss Austen—his sabre arm strong enough to strip a man from his saddle."

"Good God," I said.

"As Ewan fell, he shouted a command to poor old Mephisto—his charger—that sent me at a gallop to safety."

"And the Colonel?" I asked, breathless and horrified.

"—Was forced to surrender, in the face of almost certain death."

I pressed my fingers to my lips.

"The French officer was a gentleman, however," Miss MacFarland interjected. "He apparently admired my brother's courage. He spared his life—but sent him back through the French lines with three sabre cuts to the head and arm. Ewan barely survived the French retreat."

Only to die in the depths of Carlton House.

I felt new respect for the man I had watched sink into paralysis. What I knew of the French rout after Waterloo was all chaos: pursued by the Prussian Army from the field of battle, abandoning their gear and their wounded, the French officers meant to barter their prisoners and save their own skins. Their men, however—enraged by losses in battle—had hacked the captive English to pieces. Starving, thirsty, and bloodied, the French Army had eventually broken and run for their lives, *sauve qui peut*, whilst their Prussian pursuers cut them down. It had been an ugly scene of swift and pitiless execution.

Which begged a vital question.

"How did the Colonel escape?" I asked.

Miss MacFarland cast me a pitying look. "By his wit and daring, naturally. Such men as my brother do not wait to be *released*, Miss Austen. They see the main chance—and take it."

9

BROTHERS IN ARMS

Wednesday, 15 November 1815
23 Hans Place, London, cont'd.

I could not in good conscience prolong my visit in Keppel Street beyond the recital of MacFarland's heroics, and took my leave soon after. I had learnt much that interested, but little that enlightened me. James Dunross conducted himself towards Miss MacFarland as an affianced lover; yet he seemed more of an irritant than a comfort to the lady. Her grief for her brother had somehow divided them. I could not think that Dunross admired the Colonel, or cherished his memory, in a manner that satisfied his sister. I wondered, too, at her simple explanation of the Colonel's escape: had prowess and courage truly delivered him from French capture? Or was the history more tangled—and did Dunross know it?

What would be the effect of Matthew Baillie's information upon the household? I could not know whether the physician intended to tell Miss MacFarland her brother had been poisoned—possibly murdered. But I could imagine the fury such intelligence must unleash.

Such were the thoughts that chased one another through my head as I followed the manservant, Spence, down to the hall. My new acquaintances had bid me farewell and remained above-stairs, to pursue the rituals of mourning in privacy and peace. Which afforded me the chance to speak to Spence as he approached the front door.

"You were the Colonel's batman in the Peninsula, I believe?"

His brow furrowed; unlike the usual run of London servants, he had not been trained to impassivity. "And the Continent after that," he said. "Going on eight years we fought Boney together, when all's said and done, and if I could've died in the Colonel's place, I'd a-done it."

"Your feeling does you credit. But my friend Mrs. Parfitt taught me to expect a man of character, when she urged me to speak with you."

"Parfitt? You're acquainted with Parfitt?" he returned disbelievingly. "What's housekeeper to the Palmers across the way?"

"My nieces are the Palmers' wards," I explained.

"Not Cap'n Charles's little girls!"

"You are acquainted with my brother?"

"Austen!" He slapped his forehead. "That's where I'd a-heard the name before. I didn't think to connect you with the Cap'n, beggin' yer pardon, ma'am, and it's been a good many months since he's called in Keppel Street. Still cruising off Gibraltar, I'm thinking?"

I agreed that Charles was in the Mediterranean, and having established my respectability in Spence's mind as a woman of military connexions, endeavoured to return the conversation to his late master.

"Had you any hint of illness or . . . or other trouble . . . in the days before the Colonel's sad death?" I enquired.

"Hale as a horse he was," Spence replied. "Slept every night as sound as a baby. Could have knocked me down with a feather when Baillie brung the news. A fit! Never seen the Colonel suffer the like before. And him so cheerful when he left for Carlton House that morning, at being able to speak with Old Douro again. The Duke," he added, for my benefit.

"I see. Then your master appears to have been more fortunate than his friend, Lieutenant Dunross. The poor fellow! It is obvious his every step is an agony. But the Colonel's wounds never pained him? He required no salves or liniments, no powders or laudanum drops?"

Spence shook his head. "Not my master. Came through the battle with a mess of sabre cuts, he did, but they healed something beautiful. Dunross weren't so lucky."

"The Lieutenant's injuries were more grievous, I collect?"

"Aye. That Lancer cut to the bone."

I shuddered sympathetically. "My brother, Captain Charles, has employed camphor salve to good purpose. Do you know whether Lieutenant Dunross has ever tried it?"

"I can't say. The Lieutenant swears by yew, I reckon, like most cavalrymen—what's good for the horse being good for the rider, seemingly."

"I know little of horses," I said.

"Yew's what the stable lads use for a strained hock, in man or beast. Dunross gets it from his groom—says it sets him up something wonderful. You might tell that to Captain Charles."

I had no intention of dosing my poor brother with poison,

but I inclined my head, my thoughts racing. If yew was common in every stable . . .

But Spence was still speaking. "Lucky to have saved his leg at all, the Lieutenant was. But he owes that and his life to my Colonel."

"He must feel enduring gratitude."

Spence smiled crookedly. "I don't know about *enduring*. There are days when life's more of a burden than not. O' course, on Monday him and my Colonel was behaving like old times—before the battle came between 'em. Arm-in-arm as they went down the steps; and that's the last I ever see'd of my master."

His voice cracked and then his lips furled in an expression of belligerence. He glanced up the stairs uneasily, as tho' mindful that he was gossiping with a stranger. But his last words had piqued my interest. *Before the battle came between them.*

"I had not understood Lieutenant Dunross attended the party at Carlton House."

"No more he did," Spence returned with contempt. "Don't chuse to know his old friends in the Greys now he's sold out. Pride, I call it; wounded pride, as much as the wounded leg. Hated to be saved by a man who wouldn't have him to marry his sister."

Indeed?

Why should the Colonel have opposed his sister's marriage to an officer of his own regiment?

"And yet the Lieutenant called here, Monday, and escorted the Colonel," I persisted.

"Dunross meant to stand him a pot of coffee at Gunter's," Spence supplied, "it being in the Colonel's way to Pall Mall."

So MacFarland had drunk something immediately before his arrival at Carlton House. Unfortunate that I could not know the exact hour. I should never have said that Gunter's—which sits in Berkeley Square, west of Pall Mall—was in the Colonel's way from Bloomsbury, to the east; and it was an establishment more properly known for its confections than for the brewing of coffee. Gunter's ices were all the rage among the carriage trade in summer, and certainly it was the habit of Fashionable gentlemen to collect there. "Was the Colonel particularly fond of the place?" I enquired.

Spence shrugged. "He was a rare one for coffee, ever since our days in the Peninsula. He used to say that only I knew how to boil it right. But you'll have noticed that Dunross is a *tonnish* fellow, and nothing would do for him but to take his brew at Gunter's. Thinks it's all the crack to have his pair walked up and down in Berkeley Square whilst he takes his ease."

The choice seemed singular to my mind, nonetheless, and might bear investigation.

A slight sound from above, as of a chair pushed back, brought an expression of wariness to Spence's countenance. He reached immediately for the door.

"My respects to Cap'n Austen, if I may make so bold," he offered. "A brave, good captain by all accounts. And him so recently bereaved of Mrs. Austen."

I pressed a shilling into his palm. "Thank you, Spence. If you should wish to speak with me again, I am at Twenty-three Hans Place."

I hoped he would remember the direction if the words *poison* and *murder* ever came into his house. Particularly as I now knew Lieutenant Dunross swore by liniment made of yew.

IT WAS NEARLY THREE o'clock when my hackney coach drew up in Hans Place. The fitful November clouds had gathered and the light was poor; the peaceful lane was all but deserted. Knife grinders and muffin men were long since departed—only an early lamplighter stood on his ladder, busily tending the lanthorn a few yards from Henry's door. In Hans Place these are still fuelled with whale oil, rather than the modish gas of Mayfair.*

I glanced at the lamplighter—such men are members of the Knightsbridge Watch—but his visage was unfamiliar; and he did not employ the customary urchin to stand at his feet and hand up the oil. We two commanded Hans Place entirely ourselves. I ought to have paid more heed—to my solitude and the oddity of lighting a lamp so early—but I was still full of all I had learnt this morning.

That there was more to Colonel MacFarland's history at Waterloo than even his dearest friends could relate, I was tolerably certain. He had been taken prisoner and forced to retreat among the French lines; had he somehow acquired the interesting sketch—what I persisted in thinking of as the *Waterloo Map*—in the chaos of the final rout?

Of a sudden, I recalled the rusty stains blotting the symmetrical tears in that beguiling drawing. A knife, plunged into

---

* Gas lamps were first demonstrated in Pall Mall in 1807, but gas lighting only spread after an Act of Parliament legislated its use in 1812.—*Editor's note.*

an unknown breast—possibly that of the Frenchman who had signed his last love letter *Charles.*

Had Ewan MacFarland killed him?

And was this how the Colonel had escaped his French captors—by stabbing them to death?

It was silly of me to blench at the idea of cold-blooded murder, from a man who had fought and survived a dreadful battle. MacFarland was a soldier. He had killed many of the French before surrendering. What was it, then, that turned an act of self-defence to one of shame?

The theft of the map. If the Colonel had murdered a man for the contents of his pockets, he was no better than a brigand.

I mounted Henry's stoop and set my hand to the door-pull; behind me, the lamplighter descended to the street. As the last peal of the bell died away, I was struck a stunning blow to the head.

Fiery illuminations burst before my eyes; pain shot through my skull. I crumpled to the cold Portland stone, and knew no more.

10
THE FATE OF MEDDLESOME WOMEN

Wednesday, 15 November 1815
23 Hans Place, London, cont'd.

I can only have been insensible an instant before the front door was pulled wide. Manon shrieked—Henry told me later the sound penetrated several floors to his bedchamber—and bent immediately to drag my limp form over the threshold into the house. She assumed I had fainted, or been seized with the same illness that lately prostrated my brother.

The poor woman lacked sufficient strength to carry me up to the parlour, and to share such a burden with her aged mother must be impossible. Therefore she called loudly for Fanny. As my niece hastened down the stairs, Manon chafed my hands and removed my bonnet, at which I must have groaned with pain. The application of burning feathers beneath my nose, and a wave of Fanny's vinaigrette, brought me sharply to my senses.

"Oh, my head!" I moaned, attempting to thrust myself upright from the floor—and was immediately violently ill.

Manon uttered various imprecations in her native tongue, whilst Fanny murmured her concern. After an interval, the two of them helped me to sit. Manon fetched a tot of brandy, which Fanny administered. When I was at last able to draw breath and speak, she said, "Whatever happened, Aunt?"

"The lamplighter," I said faintly. "He struck me a *bruising* blow."

Fanny looked speakingly at Manon; she thought me out of my wits. After another sip of brandy I allowed her to support me to the anteroom at one side of the hall, where a pair of chairs sat near a table with a bowl intended for the collection of calling-cards; I sank into a seat and cradled my head in my hands as tho' it were a cracked egg.

"I must suppose she tripped and struck her head on the Portland stone," Fanny told Manon. "We must pray that the skull is not broken. Is my uncle's doctor near at hand?"

"Haden," Manon said with decision. "I shall go to him. It is only a step to Sloane Street. But first, the cold compress."

She hurried to the kitchen. I closed my eyes.

"Does it hurt dreadfully, Aunt?" Fanny slipped into the neighbouring chair and made as tho' to smooth my hair. I flinched and grimaced; she withdrew her hand.

Manon reappeared with a basin and cloth. "*Incroyable*," she declared as she gently probed my skull. "It does not bleed—your bonnet saved you that—but, *mon dieu, quelle bosse sur la tête!*"

"Naturally there is a great lump on my head," I retorted crossly. "The lamplighter did not brook his strength. Did he make off with my reticule?"

"I have it here safe." Fanny placed the article on the table. It was a smart silk one netted by my industrious mother. "Are you *quite certain* you saw a man in Hans Place?" she asked anxiously. "Is it not far more likely that you fell and injured yourself?"

"—*After* I had rung the bell? And was already standing on the stoop? That is foolish beyond permission, child. Pray, give me the reticule."

She complied without a word. I pulled at the drawstrings and peered within the bag. My small leather purse with its jingling coins remained, along with the handkerchief and needle; but Cassie's small book had gone.

What in God's name could a lamplighter want with that?

"Manon, I shall hold the compress for my aunt, if you will be so good as to fetch Mr. Haden," Fanny said briskly. "Pray tell him that Miss Austen suffered a—a—*fainting fit*, and is concussed."

The maid relinquished basin and cloth.

"Be on your guard," I told her, setting down the reticule. "That ruffian may still be about—and he has behaved most unnaturally."

Manon harrumphed, eloquent in her doubt that any man might challenge her Gallic sturdiness, and disappeared from the anteroom.

"I did not faint," I insisted as Fanny took up the compress.

"Very well," she replied as tho' I were a child. She wrung out the cloth and touched it gingerly to the rear of my skull.

I winced. "And say nothing of this to Henry. I will not have him worried."

"Then *you* must devise a reason for skulking in the anteroom," she returned. "My uncle is bound to notice your absence at dinner. He means to abandon his bed this evening, and dine at table."

I raised my head and stared dully at her. "Then be so good as to set down that ridiculous rag and help me upstairs to the parlour. I am feeling stronger now, and may attempt the steps if only we take them slowly."

For once, Fanny did not argue; perhaps she realised I should do better on a sopha. The floor swam before my eyes as I rose, but with her support I soon steadied. We had just achieved the first floor when I heard the unmistakable sound of the surgeon's arrival. He must today have been in his rooms in Sloane Street, rather than the Chelsea and Brompton Dispensary, to have appeared so quickly.

"Miss Austen!" Haden hastened up the stairs. "Do not overreach yourself. Your maid tells me you have been injured."

"We believe it possible my aunt fainted," Fanny said as she helped me to the sopha.

"I was struck down by a lamplighter," I insisted crossly.

"Indeed?"

I detected incredulity in his tone and resigned myself to general disbelief.

Fanny placed a cushion behind my back and set my booted feet on an embroidered tuffet. Haden sat beside me, his deft fingers probing my heavy knot of hair so that the pins were displaced. I guessed the lump he found to be the size of an egg.

"The skin is not broken. I do not feel a softness or shifting of the bone," he said. "We must hope the skull is not cracked. You became ill, I understand?"

"I am yet."

"That is a testament to the severity of the blow. You are fortunate, Miss Austen, that it did not fall upon your bare head—the stuff of your bonnet is rent, and you shall not wear it again—but better torn velvet than torn skin." He reached for my wrist and studied me thoughtfully. "Your pulse is tumultuous. Is the pain very bad?"

I made the mistake of nodding.

"I shall invade the kitchens and mix you a draught that may help," he said. "Pray see that she drinks it, Miss—" He hesitated, colouring as he glanced at Fanny.

"Knight," she supplied, curtseying. "Miss Austen is my aunt."

"Miss Knight." He inclined his head and turned back to me. "You must not attempt to exert yourself for the rest of the day—but neither ought you to sleep. I have known those who do, after a blow to the skull, never to wake again."

With these discomfiting words, he quitted the room.

"Did not my father call in a physician, when Uncle Henry was taken ill?" Fanny enquired.

"He did—and we may thank Dr. Baillie for Henry's recovery. But tho' Mr. Haden is only a surgeon, he is more than adequate to prescribe for my head; and he is a friend of long standing, quite at home in this house."

I did not explain that he had helped Eliza from life, easing her pain with his draughts.

"What curious acquaintances Uncle keeps, to be sure," Fanny said airily. "A very *decided* temper. I should not have expected such authority in so young a gentleman. To be issuing you orders, Aunt!"

I have learnt to recognise interest when it goes cloaked in Fanny's opinions. She has always been partial to dark men. "He is very fond of music, you know."

"Is he, indeed?"

"I am sure he should like to hear you perform on your harp."

"But should not the noise increase your head-ache?"

"So well as you play, Fanny? Not at all. The music will prevent me from sleeping. And as we have it on authority that sleep is fatal—"

"I shall fetch my harp immediately!"

I managed a smile. "Pray fetch coffee as well. I have never felt so drowsy in my life."

AND SO I WAS left alone in the parlour whilst Manon boiled coffee and Haden concocted his paregorics and Fanny perused her sheet music. I ought to have profited from the interval to order my thoughts—to divine *why* I had been attacked on my brother's doorstep—but that the brother in question descended upon me in full possession of his faculties, demanding to know the same.

"Jane, what is this nonsense I hear from Haden, that you have been struck on the head by a lamplighter? You must see that the lamps are not yet lit!"

"I do see it, Henry," I said. "If you *must* scold, pray help me to sit up. I am not to sleep, apparently, and my present position is rife with temptation."

He placed an arm under my shoulders and shifted my frame, gasping slightly as he did so.

"I ought not to tire you," I said with a sigh, "but I confess that this is better. My head does not swim so very much."

"Wait until you have Haden's draught." Henry sank into a chair and arranged his handsome dressing gown. "Now tell me how you came by that shocking lump. I was not even aware you were out-of-doors."

"I went into Keppel Street this morning to pay a call on Harriet Palmer and Charles's girls, but they were gone out. I had just returned, and sent off the hackney—"

"A hackney! How very expensive you are become, Jane."

"—and pulled the bell at the door. The only other person in Hans Place was a fellow attending to the lamp."

"The one near this house?"

"Yes. There was no one else abroad. The bell had barely ceased to ring when I collected that the man had descended his ladder—"

"*Collected,* Jane? You did not see him do so?"

"You must know how it is," I retorted indignantly. "One catches movement out of the corner of one's eye. *He descended.* And then I was struck a stunning blow."

"Possibly by a can of whale oil," my brother mused. "He robbed you as well, I suppose?"

"Without much conviction. He left my purse and stole a book of rhymes."

"How extraordinary." Henry's eyes were brighter today, and tho' sadly wasted by his illness, he appeared much like an intelligent raven, tilting his head as he studied me from his perch by the fire. "The fellow must have been mad. Haden means to go to the Watch and complain of the outrage."

"I do not think I was attacked by the Watch." I felt the back of my head tentatively. "As you say, the lamps of Hans Place were not even lit. That ruffian merely awaited my return, in a pretence of lamplighting officiousness, and fell upon me when I descended from the carriage. No doubt he had expected me to arrive on foot, so that he might achieve his misery elsewhere in Hans Place—the mews, perhaps. But being forced by the hackney to alter his plan, he gamely accosted me at your door."

Henry looked his bewilderment. "Now you would have it that he was *not* a lamplighter? But I understood it to be your chief point of insistence. Jane! Have you a fever?"

"Someone hired that man to do me injury, Henry."

My brother snorted. "Why should any person wish *you* harm?"

"Because of what I have seen." I gazed at him soberly. "Because of the Waterloo Map."

I TOLD HENRY THEN of Colonel MacFarland's final words, the yew needles in my handkerchief, and my suspicion of murder. I told him how I had examined the bay yesterday where the Colonel was taken ill, and discovered the watercolour sketch tucked into the Comte de Ségur's memoirs. I described how Dr. Matthew Baillie had begged me to translate the French soldier's letter, written on the eve of battle from La Belle Alliance.

"A map of Russia, you say? Drawn on the back of a note from Waterloo?"

"I should think it was the other way round. Buonaparte invaded Russia three years ago, recollect. The letter was written on the *map*."

"Then the French fellow must have seen both engagements."

"But he did not survive the second one," I said. "You are not *attending*, Henry. He wrote to the woman he loved, expecting the missive to be forwarded after the battle. He urged her to keep it safe—because the Emperor would have need of it, one day. Not his letter, mind, but the paper it was written upon. It is the *sketch* that is vital. I am convinced that Ewan MacFarland was poisoned because of it."

"You think he hid the map in the book, and was attempting to inform you of the fact?"

"He was staring at the shelf as he spoke to me. I should have followed his gaze, but I was too preoccupied with tending to his sickness—and besides, it was I who turned his head towards the books when he first became ill. His fixed stare might have been coincidence, as much as intent."

"But you do not think it was."

I drew a shuddering breath, remembering the desperation of the man as all faculties failed him. "Why else would a man of action, rather than learning, be found on the floor of the Library, Henry? He must have felt unwell, took fright, and put away his treasure in Ségur's book for safekeeping until he could retrieve it. Recollect that Ségur was once at the Czar's court. That was MacFarland's *aide-memoire:* A Russian map in a book about Russia."

"But because the poison took some time to act," Henry mused, "his murderer was not on hand to espy the hiding place."

Aghast, I was suddenly seized with a sinister conviction. "Unless, in fact, he was! Henry—what if the Colonel's murderer was by my side when I found the map?"

Henry snorted. "You cannot mean Matthew Baillie."

"Consider of the facts," I said urgently. "Who else should be summoned to assist MacFarland but the doctor? And who but a doctor might be forgiven for loosening all the Colonel's clothes—and going through his effects? That is one way to secure a treasure, if indeed Baillie searched for one."

"A doctor, too, might easily mistake poison for an apoplectic fit," Henry mused, "and no one should dream of challenging him."

"As indeed occurred! It was only when I *forced* Baillie to consider the yew needles in my handkerchief—when I raised the spectre of poison in the Regent's household—that he agreed to anatomise the body. Would that all murderers were safe from prying women!"

"Jane," Henry temporised, "you must see that this is a phantastical notion. What possible reason could Baillie, the *Court Physician,* have to commit *murder*?"

I was silent an instant. "The Waterloo Map must be of immense value for such a man to so forget himself."

My brother threw up his hands. "Confound it! Any of MacFarland's acquaintance might have poisoned him!"

"But *only* Baillie is acquainted with me," I observed quietly, "and you forget: I was deliberately attacked not an hour ago. Does this not look like an attempt to silence the only other witness to the map's discovery?"

Henry sank back in his chair, frowning at the fire.

"It is I who heard the Colonel's final words—and repeated them. I, who suspected poison. I, who found the sketch hidden in the book. Baillie was beside me at every turn. I *saved* him the trouble of hunting for that map, Henry! I could cry with vexation!"

"Matthew Baillie cannot have hired a man to bludgeon you to death. It is too absurd!"

"But not impossible."

"I should rather believe a lamplighter had run mad!"

"Why? —Because Baillie saved your life?"

He gazed at me wryly. "You will admit it to be a persuasive point."

"You are too intelligent a man to be swayed by a sense of obligation," I retorted. "The good doctor, being an intimate of Carlton House, is perfectly situated to slip poison into the food of any of the Regent's guests. And having risked so much in the teeth of the Royal household, he could not hesitate to despatch a meddlesome woman in Hans Place. Compared to the death of a Hero, a spinster's might be arranged with relatively little effort."

"But why should your assailant steal a book of rhymes?"

The question brought me up short, my head pounding. "To lend the entire scene verisimilitude, perhaps."

Henry stared at me, fascinated. "Your head is in worse case than I first supposed, my dear. You are not to move from that sopha until Haden has administered his draught."

11

NEWS OF THE WORLD

Thursday, 16 November 1815
23 Hans Place, London

The noxious draught was duly delivered and drunk last evening, but I benefited more from the knowledge that Haden, at least, did not think me wandering in my wits.

"I called in at the Knightsbridge Watch," he told me as I struggled with his potation, "to complain of their brutality; and was informed that the lamplighter had only then begun his rounds. He is an aged fellow named Amos Smalls, who is aided in his work by his grandson. Neither of the Smallses was abroad before five o'clock."

"I am glad to know it." I set down the draught. "I had suspected as much."

Haden studied me soberly. "I am compelled to enquire . . . have you an enemy, Miss Austen?"

How had Fanny described the surgeon? As a man of decided authority?

Any answer I might have made was forestalled by the

appearance of Fanny herself, followed by Manon and Madame Bigeon, supporting the harp between them.

"I thought it might soothe your head-ache, Aunt, if I played a few airs," she said sweetly.

"The very thing," I replied. "Mr. Haden, won't you hear the performance? Miss Knight is extremely proficient on the harp."

"I should be delighted."

"That is an excellent decision, Mr. Haden," Fanny returned, "—for my uncle has charged me with an invitation to dine with us this evening. He is even now dressing, in defiance of his doctor's orders."

"Mr. Austen is a dreadful patient. I am sure his doctor holds him in despair," Haden said as he took a chair. "Only the inducements of roast duck and Haydn's Scotch Airs can suffice to placate him."

"A bit of Haydn for a Haden," I murmured.

Fanny flashed a smile. "I had thought to offer you the latest works of Miss Dussek, which are all the rage in Kent; but you command my fingers, sir. Haydn it shall be."*

The idea that she had come to play for her ailing aunt had clearly fled; so I settled my brain and prepared to be delighted by the prospect of two attractive and intelligent young people, coming to know each other, and the tantalising smell of Manon's roast duck.

"If you are indeed the object of a murderous attack, Jane,"

*Sophia Dussek, Four favorite Airs arranged for the Harp, Book 4th or possibly Three favorite Airs with variations for the Harp, Book 1. Both were published in London around this time.—*Editor's note.*

Henry observed over breakfast this morning, "you must not set foot out-of-doors for the rest of your visit. Stay within and proof Mr. Murray's sheets. I should not like to return you to Chawton a lifeless corpse."

I considered my brother. It would seem that Haden's examination—or his interrogation of the Watch—had convinced Henry that I was of sound mind.

"I wonder if you have not stumbled on a very clever notion," I said. "My attacker intended to put me *hors de combat.* If I am so obliging as to quit the field . . . there can be no possible reason to fear or threaten me any longer. The murderer might consider himself safe."

He might act upon the map, indeed—and thus betray his motives to the world.

Henry blinked. Acquiescence in my own confinement was *not* what he expected.

"I shall do very well, tucked up here on the sopha," I added with complaisance. "No one shall hear a word from me. But *you* must write to all my London acquaintance and tell them how it is—particularly Mr. James Stanier Clarke. I had a letter from him this morning, and it would be unfeeling not to answer it."

The letter, with its characteristic seal and Carlton House direction, had given me a rude jolt when I discovered it waiting by my cup of chocolate. It began, *Dear Madam,* and continued:

It is certainly not incumbent *upon you to dedicate your work now in the Press to His Royal Highness; but if you wish to do the Regent that honour either now or at any future period, I am happy to send you that permission . . .*

He closed with the sort of humbugging modesty typical of the man, suggesting I use the considerable power of my Genius and Principles, as he put it, to *delineate in some future Work the Habits of Life and Character and Enthusiasm of a Clergyman—who should pass his time between the Metropolis & the Country—*

In other words, a Character very like Clarke himself.*

"Tell that silly fellow you've been attacked," Henry protested, "and it will be all over London!"

"True. I could not have a better intelligencer."

"Oh, Lord, Jane." My brother's eyes narrowed. "Whatever are you up to, now?"

SO UPON THE SOPHA this morning I stayed. My head-ache was nothing out of the ordinary way; my hair had been left down about my shoulders to avoid plaguing the painful lump, which was gradually diminishing; and Fanny had wrapped my feet in a shawl of Norwich wool before departing for Hatchard's in a hackney. The day was wet, which made spending it in Henry's parlour a little less tedious.

In one respect, however, my good intentions were frustrated—I received no sheets from Mr. Murray *again*, and must conclude that a shortage of paper throughout London, or a refusal to work on the part of the printers, has brought all presses to a halt! At this rate, *Emma* shall not be completed before the close of the year. I am tempted to inform Mr. Murray that no less a personage than the Prince Regent is to be honoured in the

---

* Letter No. 125A, dated November 16, 1815, from James Stanier Clarke, in *Jane Austen's Letters*, third edition (Deirdre Le Faye, ed.), Oxford, Oxford University Press, 1995.—*Editor's note.*

book's Dedication—and hope that the desire for Royal favour and its resultant robust sales, might spur his establishment to swifter action.

I submitted to a visit from Mr. Haden, who pronounced me to be going on very well, and urged me to eat heartily and partake of exercise. I assured him that I was obliged by his good opinion, but that he ought to save his words for Madame Bigeon, who insisted upon serving me gruel and wrapping me in cotton wool. When the surgeon had gone down to the errant Frenchwoman in the kitchen, I interrogated Henry as to the speed of his correspondence—he had several letters of business to write, on the subject of the Oxford militia and his dwindling bank accounts. By one o'clock, however, I had the satisfaction of reading his brief note to Mr. James Stanier Clarke—and seeing it put into the post not long thereafter.

Sir:

You were so good as to write to my beloved sister, a missive she received only this morning. I am overcome by the intelligence I must relate—I take up my pen to answer your Notice with tidings too grievous; my sister was struck down by an Unknown on my very doorstep only yesterday, and is in danger of her life. Our surgeon is in despair of her regaining sense in this world; you may imagine how this news has worked upon me. I send you the sentiments and thanks that She cannot, in regard to your kind attentions, and remain,

Henry Austen, Esq.

I expected this note to bring Mr. Clarke flying to Hans Place in earnest solicitude. I half-hoped that he should urge Matthew Baillie to physick me, in the belief that Mr. Haden was inept—and that I might enjoin Henry to observe the Court Physician for demonstrations of murderous guilt. I certainly assumed I should at least earn a tribute of hothouse flowers. But the rest of the day passed away; Fanny was returned with the latest novel by Maria Edgeworth, which she proceeded to read aloud as comfort to the Sufferer—and nobody of significance came *near* me.

I was quite put out.

"Jane." My brother strode into the parlour with something like his old vigour, a newspaper furled in his hands.

"You were not to tax your brain with news, Henry," I chided.

"Fiddlesticks. I am perfectly well. Fanny brought this from Hatchard's. Only look what has occurred!"

Fanny suspended her reading. I glanced at my brother's news-sheet. And saw my smug parcel of assumptions burst asunder.

MURDEROUS ATTACK ON COURT PHYSICIAN

I glanced up at Henry. "Good God!"

"Read it," he said.

I took the paper from his hand.

> *An event remarkable for its UNPROVOKED BESTIALITY occurred in Newman Street last night. Doctor Matthew Baillie, Court Physician to His Majesty the Prince Regent and Member of the Royal College of Physicians, was set upon by VIOLENT*

and BLOODTHIRSTY footpads, who stabbed him repeatedly about his person. A passing gentleman discovered the doctor BLEEDING and INSENSIBLE, and conveyed him to St George's Hospital. We deplore this further evidence of LAWLESS VIOLENCE encroaching on the West End, which ought to be preserved as a SANCTUM of SAFETY for our best citizens.

"So much for your suspicions of poor Matthew Baillie," my brother snorted. "He was laid low but a few hours after yourself, and in an entirely different part of London."

"What is it all about? What are you talking of?" Fanny enquired, bewildered.

"I shall explain presently, my dear," I returned. "Pray contain your curiosity a little; you shall be satisfied. Henry, I take your point—indeed, I take your point. My theories are in need of adjustment."

"I said as much last evening—" he began.

But I ignored him. "Baillie did not try to murder *himself*; therefore, it is possible he did not try to murder *me*." I set aside the crumpled newssheet. "He must have talked to someone about the Waterloo Map—shewn it, even, to others at Carlton House. I assumed he meant to go to the Duke; but the Duke can hardly have ordered my murder. Therefore, the circle of complicity has widened."

"Your *murder?*" Fanny spluttered, incredulous. She looked from me to Henry, all agog; he lifted his finger to his lips.

To whom had Baillie spoken? One of MacFarland's

intimates—Lieutenant Dunross, perhaps? Another of the soldiers present at the interesting nuncheon? Or the Regent himself?

"I would give a good deal to know whether the doctor was carrying the map when he was stabbed," I fretted. "Only think, Henry, if it should have been taken!"

"If so, his attacker may be satisfied—and this incautious bloodletting be at an end."

I touched the lump on my skull with a tentative finger. None of my blood was shed, to be sure; but my attacker had made off with my little hand-printed book. Had he been told to search my reticule for papers—or drawings? Was the object of this pointed violence to retrieve the Waterloo Map from the only two persons who appeared to know of its existence?

"Does the newspaper say anything of robbery in Baillie's case?" I snatched at it once more.

"It adds only that he was dining last night in Newman Street. He had just quitted number fourteen when he was set upon."

"Number fourteen?" I repeated, glancing up. The direction carried vague associations, as tho' I had glimpsed it once in print; or visited the premises on a forgotten occasion.

Number 14 Newman Street . . .

"You have been there some once or twice to look at pictures," Henry said diffidently. "I do not know why Baillie found occasion to dine there."

"Pictures?" I repeated stupidly.

"Yes, Jane. Number fourteen is the home of the famous painter—Mr. Benjamin West."

12
THE DRAUGHTING ROOM

Thursday, 16 November 1815
23 Hans Place, London, cont'd.

Inevitable, that a strenuous argument should be the sequel to the exchange of news. Inevitable, that a precious half-hour must be spent in dispelling Fanny's ignorance, stemming her fears, and dismissing her objections to my involvement in the Carlton House murder as girlish trifles. I was unsupported in these efforts by my brother, who insisted I ought to depart for Chawton as soon as my injuries permitted of travel. The bloody attack on Dr. Baillie had convinced him that my own was serious; he was all agitation that by remaining in London, I invited further peril.

My decision to quit the house immediately, therefore, and call upon Raphael West was vociferously opposed by both members of my family.

"West carried you into Carlton House Tuesday, and was present when you spoke with Baillie?" Henry said.

"Yes. He knows nothing of the map's discovery, however," I supplied. "He was obliged to take his leave, having an appointment to sketch the Regent. I must know why Baillie was attacked near his door last evening."

"West is unlikely to tell you anything to the purpose, Jane," Henry objected. "What can an artist know of murder and intrigue? —Or Waterloo? He cannot possibly elucidate the attack upon Baillie, even if it *did* occur in Newman Street."

Impossible to explain that Raphael West was only nominally an artist, and in actuality deep in the Crown's intrigues. But I might explode one misconception, at least. "Henry, it was as much Mr. West's activity as mine that exposed the murderer at The Vyne last Christmas. I assure you he is sanguine in the face of evil, and more than worthy of being admitted to our counsels. Indeed, I can think of no one whose aid I should rather beg, nor whose resolution I should so completely trust."

"But, Aunt!" Fanny objected. "You *cannot* solicit the notice of Mr. West, however desperate the occasion. He must first call upon *you*."

"I am too old for such missishness, my dear," I returned briskly, "and had I not abandoned it years ago, should have enjoyed a much duller life."

"Can you not simply write to this gentleman?" she suggested.

"—And lose valuable hours, awaiting his response? No, no, dear Fanny. Your Uncle Henry shall prove a valuable escort, in ringing Mr. West's bell. I shall hardly offend propriety by following my brother across the threshold. The little fact of the acquaintance with West being all *mine*, need not be published abroad."

They were dubious. It remained only for Fanny to recruit Haden, and Henry to summon Manon, for me to feel that all the forces of Nature were arrayed against me; but I forestalled these reinforcements.

"If a murderer intends to prey upon me, he shall do so equally in Hans Place as anywhere else in London," I declared. "Therefore, the sooner he is unmasked, the safer I shall be. Pray hire a carriage from the Knightsbridge livery stable, Henry, and bring it round to the mews. I shall go heavily veiled, and no one will be aware I have even left the house! Fanny may remain here in comfort, and deny me to any interested callers."

"Very well." My brother sighed. "I must submit to your will, Jane—for you shall not scruple to quit the house alone and unprotected, if I do not."

I thought it possible Henry was as tired of being tethered to a sickbed as I am.

WHEN OUR CHAISE PULLED up before No. 14 a little before four o'clock, it seemed probable that Raphael West would be abroad from home. It was the very hour that most gentlemen must be engrossed in their clubs, or hacking through Hyde Park, or in pursuit of errands and business; he might even then be at Carlton House. If we were denied an interview, I had brought with me a sealed note requesting Mr. West to call in Hans Place as soon as might be.

The gallery and home in Newman Street was familiar from past visits I had made to picture viewings: a handsome and expensive establishment of Georgian brick, rising some four storeys above the paving. We stood in front of the heavy black door and awaited a response to Henry's knock. My brother was not looking so hearty as he had this morning, and I was suddenly afraid that I had taxed his returning health. But at that moment the door was thrown open, Henry sent in his card to the son of the house, and we were admitted to an elegant anteroom off the foyer, where a fire burnt brightly.

The brisk tread of West's feet on the stairs caused the porter to recede into shadows, and we both turned in expectation.

"Mr. Austen, I believe," Raphael West said, extending his hand. "I have had the pleasure of knowing your sister a little in Hampshire; you have quite the look of her."

I was, as promised, heavily veiled, as tho' in mourning. It had cost me a good deal of pain to put up my hair; I had settled for a braided knot at Fanny's hands rather than an excess of hairpins against my tender scalp, and the result was untidy. The removal of the veils only increased this disorder. It succeeded, however, in revealing me to Raphael West's sight.

"Miss Austen!" He bowed in surprize. "How may I serve you?"

"By affording us a quarter-hour of your time, sir, on a matter of some delicacy," I said.

"Pray come up to my draughting room. It serves me as other men are served by their libraries—a place of intimacy and comfort."

He led us without another word up the sweeping staircase. It was carpeted in crimson, and the walls were lined with pictures of every description. I had been in this publick part of the house before—we were approaching the large drawing-room on the first storey, where the exhibitions of West's paintings were often held. I had seen his *Christ Rejected by the Elders* here, during a previous visit to London. But I had not then been acquainted with the son.

"You have a remarkable home," Henry ventured.

"It is my father's house," West replied. "He has lived here nearly fifty years, since emigrating from Pennsylvania. This is an atelier as well as a residence—a place where he may work and entertain, instruct his students, and exhibit his art on such occasions as the spirit moves him—but I have rarely thought it a *family* home. When I was married, I lived elsewhere in England and the Continent; but the death of my mother last year, and my father's advancing age, persuaded me to return to Newman Street to care for him."

Nothing of his own wife's death, or his daughter's marriage, or his brother's estrangement from his family—tho' I knew of all these things.

"I hope Mr. West is in good health?" I said.

"He still paints—and at his age, that is the greatest health any man could desire." West halted before a pair of doors and smiled at me faintly. "Consider yourself honoured, Miss Austen. You are admitted to a privilege few women have enjoyed."

His draughting room, as he had called it, was a square space with a range of clerestory windows high on the northern wall. These threw light into the room, and quite deliberately onto a tall, slanted desk, such as a clerk might employ in a solicitor's office, that stood in the centre of the floor. There were tables set at angles to it, strewn with lengths of charcoal and red chalk. A few worn chairs were pulled up to the fire. Scaffolding rested against one panelled wall, and various draperies—of silk and velvet and even burlap—hung from it in folds. Tall branches of candles stood everywhere, throwing out excellent light. Rolls of paper and canvas were stacked in one corner.

And at the far end was a fainting couch.

I could imagine the supple limbs of a Roman goddess languishing along its length—her skin white as marble—because a painting of a woman in just that pose rested on an easel not far from the couch itself.

I stared at it in confusion. Did he paint such figures from *life*?

"Pray sit down." West waited until each of us had taken a chair near the fire, then propped himself against the draughting desk. "You came heavily veiled, I observe. Has my father so offended the Polite World, that a lady may not be seen to call at the atelier of Benjamin West?"

"Not when the lady is meant to be dying," Henry said drily, "after a violent attack upon her person last evening."

West frowned and started from the desk towards me. "Jane! Are you much hurt? What villain presumed to touch you?"

He grasped my gloved hand between both of his own.

"I cannot say—and I assure you, I am very well. A trifling blow upon the head, soon mended. My bonnet, however, is past repair." I was babbling, my face red, and could not look at Henry—who must notice West's use of my Christian name, and the warmth of his regard.

"Trifling!" My brother snorted. "She was concussed! Foolish beyond permission to have ventured out today! But you will know what Jane is, Mr. West—determined as a thoroughbred when the bit is between her teeth. And when we saw that Dr. Baillie suffered a similar outrage after dining here in Newman Street—nothing would satisfy her but that we must know the particulars."

West released my hand and ran his penetrating gaze over my

face. "I may say you fared better than poor Baillie, thank God. I wonder if the unfortunate man will live."

"You have seen his wounds?" I asked.

"I witnessed some part of the attack. It was I who conveyed him to St George's Hospital, in a hackney. He was assailed only ten yards from our door—after dining here, and bidding us goodnight. I had lingered in the anteroom for a pipe of tobacco—my father does not like the habit, and will not have it upstairs. I heard Baillie's cries. The sound of assault is unusual in this part of Town, particularly at so early an hour as ten o'clock. Naturally I went out into the street."

It was anything but natural. London is a dangerous city. Nine men in ten should have ordered the porter to bar the door and extinguish the lights.

"The papers say the doctor was attacked by footpads," Henry interjected. "Was he robbed?"

"I saw only one man. He ran off as I opened the door of this house. But the injury had already been done. Baillie was all over blood, from a knife wound to his stomach and one to his neck. The sleeves of his coat were cut right through—he had tried to parry the blows with his arms. He could barely speak. I do not know whether his purse was taken; I confess I had not an instant to spare for such a question. My intent was to save the man's life. But what happened to you, Miss Austen? How did *you* come to be the object of violence?"

To explain the bludgeoning in Hans Place was a matter of three or four sentences.

"And this ruffian seized your book of rhymes but left your purse? That is a curious motive for violence."

"As must be any, for beating in the head of a woman," Henry observed with some heat.

"It has occurred to me to wonder if the two attacks are related," I said.

"Because you met with Baillie on Tuesday?" West did not dismiss the idea; he had seen me present the handkerchief to the doctor, and knew how the sight had worked upon him. "He told me the results of the anatomisation—that MacFarland was indeed poisoned by yew needles. Which leads the mind inevitably to murder, does it not?"

"As Colonel MacFarland appears to have had no morbid compulsion to kill himself—according to his sister, his batman, and his physician—it does," I agreed.

"Murder, and a desire to silence any accusers," Henry pointed out. "Is Dr. Baillie often in the habit of confiding in you, Mr. West?"

"Not at all! I barely know him. We only met in recent weeks at Carlton House. He came here last evening to consult my father—regarding the drawing Miss Austen discovered in the Regent's Library."

I let out a small sigh; so Baillie had indeed kept the map on his person. It was probably gone, then—and we were back to *Miss Austen*. West had recovered himself, and propriety was satisfied.

He reached for a scuttle of coals and tossed them on the fire, then settled himself into another of the chairs grouped near the hearth. "A charcoal drawing of a landscape in Russia," he continued, "overlaid with watercolour. Smolensk and Moscow noted in ink. Baillie hoped my father might recognise the artist's technique, from his days at Buonaparte's court, and put a name to the hand."

"And did he?" I asked eagerly.

West shook his head. "Deft and talented, but not an artist my father could name. An interesting item to employ as foolscap for a letter, all the same."

"It is not just a letter," I said tentatively, "or a sketch. I believe it is a *map*. The map MacFarland spoke of to me when he died. You read French, I am sure, Mr. West, so you will have noted the writer's injunction: *Keep this, as the Emperor will have need of it one day.*"

He glanced at me satirically. "It is not the Emperor who has come after it now."

"No," I agreed. "But might it not be someone French, who knew of the paper's existence? Or—or another soldier from the field at Waterloo, who was in MacFarland's confidence?"

"Or a Russian!" Henry objected. "We cannot know who is willing to kill for the paper if we do not first discover its significance. The murderer might be anyone."

"Not quite anyone." I looked at West. "Only Baillie and I knew of the sketch when I left Carlton House on Tuesday. Did the doctor say whether he showed it to anyone else?"

"No," West replied, "but he must have done. Why else would you, Miss Austen, or poor Baillie be attacked? Or your small book of rhymes and drawings, seized in error? *MacFarland's murderer knows that the Waterloo Map has been found.* He has been hunting for it. But he does not yet know where it is."

West rose and strode to a sideboard placed against the wall

opposite our fire; a decanter of brandy stood there. He poured three glasses and offered them round.

I never drink brandy. It is medicinal in the Austen household. But this smelled heady and powerful, a concoction I could not refuse. And after all, I reasoned, I was recovering from a blow to the head. I took a sip, and felt fire course down my throat.

"Cognac," Henry murmured.

"Mr. Austen, I know nothing about you," West said, "but as you are this lady's brother and intelligent enough to detect French brandy when you taste it, I shall trust you so far as to speak plainly. You did well to come to me today. We must assume this drawing, or map, or love letter—whatever it is—is a document of paramount importance to a very dangerous man. We must move, therefore, before he strikes again—or run the risk of losing all our lives."

"Your person is not at risk," Henry protested. "You may withdraw from the affair this moment, Mr. West! Your excellent father could divine nothing from the drawing. Was Baillie robbed of it last night?"

"He was not." West set down his empty glass. "Which is why I cannot draw back from violence, Mr. Austen. Baillie placed the map here, in my father's picture vaults—and put all the Wests at risk, in consequence."

13

AQUARELLE

Thursday, 16 November 1815
23 Hans Place, London, cont'd.

He led us to the rear of the house along a carpeted hall smothered in quiet. We passed a dining room with a magnificent set of French windows draped in gold and a more intimate saloon that held a pianoforte. The ghost of his late mother lingered there, perhaps, along with the portraits of her on the walls. My eyes found one of these: a Madonna and child in a round frame. Raphael West as an infant, and his mother captured forever in supple beauty—

All was silent and untouched in these elegant rooms, however—as tho' the painter's world had already become a museum. I felt a twinge of compassion for the man beside me: a widower returned to the ground of childhood, and finding it vanished into dust.

"My father," he murmured, "sleeps hardly at all during the dark hours and lies abed long into morning. It is one of the liberties of the aged to ignore the clock. Each of us in this household is under strict instruction not to disturb him. Hence the air of desertion throughout the upper storeys; the servants are banished until my father rings." He halted by a simple panelled door. "The back staircase. It is rather narrow, Miss Austen, and we must descend to the cellars; I beg you would mind your steps."

I glanced at Henry. "Shall it tire you too much?"

"If you think to leave me behind whilst you examine this fascinating document, you are entirely beside the road, my dear," he said firmly.

We descended, West to the fore and my brother behind.

The back stairs were no doubt employed by the domestic staff, and thus were well-lit and carpeted with drugget. I was reminded all the same of a previous occasion when I had followed Raphael West into a narrow passage—the concealed tunnel that led from The Vyne to an icehouse at some remove from the great house.* Then, I had followed in trepidation, and knew not whether to place my trust in the gentleman carelessly throwing himself down the present flight. How deeply the passage of time may alter one's impressions and emotions! I viewed him now with as much approbation and gratitude as my Lizzy Bennet regarded her Darcy, after the restoration of poor Lydia.

"That leads to the kitchens," he noted as we passed a green baize door set into the wall of a landing. He took up a lanthorn that sat near it and lit it from one of the stair passage candles. "Only one more flight."

We followed him ever downwards. The final flight of stairs was unlit, and West's lanthorn a comfort.

"I had no notion your father set aside his pictures!" Henry

---

*See *Jane and the Twelve Days of Christmas* (Soho Press, 2014).—*Editor's note.*

commented a trifle breathlessly as we reached the cellars at last. "I should have thought them in such demand, that to hide them away were to hide a fortune!"

"Exactly," West replied. "My father is a Philadelphian, Mr. Austen—which is to say, a man schooled in a thrift that should put a Scot to the blush. He is certain his treasures will fetch a king's ransom once he is gone. These vaults are his private bank—his provision for his family, when he may provide for them no more."

The ground was flagged in stone, the ceilings arched like a crypt. I expected the atmosphere to be chilly, noisome, and damp, from the cesspools that riddle the earth beneath most of London—but was surprized to discover that the air was indistinguishable from that in the rooms above.

"The cellar is heated," Henry exclaimed.

"Moderately so, yes. My father employs a Belper stove for the purpose."* West led us forward, set the lanthorn on a small octagonal table, and opened its glass door. Using a spill from a collection provided on the table, he carried flame from the lanthorn to oil lamps set into the walls. Light leapt from one to another, further revealing the arches all around us. It was a lovely moment, recalling the rise of a curtain on a Covent Garden stage.

"Come."

---

* This was a heated-air system devised in 1805 by William Strutt (1756–1830), and variously known as a cockle or Derby stove. Strutt was an architect, inventor, and fellow of the Royal Society, credited with numerous technical advancements of the early Industrial Revolution. The Belper stove was an iron box encased in a ventilated brick structure that warmed air before moving it through vents to interior rooms.—*Editor's note.*

We proceeded down the central passage. There were iron grilles to left and right, enclosing the archways; behind them, I glimpsed raised wooden racks burdened with shrouded shapes: paintings of various sizes, wrapped in silk. West halted before one of these, and removing a set of keys from inside his coat, set one into a heavy lock. The grille opened inwards on well-oiled hinges, and we followed.

"Does he ever fear the danger of fire?" Henry asked in a hushed tone. There was just enough of the sacred—or the illicit—about the scene to urge a whisper.

"The entire household is under strict orders never to descend to this level with an open flame," West said. "That said, every artist's nightmare is flood or fire. It is my father's belief that if the household above were ever damaged, these vaults might protect his life's work. He thinks it probable they date to Roman times. When he purchased the property in the last century, he discovered ancient drains set into the stone at our feet, leading to the river."

"Did Matthew Baillie know of this, when he came to you last night?" My voice sounded overloud in my ears.

"No, and we certainly did not conduct him on a tour. The knowledge of this place is closely-held. Some few of my father's students—many of them now returned to America—are aware of its existence, as copies of their paintings are preserved in these vaults."

"Copies?"

"—Insurance against the uncertainty of shipping cargoes across the Atlantic, in times of persistent war. Here is one!"

He reached for a shrouded rectangle and carefully removed

its wrappings. It was a portrait of a young man, taken I should guess about a dozen years ago, from the stile of dress. He was bespectacled, sensitive in appearance, with a thoughtful look. His left hand was loosely clasped around a potted flower.

"Rubens Peale, with a geranium, by his brother Rembrandt," West said. "You will note the propensity of American painters for naming their sons after European Masters."

This was a gibe at himself. Benjamin West had long been apostrophised as "the American Raphael." It was no coincidence his firstborn bore the same name.

"But I digress." He enfolded the portrait in silk once more. "Here is what you have come to see. My father placed it between two panes of glass, with weights set at the corners, in an effort to soften the creases."

West set his lanthorn on the edge of the nearest wooden rack. Henry and I bent over the glass frame laid out on its surface. The Waterloo Map was as I remembered it: a fanciful sketch of onion domes and brown hills, with the haunting features from an icon in one corner. Martyred man or pierced Madonna? I could not say.

"And Dr. Baillie imagined your father might detect the hand of the artist?" I enquired. "Is technique so distinctive, then—as, for instance, the hand of a particular correspondent might be?"

"Of course it is, you silly woman."

I looked sideways at Raphael West in surprize, but it was not he who had spoken. We three turned as one and confronted a slight, eel-backed figure in an ancient periwig, a second lanthorn held aloft in his wizened hand.

"Father," West said.

"Raphael." The elderly artist inclined his head, and swept his piercing gaze over his son's companions. "What can possibly have possessed you, to bring two such shabby-genteel persons poaching in my personal preserve? From the look of them, they could not meet the price of a quarter-length portrait between them, if they worked an entire year."

"Father, may I introduce my particular friends, Mr. Henry Austen and Miss Jane Austen," West returned imperturbably. "You may recall that I made the acquaintance of Miss Austen in Hampshire last Christmas, whilst staying at The Vyne."

"I remember nothing of the sort." Benjamin West set down his lanthorn with a decisive ring and advanced upon us. "What I want to know, sirrah, is how often you invade these precincts without my express consent or knowledge—and how you pilfered the keys!"

Such a speech, to a boy of sixteen or twenty, might have been humiliating enough; but Raphael West will not see forty again. To witness him harangued by a man half his size, and possessed of twice his fury, was discomposing in the extreme.

Rather than flaring to meet his father's passion, however, West merely grasped the old man's hand with the ease of affection. "You gave me the keys yourself, Papa," he said gently, "when you could no longer recall where you had placed them. Now, pray attend, dear sir. We have need of your wits and wisdom. Miss Austen discovered this intriguing sketch at Carlton House. You remember Dr. Baillie, who showed it to you last e'en?"

"I do," the artist said querulously. "Baillie. Carlton House. French sketch. Wanted to know who'd done it. Couldn't tell him."

"Exactly, sir. Would you indulge me and my friends, and glance at it again? Recollect, we are talking of years ago. When you were last in France, at Buonaparte's court."

There was a hesitation, I thought, on the father's part, and a clouding of the piercing gaze. I apprehended, suddenly, that Benjamin West—tho' still capable of painting—lived in that dubious half-light of the mind that so often assails the elderly. At times he commanded his faculties; at others, he did not. No wonder Raphael had returned to his childhood home once his mother died—as safeguard against a parent's infirmity. The patience required must be enormous. Benjamin West reigned as absolute master in his domain, and yet was incapable of mastering himself. A perpetual dance of indulgence and accommodation, wilful blindness to slights and the comforting of improbable fears, must be Raphael West's trying lot.

Then the frail figure stepped forward, imperiously shouldering Henry and me aside. He drew a pair of spectacles from his coat and commanded, "More light!"

Raphael West brought the second lanthorn to bear upon the sketch, and his father bent over it.

"Aquarelle," he murmured, using the French word for watercolour. "Not the usual thing among Buonaparte's people. Not Jacques David's style, nor Girard's. Preferred oils. Prefer 'em meself. Aquarelle deuced tricky. Not many people good at it. Not many like this. Usually done on ivory, not paper. This is deuced well done. Colour not laid on too heavy, delicacy in the brushstrokes. Who was that young buck, Rafe, always bowing and scraping to the upstart Cits in Little Nap's Court?"

"A watercolourist, sir?" Raphael West asked.

"Of course a watercolourist!" the old man shot back. He snatched off his spectacles and glowered at his son. "Good God, man, he painted a miniature of your Charlotte. Used to drink with him in taverns of nights, when you weren't trying to seduce his wife. *Think*, clodpole!"

"You cannot mean Isabey?" Raphael West declared.

Both of the Wests appeared to have forgotten the Austens altogether.

"That's it! *Isabey*. Had some other names, too, but I don't care to recall them."

"You think Isabey painted this? But he was hardly at Waterloo." Raphael West glanced at the sketch. "Much less Moscow! Isabey, to leave the signal comforts of Paris for all the depravations of campaign! Never, sir. You are dreaming. Last I knew, he had thrown in his lot with the Bourbons—and was painting pictures for Louis XVIII."

"Then it's School of Isabey," Benjamin West muttered. "Nobody else does *aquarelle* in that fashion. Give you my word, Rafe. Some feller who learnt his trade at Isabey's knee."

"Might the name *Charles,* signed on the reverse, offer a clew?" I enquired.

The dim eyes slid around to mine. The old man's mouth curled in contempt. "Don't pretend to know Isabey's lackeys. More Rafe's set in Paris than mine."

And from all Raphael West had told me, his Set had been inclined to spies and revolutionaries, however much they were passionate about paint. A perfect grouping to produce the Waterloo Map, and hold it against the Monster's return.

The Wests had removed to Paris during the years of peace

that followed the Treaty of Amiens. They had quitted the city in 1805 or thereabouts, once Buonaparte crowned himself Emperor, disappointed in their hopes of a truly democratic rule. The French years seemed to have been their last flicker of republicanism. Both were now English subjects; the father even yearned for a title.

It was the son's revolutionary friends, however, who had embroiled Raphael in service to the Crown. Once returned to England, he had been pursued by those who administer the Secret Funds—my late Lord Harold Trowbridge among them—and persuaded that his family's best protection lay in his devotion to the Government's ends. He could be branded a traitor to English sympathies, and exiled to the United States—or he could inform upon his French acquaintance. As Buonaparte's threat to Europe and England waxed through the years, Raphael's French Set rose in power and influence. His connexions and insights, his easy movement between the worlds of Art and Policy, soon became invaluable.

He was a master of plausible lies. His life and security, not to mention that of all the Wests, were built upon the talent. And yet not since Lord Harold had I known a man of such canniness—or private principle. I did not hesitate to trust his judgement.

"And the figures?" I interjected swiftly. "The curious mathematics penciled at the bottom of the sketch?"

Benjamin West peered at them narrowly in the lanthorn light, his lips moving as he parsed the numbers. Then he sighed wearily. "Cypher, of course. Buonaparte was mad for 'em. Now leave off your questions, woman, and let an old man find his couch!"

That quickly he seemed burdened with years, his shoulders sagging and his fingers fumbling for his coat pocket. There was a sharp clatter of metal on stone; the spectacles had slipped from his hand to the cellar flags. Pray God they had not shattered!

Raphael West stooped swiftly, the gleam of gold revealed by lanthorn light. With infinite care he retrieved the spectacles and tucked them into his father's coat pocket. "Shall I escort you above-stairs, sir?" he asked solicitously. "You ought to rest a little. There is the reception at Somerset House this evening, recollect, and you would not wish to faint from weariness."

"Somerset House," the elderly man said sharply. "Somerset House! Whole world paints there, Rafe. Lots of 'em Frenchies. Copying my work. No stile of their own. Thieves, the lot of 'em."

"You ought to be flattered, sir. The World will always acknowledge its Masters—even if only by imitation."

"Thank'ee." The artist glanced around at us with that sudden, swift reversion to vagueness. "These your friends?"

"Indeed," West returned in a soothing tone. "Mr. Austen shall lend you his arm, whilst I lock up your treasures."

Henry, bless him, stepped forward without a word and supported Benjamin West as he wandered in a bewildered fashion from the vault. Raphael West clanged home the iron grille. I stood between the two parties, uncertain what exactly had been learnt.

"I shall just see my father into the hands of his valet," West murmured, "and then we shall hold a Council of War. May you spare another half-hour to this business?"

"Certainly," I assured him, and followed my brother to the stairs.

14

COUNCIL OF WAR

Thursday, 16 November 1815
23 Hans Place, London, cont'd.

"A cypher," my brother mused as we collected once more around the draughting room fire. "Then the sketch is almost certainly a secret message or map. But I know little of such things—does not one require a *key* to read them?"

"I confess that I do not know what a cypher is at all," I said vexedly. "I have been taught to consider the word as meaning *nothing*, or of marginal significance, as when one describes a tedious acquaintance as *a complete cypher.*"

"I pray you do not know many of those," West said seriously, "as they should be an unconscionable waste of your time, Miss Austen. But the sort of cypher I mean cannot have come in your way before. They are most often the playthings of military men, and hide the truth of vital communications. Consider how valuable the French should find Wellington's orders, if they fell into their hands—or what pains Grouchy and others must have taken, to protect French communications from the British! As gentlemen, the English do not often stoop to such subterfuge; being rogues, the French are masters of it."

"But this cypher is composed of figures," I said in puzzlement. "Not words."

"True; to read it one requires, as your brother observed, a key."

I looked all my bewilderment.

West leaned forward in his armchair. "Your father was a clergyman, I believe?"

"Indeed."

"Did he take pupils in Latin and Greek? —Cloddish fellows requiring to be crammed, before sitting the entrance examinations for Oxford?"

I caught Henry's eye and smiled. "One of the great regrets of my father's death is that Greek has vanished from my life. I understood not a word, but the cadence and inflexion of his quotations were delightful."

"No doubt your father was required to write down two lines of symbols for his pupils' instruction," West continued. "One comprised of good English letters—*a, b, c*—and the other of Greek ones. Ά, β, γ, and δ, for example. His students might consult the first, to comprehend the second."

"A key," I said.

"In the case of your sketch," Henry added, "a number might equal a particular letter. *A* might be 1, *B* 2, and so on. The word *cat,* thus expressed, should be the figures 3, 1, and . . ." He paused for an instant, counting on his fingers. "15."

"How tedious! The composition of a single paragraph should run to pages! Is it possible you have already hit upon the Waterloo key, Henry?"

"The figures are too concise and too varied for that to be likely," West interjected. "I suspect, rather, that each group of numbers in our cypher stands for a single word. And without knowing where to begin . . . the possible combinations of numbers and letters being infinite . . ."

"How is one *ever* to make it out?" Henry exclaimed.

"Lacking the key, the mystery is secure in the mind of its creator." West rose and paced moodily about the room. "But I would remind you, friends, that such trifles need not concern us. *We know the key exists.*"

I looked in consternation at my brother. I knew no such thing.

West wheeled and studied us intently. "*The key is in the killer's hands.* Why else should he have poisoned the Colonel—or attacked the two people who discovered the map? Why make off with your book of rhymes, Miss Austen—no doubt to his subsequent disappointment? *Because, possessing the key, he now requires the cypher.* And I do not think he will stop at anything to secure it."

We three were silent for an interval. The coals in the hearth before us glowed red, and hissed with a gust of wind that came suddenly down the chimney. In all the excitement of *aquarelles* and cyphers, I had forgot there was a murderer at large.

"You must return to Chawton, Jane. The risk is too great," Henry said heavily.

"Nonsense."

I had certainly thought the sentiment, but it was West who expressed it.

"Between the two of us, Austen, we may keep her safe until

her latest novel is printed," he said. "A very little while may see the end of this affair. We have allowed ourselves to be diverted by the secrets of the map—we have ignored Ewan MacFarland. Find his murderer, man, and we shall know all at once!"

His tone was vehement; but Henry answered with weariness.

"I cannot allow my sister to be exposed to further danger."

"As the lady in question," I retorted tartly, "I agree with Mr. West. We waste our energies in diversions of no import, Henry, when we ought rather to be considering who killed the Colonel. I may offer you one possible suspect, Mr. West—Lieutenant James Dunross."

I told both men then of my visit to Keppel Street yesterday. The injuries visited upon my skull had very nearly banished all memory of Miss MacFarland and her household; but there remained the words of the batman, Spence: MacFarland had opposed the Lieutenant's marriage to his sister. The Lieutenant, in turn, was hard-pressed to call the Colonel a hero for his actions at Waterloo. And yet, they had drunk coffee together at Gunter's on the way to Carlton House, the last morning of MacFarland's life . . .

"He might well have slipped poison into the Colonel's cup then," West agreed, "but a lame man, however young, could not have run from me last night. Dr. Baillie's attacker fairly flew down Newman Street."

"The ruffian who bludgeoned my head was hardly James Dunross," I countered. "But a lame man may hire others to do his dirty work."

"How did the Lieutenant learn of the map's discovery?" Henry asked. "He was not at the Carlton House nuncheon, you say; and the batman insists that he no longer notices his friends among the Scots Greys. Is he at all acquainted with Baillie?"

"I do not know. The doctor might have told Dunross or Miss MacFarland about the map, however," I admitted, "if he returned the Colonel's body to Keppel Street for burial yesterday. He had not yet done so when I called."

"Did you describe the sketch to Miss MacFarland whilst you were there, Jane?" Henry persisted.

"I did not even mention the word *poison,* believing it Dr. Baillie's place to relate the results of his anatomisation." I cast my battered mind back for an instant. "I *did* repeat the words *Waterloo Map*, as being the last MacFarland uttered. That cannot have told his sister or Dunross much. Indeed, they both suggested only disappointment at the phrase."

"We must return," said Raphael West, "to the critical facts. It is probable that one of the Regent's guests at Carlton House dosed the Colonel's nuncheon on Monday. The same person learnt of the map's discovery from Dr. Baillie on Tuesday. On Wednesday, he or his associates attacked both Baillie and Miss Austen. We must put a name to that person, and soon."

"You, Mr. West, are the only one of us who possesses an *entrée* to Carlton House," I said. "Can you obtain a list of Monday's guests?"

"I can," he replied. "MacFarland's killer is almost certainly among them; but we cannot know *which* of those guests Baillie told of the map on Tuesday."

"Surely we might ask Baillie that himself?" Henry cried.

"You forget." I laid my hand on my brother's wrist. "The doctor's throat was stabbed. He may not yet be able to speak."

West had ceased his restless pacing and taken up a position near the fire, one glossy boot propped on the fender. His countenance was brooding.

"The map itself may speak for Baillie, if only we may learn to read it."

"But without the key . . . ?"

He glanced at me. "There is one person who knows a good deal of cyphers," he said, "and the Regent's nuncheon was given in his honour. We must inform the Duke of Wellington of his Hero's murder—and show him the Waterloo Map."

"JANE," MY BROTHER SAID as we rumbled towards home in a hackney, "I am divided in my mind whether we ought to admit Fanny to our confidence."

Or send her packing back to Edward in Kent.

Naturally the problem had presented itself. I, too, was divided. It is one thing to apprehend and accept danger for oneself—another to thrust it upon an innocent young lady.

"She is no longer a green girl," I said tentatively.

"But neither is she ours to risk," Henry replied. "If she is to remain, she must be informed of her danger. The choice must be hers, to stay or to go."

"You know what she shall chuse! Any woman of spirit should do the same!"

"Yes—but at least I shall have a plausible excuse for my brother, if his dearest child is stunned or stabbed," Henry argued.

"Very well. We have already told her of murder; we shall relate the rest of the particulars to her this evening."

But upon our arrival at Hans Place, we found that Mr. Haden had descended before us, intent upon ministering to both his Austen patients; and finding them inexplicably gone from the house, had required little urging to stay and listen to Miss Knight's harp.

It was the modish airs of Sophia Dussek, and not Haydn, that held the surgeon wrapt this evening; and between observing his transported looks as Fanny played, and ordering an early dinner from the Frenchwomen in the kitchen (for I found that I was famished, and Henry overly-tired from his excursion into Newman Street), there was neither leisure nor occasion for talk of a serious kind. The shadow of Death passed over our house this e'en, banished by laughter, good food, and music. I accepted Mr. Haden's scolding, for having abandoned my sopha too soon, and his paregoric draught at bedtime.

All the residents of Hans Place slept deep and sound throughout the night, our peace unbroken by the possessors of cyphers.

15

ORDERED TO THE REAR

Friday, 17 November 1815
23 Hans Place

It had been agreed, yesterday, that Raphael West should despatch a brief letter to Wellington's secretary to request an interview. Having sketched the Duke, West was known to Wellington's suite, and should certainly be afforded an answer. The result of this correspondence could hardly be learnt from the early post, however; so I enjoyed a breakfast free from anticipation.

My insouciance was rewarded, as insouciance often is. I had hardly sat down to my toast when Manon appeared, followed by an urchin of rough appearance and indescribably blackened hands, bearing a corded parcel from Mr. John Murray's establishment. *Emma,* at last! —Or as much of her first volume as has yet been printed.

An enclosure from Murray begged me to forgive him for the unconscionable delay, as a lack of paper of suitable printing quality throughout the Metropolis had set behind his work some weeks. He offered, as olive-branch, an edition of Miss

Williams's *Narrative of the Events which have taken place in France* for the delectation of the Hans Place intimates, a work not yet available to the publick.

Miss Williams's book seemed to spring like Venus from our discussions in the picture vault yesterday. Being a lady's account, it is sure to treat of French fashions and Society, more than French politics or cyphers—but as a lady's interest is never far from *Art*, I consigned the volume to Henry, with orders that his reading should pay strict attention for references to the unknown Isabey or his possible School.

For my own part, I intended to retire with *Emma*.

Henry, however, was applying his spectacles to his own correspondence, a faint line between his brows.

"Do not say that your bank is proving tiresome, again!" I poured out his coffee and proffered the cup.

"If the present course continues, it shall in all probability fail," he returned equably. "But I am not reading of that. This is a letter from Mr. James Stanier Clarke—in answer to my missive of yesterday."

I had quite forgot that I had been reported as at death's door.

"He says all that is proper, regarding your shocking violation," Henry continued. "I shall not sport with your patience by reading *that.* He concludes, however, in the devout hope that *no sudden taking-off on the part of Miss Austen will preclude the dedication of her latest Work to His Royal Highness, the Prince Regent, whose heart is entirely animated by the Prospect.* He actually urges me to rifle your desk, in the hope of finding the Regent's praises already composed."

"Mr. Clarke never used the word *rifle,*" I said indignantly.

"Perhaps not." Henry glanced up. "His fist is dashed awkward to make out, Jane. Could it be *ruffle*?"

I snorted. The ridiculous little man had hardly spared my tragedy a thought. No lament for the untimely passing of Genius. Not so much as a single lily from the Regent's succession-houses, in tribute to a maiden plucked in her youth. I gathered my dignity and rose from the table.

"Pray send him whatever lines you think proper, Henry. I am sure you may compose a tolerable piece of Royal flattery more readily than I. You may tell Mr. Clarke you discovered the dedication clutched next my heart—or hidden beneath my bed-pillow. Perhaps *then* he will be sorry."

"AUNT," FANNY MURMURED AROUND the parlour door-frame perhaps an hour later. "There is a man come to the servants' entrance, endeavouring to see you. Madame Bigeon will not admit him, in the apprehension he means to bludgeon you."

I set down my pen and turned from the little deal table that served me as writing desk in Henry's abode. I had just reached the point in my excessively gratifying narrative where Knightley observes to Mrs. Weston that he *should like to see Emma in love, and in some doubt of a return*. Much the same might be said of dear Fanny. She has always seemed too cool for her heart ever to have been engaged. I wonder if she will recognise some part of herself in my spoilt and engaging Miss Woodhouse?

"Does the man look like a murderer?" I asked.

She considered. "I have only the one experience from

which to judge, to be sure—but I should have said that he is a servant."*

I rose from my sheets and followed her downstairs.

The fellow waiting near the kitchen door was hardly my ruffianly lamplighter, but of scrupulously neat appearance.

"Spence!" I inclined my head cordially to the batman. "Pray step inside—it is far too inclement to be standing about in the area."

"As to that, ma'am, I've known far worse outside of Badajoz," he replied. "I've no wish to disturb; but you did say as I should remember your direction if ever I thought to speak to you—about the Colonel, God rest his soul, and Miss MacFarland, and that there Dunross."

I held the kitchen door wide, despite Madame Bigeon's disapproval. The Frenchwoman threw up her hands and retreated in dudgeon to the cellar.

"I shall be quite all right, Fanny," I told my niece. "This is Mr. Spence, who lives in Keppel Street, and is a little acquainted with your Uncle Charles."

She looked askance—Spence's accent betrayed he was no gentleman, and quite undeserving of the title *Mister*—but forbore to question me. "Very well. If you will like to undertake our walk to Grafton House in a quarter-hour, I shall be writing letters above-stairs."

With this parting hint to the batman that her aunt was not entirely undefended, Fanny took herself off. I drew a plain

---

* Fanny refers obliquely here to her previous encounter with a murderer in *Jane and the Canterbury Tale* (Bantam, 2011).—*Editor's note.*

wooden chair up to the scrubbed oak table and sat down. Spence, however, remained on his feet in a gesture of gallantry and deference.

"You told us t'other day how you found the Colonel," he began, "but not how he died. 'Twas poison! The sawbones, Baillie, told us—after he was done cutting up my master's body."

"I am sorry to hear it," I said. I did not wish him to know I had deliberately withheld the truth. The intelligence of murder had not been mine to give. "Your mistress must be deeply distressed."

"Fair beside herself." Spence shifted uneasily. "As you'll see when I tell you. I've been turned off, ma'am, and without a character. Turned off! After all the scrapes the Colonel and I came through together."

"But that is shocking!" I cried. "What possible reason could Miss MacFarland find, to treat you so unhandsomely?"

"Dunno. She wouldn't speak for herself. It was the Lieutenant who ordered me to the rear, in a manner of speaking. Told me I was no further use to the lady, as she'd be married soon and shutting up the house."

That might be true, I supposed. "But why did she withhold your character?"

"Dunross said as she'd no opinion of my service, being only a batman and not a butler. Said I ought to take up the Army again, as striking camp and grooming a trooper is all I'm fit for."

It was a bruising appraisal, harshly delivered. At a time when Wellington's Army was being discharged *en masse*, Spence was unlikely to find a foothold even among his old cavalry mates. Miss MacFarland had turned her brother's loyal servant upon the world without the barest provision. What had Spence done, to merit such careless treatment?

Or what, perhaps, had he *known*—that made a swift dismissal expedient?

"What I came to enquire, ma'am," he persisted, "is whether your brother, Captain Charles, is to be turned on shore any time soon? And if mebbe he'll be setting up his own household? I can promise to work hard and faithful, if he's wishful of a manservant."

The request was so pitiable I bit my lip. "I have not had a letter from Captain Austen in some weeks," I said truthfully, "but if you will provide me with your direction, Spence, I shall make it my business to write to him today. I cannot promise an early return of news, as the mails at sea are so uncertain."

"Thank'ee, ma'am. I don't suppose you've need of a strong back and quick hands here in Hans Place? I can promise you not to meddle with the Frenchwoman, as her kind and mine have never seen eye-to-eye."

I shook my head regretfully. "This is my brother's household, not mine, and he has all the servants he requires at present."

"Which is as expected," Spence replied. Very much on his dignity, he bowed and turned towards the kitchen door.

"Spence, stay a moment," I said impulsively. "Were you surprized to learn that the Colonel was poisoned? Can you think of any reason he should have died in that way—or of anyone who might have sped his taking-off?"

He stopped short, his gaze fixed on the doorframe. There was an uneasy pause, filled with thought and regret.

"There's many as hates a Hero, ma'am," the batman said tightly. "And my Colonel was certainly a Hero."

"Were you with him at Waterloo?"

"—Holding his third mount behind the lines. The first two were shot out from under him. And if I'd been beside him when he lost the last," Spence flared, "he should not have surrendered, nor found himself a prisoner of the French."

"Did he ever tell you how it was, those terrible hours in enemy hands?"

The batman shook his head. "Not a word would he speak. Discovered me with what was left of the Greys in Brussels, two days after the fighting ended—the bulk of the British forces having retreated there. Fair crazed the Colonel was, from no sleep and living rough. He'd walked back into the city behind the Prussian baggage train—they're the ones as chased the French, as you'll probably have heard. Walked nine miles, I might add, *without* his boots! The French had stripped 'em off him straightaway." The batman's voice broke suddenly, as tho' the image of his Colonel's bruised feet was more harrowing than he could bear. "*Hoby's* boots, what I've shined with blacking and champagne time out of mind! Bloody soles, the Colonel had, ma'am, and blood on his hands."

"How dreadful! The march alone should qualify him for Hero," I said soothingly. "And yet he told you nothing about how he freed himself from the French?"

"Only as the coves looted some wine in Braine l'Alleud, and he slipped away whilst they was snoring," Spence confided.

"—Seizing his chance, as Miss MacFarland observed. And how did he seem to you, Spence, in the months after the great battle? Was Colonel MacFarland able to be comfortable in London, without the cavalry to give him direction?"

There was a brief silence. "It's been hard on any number of us, ma'am," the batman said, "living alongside regular folk, who've no notion of pickets in the brush, waiting to send a lead ball into a man's heart. 'Twas hard on the Colonel. Only the map gave him comfort. It trained his interest, as it were, when nothing else could."

I felt the breath stop in my lungs. "The map?"

"Aye. He spoke of it, seemingly, when you found him. My mistress said they were his last words. *Waterloo Map.*"

"Yes," I whispered. "You knew of it, Spence?"

"O' course. Showed me it a hundred times if he showed me once. A picture with a letter writ on the back."

"And Miss MacFarland. She knew of the map?"

Spence shook his head. "It was the Colonel's great secret. But after you'd paid your call and gone, the mistress did come to me. Couldn't understand why the Colonel said *Waterloo Map* when he was took ill. Hoped he'd have thought of *her* in his death-throes, and given his blessing on her marriage. Which he never would."

This seemed in keeping with Miss MacFarland's behaviour Wednesday as I recalled it. "Was Lieutenant Dunross equally ignorant?"

"Not him!" Spence cried. "I'd have said it was the map divided him from the Colonel. But I might not have the right of it, ma'am. Neither man would speak a word about what lay between 'em. Fair drove my mistress wild, trying to get to the bottom of their coldness."

And yet the Lieutenant had evinced little by way of emotion when I had uttered the Colonel's final words. If he knew of the Waterloo Map, he was successful in his studied indifference.

"Did Lieutenant Dunross ask you about . . . this paper, after the Colonel's death?"

"Aye, and he did. Wanted to know if I'd took it," Spence said indignantly. "When he knows I can't even read!"

I digested this. Illiteracy may have been the batman's friend. He had seen the map, but had no notion of what it said; this may have preserved him from violence.

"I told him the Colonel kept it always in his breast pocket," Spence continued, "but Dunross flew into a passion and said it weren't there. Baillie'd brought the Colonel's body home, you see, and the paper couldn't be found among his things."

So Dunross had searched. And was foolish enough to betray the fact.

I began to wonder at his motives for consoling his bereaved young lady. Did he linger so many hours in Keppel Street, in order to turn over the rooms?

And all the while, it was Dr. Baillie who had the map on his person. Baillie, who was attacked Wednesday night, mere hours after bringing the Colonel's body home.

"When were you dismissed from Miss MacFarland's service, Spence?" I asked.

"Wednesday. The very day you called, ma'am," he said. "Baillie'd been and left. I'd just seen the Colonel's corpus laid out decent in the parlour, and set flowers near his bier, when Dunross spoke his piece. I was to gather my things and be gone, whilst he was there to see me do it, and dinner not even laid for my mistress."

I could summon nothing in response to this outrage except, "So late in the day! Where did you go, Spence?"

The batman's eyes slid away from mine. "I've a few friends left. And some blunt put by. Don't you worry yourself about *me*, ma'am."

I had enough familiarity with my nephews' schoolboy cant to know that *blunt* meant coin. But I felt certain Spence was hardly plump in the pocket.

"I have thought of the very thing to suit you," I said firmly as I rose from the kitchen table. "A gentleman of my acquaintance is sure to have need of a manservant. Mr. West, in Newman Street. Are you at all familiar with Belper stoves?"

"With *what,* begging your pardon, ma'am?"

"I am sure he shall soon put you in the way of it," I assured him. "Now. Be so good as to remain here in the warm, Spence, whilst I write a few lines of introduction to Mr. West."

16

VIOLET IN SPRING

Friday, 17 November 1815
23 Hans Place, cont'd.

I have said that Grafton House is a place of misery; but like most sources of suffering, it offers manifold delights to the innocent and unsuspecting. I have been taken in by its blandishments for years. No lady of my acquaintance would think of visiting London without submitting to its temptations; and Fanny, being more than willing to part with her pin-money, was straining at the leash. It was my penance to accompany her there this morning, for having banished her from my interview in the kitchen. She profited from our two-mile walk into Town by interrogating me about the batman, Spence—and having secured Henry's unwilling complaisance, I felt free to tell her All.

The history was complicated enough to bring us right up to the corner of Grafton and New Bond Streets. Here, the crush of carriages awaiting their mistresses delayed us some moments; the crowd of ladies standing near the entrance of Wilding & Kent, the linen-draper we sought on the Grafton House premises, made it almost impossible to gain the threshold.

"I am excessively glad I persuaded Papa to part with me these few weeks," Fanny said thoughtfully. "There is nothing to equal your intrigues, Aunt, in a Canterbury neighbourhood. Will you forgive me if I say I am eager to meet Mr. Raphael West? The stile of his father's painting is outmoded, of course—any creature of taste must prefer the naturalism of a Lawrence—but Mr. West has won your esteem, and must therefore be of interest to all who care for you."

"Do not be assuming we share any extraordinary degree of friendship," I said hastily. "He is a very gentleman-like man, and must always treat a lady with deference; but I do not think he cherishes any peculiar regard."

I said this for myself as much as for Fanny; for indeed, Mr. West occupied too large a share of my thoughts to be entirely safe. It was his eyes I saw in my own mind, when I settled myself for sleep.

"Pish," Fanny said airily. "He reads your novels. He admits you to his confidence regarding the murder and the map. This is the highest mark of esteem possible—when a gentleman acknowledges the worth of a lady's understanding."

I had known one such man before, and lost him. I could not endure the temptation of another. "I believe it was *I* who admitted *West* to *my* confidence, regarding the murder and the map, Fanny."

"Had my intellect met with half so much respect," she persisted, "from even *one* of the young men of my acquaintance, I should have been married long since."

Being unequal to an answer, I hastened to the opposite paving and Grafton House.

Wilding & Kent is an enormous establishment, even by London standards. For those who are incapable of meeting the extortionate cost of a modish dressmaker (who reserve their Genius for the titled and the Great), the Grafton House emporium is a practical and thrifty answer. Here one may purchase bugle trimming at two shillings, four-pence the yard; silk stockings for twelve shillings the pair, cotton at four; white silk handkerchiefs for much cheaper than one will pay at Crook & Besford's—which is far less crowded for that very reason; worsteds; woollens; crewels; muslins; figured cambric; all manner of shawls and feathers; sarsenet and lace; and Irish linen at four shillings the yard. The relative cheapness and quality of the millinery are so fixed in the minds of the Metropolis's ladies, that unless one broaches the Wilding & Kent door when most of London is still abed, one is obliged to wait full half an hour for attention.

On this occasion, we were arrived at Grafton House a little after one o'clock—and from the press of ladies circling the broad tables overflowing with bolts of brightly-coloured stuffs, we might expect a tedious interval before putting in our orders. We were meant to purchase enough ells for Eleanor Bridges's purple gown, and her brothers' linen shirts. Fanny's attention was divided, however, between a ravishing sea-blue silk for evening wear, an embroidered one of royal purple, a velvet in deep violet—and the mysteries of the Waterloo Map. The cacophony of female voices all around us served as a convenient screen for private conversation.

"I collect that Mr. West's exertions are all on the side of naming the murderer, before he should strike again," Fanny mused as she held the sea-blue silk against her bodice, and endeavoured to view it in a pier glass overwhelmed by other ladies. "But for my part, I should like to know more of the cunning sketch."

"In order to penetrate the cypher?"

She shook her head. "I refer to the romance, Aunt! The letter on the obverse! Has no one thought to consider of the poor lady, who never received her lover's parting words?"

Oh, God, that I might have kissed you one last time . . . Trust Fanny to go straight to the heart of the intrigue. An unknown named Charles had penned those words; presumably he had died not long thereafter, and the Waterloo Map fell into Colonel MacFarland's hands. His *bloodied* hands, as Spence had described them. How had the map come to the Colonel?

"If the letter writer also painted the sketch," Fanny persisted, "would not it behoove us to learn his name?"

"Perhaps," I said. "But we cannot assume that artist and letter writer were one and the same."

"Why ever not?" She turned from the thronged glass in frustration. "He clearly understood the map's purpose. He wrote to his Beloved in part to urge her to *keep the paper*, because the Emperor would have need of it one day. The sketch was uppermost in his mind on the eve of his death. I am sure he is the author of the cypher as well as the farewell letter. Perhaps it is a *Frenchman* who wishes to get it back!"

I stood still, a length of gold spangle drifting through my fingers. Fanny had said something of importance, I knew; something that tugged at the mind, and took me back to the picture vaults beneath West's house. We had been determined to discover MacFarland's enemy in his murderer—but what if we sought instead the dead artist's *friend*?

School of Isabey.

I could not summon my errant thought; the air in Wilding & Kent was close, and my concussed head ached. I resolved to consider Fanny's words in the hackney we must hire to take us and all our bandboxes home. In the meanwhile—a clerk in neat black suiting and a long white apron was approaching us. We dared not escape his attention, or we should be idling here another hour.

"I cannot decide whether Eleanor Bridges will like embroidered silk or velvet more," Fanny mused, a hand caressing each. "One is so *truly* purple; but the other is far more attractive, for being rather *less*."

"Then buy Eleanor the purple and take the violet yourself," I advised. "A girl is never so happy in her friend's appearance, than when she displays a superior taste."

It is my experience in life that when one is particularly eager in anticipation of an event, one is doubly sure of a disappointment. Parties have been made up and boxes secured, for the performance of a Mrs. Siddons or a Kemble, only to be met with illness or mischance or the substitution of a pantomime. Cards of invitation have been sent and received, with mutual satisfaction, only to have the encounter put off by dubious weather or colic among the carriage horses. Lizzy Bennet approaches the Netherfield Ball determined to dance every dance with Mr. Wickham—and discovers the blackguard has fled the village, from a fear of encountering those who know him best.

By this estimation, Fanny ought to have been disappointed in her desire to meet Raphael West.

The entirety of her fortnight's visit ought to have passed away, without a glimpse of the man or a line from his household. She might then have brooked her frustration at the denied treat, by observing her Aunt's depression of spirits and withered hopes. A chord of silent sympathy should have strengthened the affection between the two. But in an episode unique in my experience, Fanny's eagerness was rewarded almost as soon as it was expressed. We arrived back in Hans Place to discover Mr. Raphael West sitting with Henry by the parlour fire.

The gentlemen rose with celerity as we approached, and secured places near the hearth for our revival; for there is nothing like a hired chaise for discomfort and draughts, no matter how clement the weather. Before we seated ourselves, however, I recollected my smiling niece.

"May I have the pleasure, Fanny, of presenting Mr. Raphael West to your acquaintance? Mr. West, my niece Miss Knight, of Godmersham Park, Kent. She is arrived like an angel of mercy, complete with celestial harp, to nurse her ailing Uncle."

Mr. West bowed, and kissed my Fanny's hand, with one of those penetrating looks from his dark eyes that must put every maiden to the blush. Having met them for a year, I was accustomed; but I observed Fanny's cheeks to flush the faintest rose.

"I am come in part to thank your aunt for the unexpected appearance of a most desirable manservant," he observed. "I commend the swiftness of your understanding, Miss Austen, in despatching Spence to Newman Street; he is certain to be useful, not only in my present endeavours but, I daresay, in future ones. There is nothing like a manservant who is well acquainted with both horses and firearms. For the present, I am content to instruct him in the mysteries of Belper stoves."

"I have been urging West to dine with us," Henry cried, "but he insists he may stay only to issue an invitation. He has secured an audience with no less a personage than the Duke of Wellington, Jane—you will know that he has lately been painting His Grace at Carlton House—and pays us the very great honour of hoping we shall accompany him!"

This arch attempt at veiled communication—a hint to West that not *all* in the room were privy to his intelligence—was immediately put to a rout by Fanny, who cried, "Famous! So you shall learn the truth of the cypher from the one man likely in all of London to command it! I wonder if the Duke will recognise the significance of the drawing as well, Mr. West?"

By way of answer, the painter raised his brows at me. I was acutely aware of having committed an indiscretion, in relating so much of a privileged nature; I might be suspected of *gossip*, in a matter of life and death. I lifted my chin, therefore, and met the challenge directly.

"I have apprised Miss Knight of the danger she undertakes, in remaining with us in Hans Place," I said. "I could not expose her to violence and murder, in all ignorance, as my brother and I are responsible for her care whilst in London. I may assure you, Mr. West, that Miss Knight is a creature of decided understanding and absolute discretion—tho' her present enthusiasm may have produced quite a different impression."

"Very well. As for your surmises, Miss Knight," West said smoothly, "I should be astonished if the Duke of Wellington understood the sketch's import; tho' familiar with many ravaged and desperate parts of the world, he has not yet been to Russia, and certainly not during the Emperor Napoleon's disastrous campaign. But I collect you have your own thoughts upon the subject of cyphers. May I know them?"

Fanny seated herself with a pretty air of satisfaction at being treated as a member of the company. "I am more interested in artists, Mr. West. Watercolourists, to be precise. My aunt and I were agreeing only now, on our way home, that my own poor talents might benefit a good deal from a visit to Somerset House."*

"Somerset House?" West repeated, with a look for me. "A great many persons must admire the paintings exhibited there, to be sure—"

"And copy them," Fanny supplied. "An admirable pursuit for a young lady, do not you agree? I might reasonably be thought to avoid any dangers attached to Hans Place, if I were to spend my mornings before an easel and an Old Master, attempting to seize a likeness that is not thoroughly contemptible. When the stiffness in back and neck becomes insupportable, I might take a turn about the room, and admire the work of others—"

"—Or request their opinion of your own," I suggested.

---

* Erected on the site of a former Tudor palace on the Strand, Somerset House was home to the Royal Academy, of which Benjamin West was president in 1815. The academy held an annual exhibition of more than a thousand works of art each spring; Jane Austen attended it on May 24, 1813, joking in a letter to her sister that she had hoped to find a portrait of Mrs. Darcy there, but for the fact that Mr. Darcy disliked having his wife exposed to the publick eye. Somerset House's Great Exhibition Room was lit from above by a lanthorn skylight, which made it ideal for the viewing of pictures. After 1836 the Royal Academy and its collections moved to the National Gallery and then to Burlington House.—*Editor's note.*

"Indeed, if you were to receive instruction from any likely painters in *aquarelle,* your artistic education should be complete. I understand a number of French artists attached to the Napoleonic Court have lately fled Paris, being loath to accept the patronage of the Bourbons. Is not that true, Henry? For I know you have been reading Miss Williams's recollections."

"Jane—" my brother attempted.

"What better place for them to congregate, than the Royal Academy? I should not be surprized if Fanny were to meet with a member of even the School of Isabey there."

A brief pause greeted this pronouncement. Then West rose from his chair and turned restlessly before the fire. "Like Dr. Baillie, you believe it necessary to identify the painter? I had thought we were agreed that it was the murderer of Colonel MacFarland we meant to pursue."

I exchanged glances with Fanny, who was bursting to express her views. A slight shake of my head, and she bit her lip.

"Certainly we are in pursuit of a poisoner—a dangerous person who will kill to obtain the map," I agreed. "But we have been assuming, all along, that the murderer is an enemy of MacFarland's, and that the clew to his identity lies in the Colonel's past. What if the murderer is a *friend*, rather, of the man who painted the sketch? —A follower of the deposed Emperor, perhaps, whose loyalties still lie with Buonaparte's France?"

West's brows drew down over his blade of a nose, but he said nothing. He came to a halt before the fire, revolving the idea.

"Surely West himself may survey the rooms of Somerset House," Henry protested, "and detect any painter who might share the stile of the Waterloo Map. Such a search need not involve Fanny."

"But Mr. West carries everywhere the *cachet* of his formidable father," Fanny interjected, "inspiring awe as much as intimacy! —Whereas a young lady, gently reared, is bound to excite a simpler notice; and inspire confidences Mr. West cannot."

West wheeled on Fanny. "You mean to sit in the Great Exhibition Room and pretend to paint, do you?"

"Tomorrow morning, if I may," Fanny replied. "Although I should not use the word *pretend,* Mr. West. My friends consider me fairly adept with charcoal and chalk."

"Watercolour is another matter entirely."

"Which is why I shall require your permission—a note of introduction—to gain the exalted rooms of Somerset House. I should never be mistaken for a proficient."

West studied her with a spark of amusement. "I shall do better than that," he said. "I shall make a passable copy of the Waterloo Map—merely the picture and not the cypher, mind—for you to take with you tomorrow. You might usefully consult it before you survey your rivals' art in search of the *School of Isabey.* Stile is a subtle quality, Miss Knight—it demands a trained hand and eye. But if you can successfully detect it in others, your adventure may prove of use."

"My Aunt assures me," she said, with a droll twist to her mouth, "that I possess superior taste. Your hunt could not be in better hands, Mr. West."

THE PAINTER TOOK HIS leave of us, despite protestations that we wished him to stay. I led him down to Henry's front door, and was rewarded by the sudden grasp of my hand in his. He raised it to his lips. A warm flush swept over me; the softness, and yet the decidedness of that caress—

"You will understand why I must go," he murmured, "when I tell you that I intend to see Dr. Matthew Baillie this evening. I am allowed to visit only after six o'clock, when the regular business of St George's Hospital is done. My hope is that the fellow may have recovered speech, and will tell me something of his assailant."

I nodded, my throat too tight for words. He retained my hand an instant, his eyes fixed on mine, then turned resolutely through the door.

I am a liar if I said I attended to half what was said, for the remainder of dinner.

17

OLD DOURO

Saturday, 18 November 1815
23 Hans Place

The Duke of Wellington is at present the Governor of Occupied Paris, where he has remained with few interruptions these five months since the Battle of Waterloo. When in London for consultations with the Government or His Royal Highness the Prince Regent—or to be sketched by a West for the purposes of posterity—he lodges with his elder brother, Richard, the Marquess of Wellesley, rather than in the country with his wife.

Richard Wellesley is one of the greatest and yet most puzzling men of our Age. When only forty, as Governor-General, he presided over the expansion of British rule in India to what may justly be called an empire—and suffered an enquiry for it in Parliament. He served as Ambassador to Spain whilst his brother waged war in the Peninsula. When Castlereagh and Canning met in a duel, and were obliged to resign from Spencer Perceval's government, it was Richard who ascended to the post of Foreign Secretary—only to leave it when Perceval was killed by a madman. He is a brilliant speaker, yet suffers periods of utter mental blankness, without warning or recollection, that prevent his saying so much as a word.* He has fathered five children on a former Paris Opera dancer named Hyacinthe, who speaks no English, and whom he only made his Marchioness long after she was past child-bearing age. As a result, he possesses a numerous family—but no legitimate heir.

Wellesley is renowned as a drunk and a rake; he is frequently held at swordspoint by his creditors; and as the head of an Anglo-Irish noble family, his unprofitable acres are heavily mortgaged. Naturally, therefore, he bought the lease to Apsley House from the Crown some years since, and set about renovations in an extravagant stile. Apsley House is a magnificent Robert Adam structure fronting Hyde Park Gate, and is known as No. 1 London, accordingly.

It is most particularly No. 1 when Richard Wellesley's brother, the Duke of Wellington, is in residence.

Raphael West collected his Austens in Hans Place this morning, in a handsome closed carriage pulled by a pair of chestnuts. I recognised the conveyance from my first encounter with Mr. West—his coachman had collided with my brother James's cart in a snowstorm last December. The coachman having failed to recognise *me,* however, I forbore to mention the incident, and settled myself gratefully against the velvet squabs of the interior. I had adopted the same costume I wore to Carlton House for this call upon the Duke—my Prussian blue carriage dress and

* These blank periods afflicted Richard Wellesley in public, including in Parliament, and may in fact have been a form of "absence seizure," or epilepsy.—*Editor's note.*

dull bronze bonnet, with Eliza's sable muff; and I flatter myself that I looked as much a lady of Fashion as any who might mount the steps of Apsley House.

"How went your interview with Matthew Baillie?" I enquired, as we rumbled away from Henry's door.

"Well enough. He is expected to live, although his doctor fears the influence of fever and infection. He is to remain in St George's another week, at least."

"You met with Baillie?" Henry interjected. "Is he mending? Can he speak?"

"He can," West replied. "The stab wound to his throat is stitched and healing, but quite painful. I put two questions to the Court Physician—did he recollect anything at all of his assailant, and did he know why he was attacked—but he merely shook his head in answer. When I pressed him, he croaked out that he was the victim of a footpad. His purse, it seems, was stolen."

"He said nothing of the map?" I demanded. "Nor of MacFarland's poisoning?"

"He asked only if the paper he'd given me was safe," West returned, "and when I told him it was, he lay back upon his pillows in some relief. I observed that he was tired, but persisted long enough to ask if he knew of anyone who might do violence, to secure the sketch he had shewn me. Baillie only shook his head, and begged me most earnestly to present the map to His Grace, the Duke of Wellington. I assured him I should do so this morning."

"And with this we must be satisfied," I observed. "Let us hope the Duke is more forthcoming."

"We are granted a quarter-hour of his time," West advised as the chaise rumbled towards Knightsbridge and the Brompton road. "I hope you will not mind it, Miss Austen, if I speak for us all at first. Once His Grace is accustomed to the notion that we are come on a matter of cyphers, and not my father's commission, he may afford us more time to speak."

"Of course." As I could not hope the Duke of Wellington had looked into anything so paltry as a *novel* during his years in the Peninsula or whilst presiding over the Congress of Vienna, I felt certain he should have as little to say to me as I should to him.

"For my part, I am dashed fortunate to be included at all," Henry said. "I ought to have driven out with Fanny to Somerset House, and played chaperon in the face of encroaching artists."

Raphael West had presented Fanny with a remarkably deft copy of the Waterloo Map, *sans* cyphers, upon his arrival this morning. He had also lent my niece a sketchbook scrawled with charcoal by his own hand; an easel; a paintbox from his stores filled with rags and brushes; and a box of watercolours already well-used, so that she should not look like a complete novice. Moreover, he had spared a few moments for her instruction in Henry's ground floor anteroom, removing his coat and setting brush to paper in a manner that reduced Fanny to wordless admiration.

"The great danger in watercolour, as no doubt you know, is the tendency to muddy one's paints," he began. "That may be avoided by a frequent resort to your water and rags, and a care for the cleanliness of your brush."

Fanny maintained a respectful silence, her whole being trained on the artist's hand as it moved over the heavy laid paper.

"You are searching for a particular manner of painting, Miss Knight, that was practically invented by my friend Isabey," West continued, as he swiftly filled in shades and color with a sure but delicate brush. "He began life as Court Painter to Marie Antoinette, and specialised in miniatures. He is extremely adept at painting on ivory with a fine brush, and so far as *aquarelle* is concerned, possesses the hand of a master. Having said so much, I will add that he survived the Revolution by apprenticing himself to Jacques Louis David—and sketching some two hundred members of the Assembly. Having evaded the guillotine, Isabey adopted the Napoleonic Court, being a favourite of Josephine's. He served as drawing-master to her children, Hortense and Eugène. This was about the time that I was acquainted with him; we have not met in ten years. It is my understanding that at present he is portraitist to Louis XVIII. In this, we may read a treatise on survival."*

"But what is his *manner*?" Fanny asked vexedly. "Do you refer to his preference in subject, Mr. West, or the way he paints?"

"I refer to what the French call *technique*," he replied. "We should use the word *stile.* Isabey's is as distinct, to my eye, as your signature should be to your aunt's."

"But that cannot help *me*," Fanny argued. "I know nothing of painters."

* Jean Baptiste Isabey (April 11, 1767–April 8, 1855) was a French painter born in Nancy.—*Editor's note.*

"Nonsense," West retorted impatiently. "I am sure you may detect one of Sir Thomas Lawrence's pictures out of a hundred other portraits, just as you should probably know one of my father's. We are rarely cognizant of our own discernment, until it must be applied. Begin by glancing at the copy of the Waterloo Map."

Fanny did so, with greater attention.

"Isabey is known for his lack of ornament," West noted, "and even of background—spurning all trifling groupings with his portrait subjects, such as jewels and draperies, dogs or flowers. Moreover, his brushstroke is extremely delicate—the paint is never laid on too heavy. He prefers to capture solely the visage of the person he paints, fading into delicate tints that blend with the cream of his paper. It is as tho' the subject emerges from a cloud. Or, as my father may have seen when he studied the original of this map—as tho' the hills around Smolensk have emerged from the smoke of Buonaparte's cannon . . ."

Fanny lifted her eyes from West's copy. "The features of the icon might almost be a miniature," she observed. "And yet you are sure that Isabey himself did not paint the original?"

"He certainly did not accompany Napoleon on his invasion of Russia," West replied, setting down his brush and reaching for his coat. "And now, Miss Fanny—if you will forgive me—your hackney awaits; and your aunt and uncle have a pressing engagement."

THE MARQUESS OF WELLESLEY'S grand London home is of red brick, with five bays giving out on Piccadilly; Mr. Robert Adam designed it around an existing stable-block, which may account for its rather irregular pattern.* I had often passed the noble structure on foot, and wondered about the lives of its inhabitants—whether the French marchioness, Hyacinthe, whom nobody in London will receive due to the little nothing of her having borne five illegitimate children—is made miserable by her isolation; or whether being allied to Richard Wellesley is compensation enough for the lost pleasures of an opera-dancer. To pass through the portals of No. 1 London must inevitably stir my heart; admission to the Duke of Wellington's presence should prove sadly flat by way of comparison.

The entrance hall was lofty and spacious, dotted with busts from antiquity and marble-topped tables; these had carved gilt legs resembling Egyptian caryatids, altogether startling. A massive portrait of the Marquess as Governor-General of India—merely an earl at the time—dominated the room; his handsome face sported the Wellesley nose, his gaze held all the usual Wellesley arrogance, and his foot rested on a tiger skin.

An oval staircase, studded with columns, rose before us; to left and right were a study and a drawing-room, for No. 1 shares with Carlton House a predilection for putting its principal chambers on the *ground floor.* My expectation of meeting the Duke in one of these, however, was frustrated: for from the elegant drawing-room to our right emerged a figure in the uniform of the 1st Guards—which are now to be known as the Grenadier Guards, from having defeated Napoleon's troops of that name at Waterloo.

---

* In her descriptions of Apsley House, Jane refers to the state of the building prior to 1816, when the Duke of Wellington bought the lease from his brother and renovated the entire structure beyond recognition. Apsley House today is administered by the National Trust, and is very much as the Duke of Wellington knew it.—*Editor's note.*

Raphael West stepped forward. "My lord."

"Mr. West!" the soldier cried. "It is a pleasure to see you again."

As he approached us, I observed that one sleeve of his blue coat was pinned neatly to his breast; he had lost his right arm.

"My lord, may I present Miss Jane Austen and Mr. Henry Austen to your acquaintance? Lord FitzRoy Somerset," West said.

The youngest of the Duke of Beaufort's eight sons, Lord FitzRoy is one of the most distinguished of the officers on Wellington's staff, and one of the very few who emerged alive from Waterloo. Tho' only in his twenties, he is a veteran of innumerable battles, having served the Duke throughout his years in the Peninsula, during the Hundred Days, and then at the Conference in Vienna—a skirmish of a different sort. When his arm was amputated in Belgium last summer he demanded it back from the surgeons, so that he could retrieve a ring his wife had given him; it is that kind of dash that distinguishes Wellington's staff.

"I have told all my acquaintance about the handsome portrait you have made of me, West." He smiled at us charmingly. "I am to appear in Mr. Benjamin West's great painting of Waterloo, you know. Lady FitzRoy demands a copy of my head as forfeit, for all the time I have been absent from Paris!"

"You may have anything you wish, my lord, with my thanks for securing this interview," West said seriously.

"Nonsense. Allow me to convey you to the Duke—he is in expectation of you. May I commend you on your timeliness, West. Old Douro abhors a laggard."

It seemed there were principal rooms above, as well. We followed Lord FitzRoy up the colonnaded stairs to the first floor, and into a drawing-room with an Adam ceiling done in plaster and primrose, a decidedly unmilitary room—but I could imagine the mysterious Hyacinthe drinking ratafia in it, swathed in a gown of blue gossamer.

Standing by the hearth with one gleaming boot on the brass fender was the very fellow whose profile I had last glimpsed at Carlton House; and unremarkably, in a day-gown of striped French twill with grouse-colored velvet facings, her magnificent guinea-gold hair massed in curls about her perfect countenance, was Lady Frances Wedderburn-Webster. The Duke's latest flirt—and a formidable social force. The papers had reported the twenty-two-year-old was in Brussels on the eve of Waterloo, and despite being in the family way at the time, attended the Duchess of Richmond's ball. Half the British aristocracy had done the same, waltzing as Buonaparte crossed the Belgian border.

"Good morning, Your Grace. Lady Frances." Lord FitzRoy bowed low. "I have brought Mr. Raphael West to you, as instructed."

"Have you, by God. Hallo, West," the Great Man said—and strolled forward with his battlefield gait. Having spent most of his life astride a horse, His Grace may be forgiven a tendency to bowleggedness.

The Duke of Wellington is said to disappoint, among those who share his exalted station, due to his commonplace manner and his braying laugh. The Fashionable of the *ton* have made such a demi-god of the man, in their fervour to seize a Hero, that they know not what to do when confronted with a human being. Arthur Wellesley has spent his life living rough; he is accustomed to drinking poor coffee by campfires at two o'clock in the morning and drinking raw red wine in villages whose names no one has heard of, much less can pronounce. He has slept countless nights in canvas tents throughout India and Spain and Portugal; has been shot at by nameless marksmen in the hill country around Oporto; has thousands of deaths of young men on his conscience; and has outmanoeuvred the best diplomats of Vienna and Moscow by deploying the men he calls his *family*: young aides-de-camps like Somerset, who have mastered grace from childhood and know very well how to waltz. It should not be considered wonderful that he is awkward in Society and abrupt in his speech; he is the consummate Englishman of Empire: a doer, rather than a talker.

Being commonplace people enough, we Austens took his measure immediately.

Raphael West wasted none of the Duke's time. Somerset had hardly departed, closing the drawing-room doors behind him, before West launched into speech.

"We are grateful for your time and attention, Your Grace, and shall not abuse it," he said with a bow for Lady Frances. "May I present Miss Jane Austen, and Mr. Henry Austen, her brother, to your acquaintance?"

"If you must. What is this about, West? Have you marred the daub you made of me at Carlton House?"

The Duke did not even glance at us. And I carried a sable muff! I felt as exposed and unloved an object as a rainswept mongrel puppy discovered in a ditch.

But West said swiftly, "Murder, sir. Of a man you taught

us to regard as a Hero. I speak of the death of Colonel Ewan MacFarland of the Scots Greys. You will recall that he expired so recently as Monday, after your Carlton House nuncheon."

Wellington's brows drew down over his imperious nose and he stared accusingly at West. "You think I killed him, I suppose! I understood it was an apoplectic fit."

"The Court Physician, Matthew Baillie, has determined that the Colonel was poisoned. Baillie himself was recently stabbed in the street—the day after performing the Colonel's anatomisation—and is at present clinging to life in St George's Hospital."

"Is he, by God? I read of the attack in the papers, but did not realise . . . Oh, very well. Sit down, all of you," Wellington commanded. "Fanny, you ought to leave us; the present discussion is too distressing."

Lady Frances merely lifted her chin and gazed limpidly at the Duke; he sighed, and motioned the three of us to a settee.

We sat.

I confess I felt as tho' I had been brought before an Inquisitor; I was devoutly thankful that West intended to speak for us all.

"Poison, by God," Wellington mused. *By God* appeared to be his constant resort; having cheated Death on so many occasions, perhaps he credited Providence. "Why should anyone kill MacFarland? There was no evil in the man."

"Just so."

"And what has it to do with me?" the Duke demanded.

"Colonel MacFarland was discovered *in extremis* by Miss Austen, in the course of her visit to Carlton House," West began. But his words were cut short by Lady Frances.

"*That* is where I have seen you before!" she exclaimed. "I never forget a gown, and that dull bronze braid on Prussian blue is exactly suited to a lady of your years. You were with stuffy old Clarke, the Court Jester, and you came through the Blue Anteroom. A few days ago, was it not?"

"Monday," I managed. "The day Colonel MacFarland was murdered."

I might have said *died;* but it seemed important to support the line Raphael West was taking.

"How extraordinary." Lady Frances stared at me, her clever blond mind working. "What brought you to Carlton House, after all—and in Clarke's company?"

"I am to dedicate my latest novel to the Prince Regent."

"A novel!" Lady Frances rose from her chair and crossed to our settee, forcing Henry to his feet and taking his place beside me without a second glance at my brother. "Do not tell me you are an authoress! I adore novels above all else! Arthur is always twitting me upon the subject, I declare! Are your books dreadfully horrid? Have I read any of them?"

I felt myself to be at a loss.

"You may perhaps be acquainted with *Pride and Prejudice,*" Henry volunteered, "or *Sense and Sensibility,* which came before it, or *Mansfield Park,* which has recently delighted discerning readers with its instructive and moral sensibility."

"Lord!" Lady Frances cried. "How I loved Lizzy Bennet! All of my acquaintance have read *Pride and Prejudice*, to be sure! But I confess I did not admire *Mansfield Park* at all; I wished to drown Fanny Price in the nearest pond."

"That is a sentiment I have heard frequently expressed," I

admitted. "My readers seem to prefer Mary Crawford, reprehensible as she is."

"A delightful creature," Lady Frances agreed, pressing my hand with considerable emotion. "I might almost have seen myself reflected in her every word and action—tho' I believe she was meant to be dark. I am excessively gratified to make your acquaintance, Miss Austen! But what has an authoress to do with poor Ewan MacFarland? We all wept over his death, of course—it is a sad thing to lose a Hero—but why do you believe the Duke poisoned him?"

By way of answer, Raphael West drew the Waterloo Map from his coat and presented it to Arthur Wellesley. The Great Man stared at it for an instant, his piercing gaze roving over the sketch. "Smolensk," he said. "Moscow. What is this thing, West?"

"MacFarland's mind was fixed on that paper as he lay dying," West returned. "His final words to Miss Austen were *Waterloo Map*."

"Were they, by God?"

"Pray read the obverse, sir."

Wellington was put to school in Belgium as a youth; French is his second language. He scanned the lines of the parting letter and his frown deepened. "But this was penned from La Belle Alliance, on the eve of my battle!" He glanced up. "*The Emperor will have need of it one day*? The fellow refers to the sketch, of course, which he presumed would be despatched to his lady if he did not survive. Was this found on MacFarland?"

"It was not. Miss Austen discovered it hidden in a book in the Regent's Library, the day *after* MacFarland died."

The Duke's dark eyes grazed my own. "He had placed it there, perhaps, before the poison destroyed him. I wonder if he took this from the Frenchman who wrote it. Fellow was despatched by a bayonet, by God—the cuts in the paper are three-sided. Being a cavalryman, MacFarland did not carry a bayonet—a sabre was his weapon—so he didn't do for the Frenchman."

"Not on the battlefield, perhaps," West said. "But I understood the Colonel was sent back behind French lines, a surrendered prisoner."

"Think he killed his man then? And took this map? I should not have thought MacFarland a looter, by God—"

Over a lifetime of hard campaigning, Wellington had learnt to grasp essentials; he cut straight to the heart of the matter, then thought two steps beyond.

"Observe the figures at the bottom of the sketch, Your Grace," West said.

"Already have," the Duke replied, turning the paper over once more. "Saw them straightaway."

"Is it some sort of cypher?"

There was a silence. Wellington was no longer looking at the map; he was staring at Raphael West. "What do you know of cyphers?"

"I have encountered them in recent years through my acquaintance with Sir Joseph Banks," he said smoothly.

"Ah." The silence deepened. Sir Joseph was president of the Royal Society, an intimate circle of the most distinguished scientific minds of his day. The Royal Society shared the premises of Somerset House with the Royal Academy, which might account for West's acquaintance with Banks; but Wellington must be aware, as was I, that Sir Joseph also administered the government's Secret Funds—which were spent almost entirely on *spying*. It was Lord Harold Trowbridge who had informed me of the fact, being a member of Banks's stable—and responsible, I knew, for West's recruitment to the same work.

"Fanny, I really must insist that you leave us for a little," Wellington said. "If you will be so good as to conduct Miss Austen and her brother to the Library? You might order tea. Mr. West and I shall be only a few moments."

"You are very mysterious, Arthur." Lady Frances sighed; but she rose and smiled expectantly at Henry and me.

We dutifully followed her like errant children to the drawing-room doors.

"Send FitzRoy to me, if you please," the Duke barked.

Lady Frances merely waggled a hand in reply.

I HAVE NEVER BEEN so thankful for my brother, as when I sat down to drink tea in the Marquess of Wellesley's Library, which Lady Frances confided was the one room the Marchioness never entered. If I was disappointed in being denied a glimpse of the remarkable Hyacinthe, the emotion soon gave way to admiration for Henry's degree of address. Tho' hardly raised among The Great, his life in the late Eliza's company has taught him to be easy with every station; he possesses just that degree of deference and intimacy that most truly marks the gentleman. Lady Frances might be an acknowledged leader of the *ton*, but to Henry she was also a pretty young woman who expected attention—which he certainly knew how to supply. They were soon enjoying a comfortable coze, whilst the tea things were brought in on a silver tray. Lady Frances poured out; and hardly had she proffered me a cup, than the Duke and West appeared.

"The Duke shall be fixed in Paris some months, of course—perhaps another year, until King Louis is assured of a stable hold on government—but he really ought to be thinking of leasing a London house," she was saying as His Grace swung through the Library door. Lord FitzRoy and West were behind him. "Shouldn't you, Arthur?"

"This one suits me."

"But you cannot always be imposing on your brother! A gentleman of your position requires a liberal and numerous household."

"He requires new window hangings, is what you mean, Fanny." The Duke's gaze roved indifferently over the silk draperies that lined the Library, admittedly a trifle worn. "Richard has a shocking disregard for appearances, by God. Perhaps I shall toss him into the street and make something of this place. I like the address."

"Tea, Lord FitzRoy?" Lady Frances enquired. "I declare, I have not seen you this age! How does your pretty wife get on? How does Paris suit her?" Without waiting to hear the answer, she turned to me. "Lord FitzRoy was recently made aide-de-camp to the Regent, you know, but he still serves as the Duke's secretary during this Occupation, and like everyone else is gone to be happy in France! I believe I shall take a house in Paris myself, after Christmas, when what remains of Society has buried itself in the country."

"Then you may chuse the silk for the draperies, Fanny, in your visits to Lyons."

In such politenesses and sallies, our visit wore away, and we learnt nothing more to the purpose regarding the Waterloo Map. As I followed Lord FitzRoy Somerset to the door of Apsley House, however, I was much struck by this evidence of Wellington's good feeling: He had chosen to place at his right hand, a man who no longer had one to write with.

18

A PAINTER'S EYE

Saturday, 18 November 1815
23 Hans Place, cont'd.

"Forgive me for that unwonted exile," West said as we made our way back up the Brompton road. "The Duke is chary with information, as any man must be who has held the fate of Europe in his hands. He did not wish to speak of the cypher before strangers; my own guarantee was the mention of Sir Joseph's name."

"I confess I cannot see why," Henry objected. "What does a natural philosopher like Banks have to say to the present purpose?"

"His opinion is one the Duke has learnt to value," West offered, with a quick glance at me. "I will not relate all the particulars we canvassed but will tell you the Duke recognised something he called the Great Paris Cypher, which was much in use in the Peninsula. Indeed, he thinks it was expressly devised by Buonaparte's people for the conduct of that war. Most of the French communications intercepted by British forces were cloaked in it; but a member of Wellington's staff penetrated the cypher with effort and time. Each figure stands in place of a word. Even after the passage of many months, the Duke was able to recall a few of the simpler ones on the Waterloo Map. They are in French, mind, but he recognised the figures for *de* and *et.*"

"That helps us not at all," I protested.

"Not very much in itself, perhaps," West agreed. "But he told me the name of the man responsible for breaking the cypher—a Major Scovell. He is attached to the Occupation forces in Paris, but is at present in London, having come over with Wellington for these sittings at Carlton House."

"God in Heaven!" I cried. "Then we might know the meaning of the thing in a very little while!"

"The Duke intends to call upon Scovell at Stephen's Hotel this very day," West agreed, "and ask him to study the map.* Wellington believes, as we do, that once the cypher is understood, we may explain MacFarland's death—and the attacks upon yourself and Baillie."

"You gave Wellington our paper?" For some reason, I could not feel easy; indeed, what I felt bordered on outrage. "You believe Apsley House more secure than your father's vaults?"

"I believe the Duke is a better guard," West returned. "There can be few men in the world more worthy of trust."

That was true. I was unreasonable. It had never been likely that Wellington would allow a cyphered paper found near one of his murdered officers, out of his own hands; West had no choice but to relinquish the map, as he must have foreseen before ever

* Stephen's Hotel, in Bond Street, was patronized primarily by army officers and gentlemen in Austen's day.—*Editor's note.*

we entered Apsley House. I ought to feel some relief. We might all move in greater safety now the object of a murderous desire was in Wellington's charge.

But I doubted whether the Duke would tell us who killed Ewan MacFarland, now that he controlled the enquiry. He was never one to share a command.

WE WERE BACK IN Hans Place by two o'clock, and discovered our good Mr. Haden on the point of leaving his card, and inclined to regard Henry's activity as dangerous in the extreme.

"Having witnessed the suddenness of your decline in recent weeks," he said, "I should not wish you to precipitate a relapse. You cannot be sure of your strength."

My brother was looking decidedly weary, and I promised Haden I would prescribe pork jelly, beef tea, and rest for the remainder of the day. There could be nothing further to occupy Henry until Fanny returned from Somerset House and her researches.

"Miss Knight is gone out?" Haden enquired as he parted from us. "And quite alone?"

Such care as he takes of all of us! The man requires a wife . . . and children, perhaps . . . a numerous family, who might benefit from the depth of his anxiety and concern. It is wasted on a party of Austens.

I HAD WORKED MY way through most of the first volume of *Emma* by the time Fanny's hackney rolled to a halt in front of Henry's door. I broke off from the sentence *It was rather too late in the day to set about being simple-minded and ignorant,* and took up a position by the parlour window. No errant lamplighter bludgeoned my darling as she descended the carriage-step. The driver was so obliging as to hand out her easel and paintboxes to Manon, who was already on the paving. I must believe that each time Manon now hears a carriage halt before our door, she races to the threshold in anticipation of bloodshed.

I left Mr. Murray's sheets neatly stacked on the small table near the window in Henry's snug parlour, and hastened downstairs.

"My dear," I exclaimed as Fanny swept into the hall, Manon staggering behind with the easel. "How have you fared, alone in London?"

"Brilliantly, Aunt," she said with satisfaction. "Is Mr. West here, by any chance?"

"He is not. He was required at home after our visit to the Duke; something about his father, I collect."

"Ah." Some of the luminous beauty faded from her countenance; and I felt a sudden stab of fear. I could not bear Fanny to be made unhappy by a reckless passion for an artist twice her age. Particularly an artist I myself favoured.

"No matter. I may tell him about it when we next meet."

"About what?"

"The extraordinarily varied acquaintance I have made, in a few short hours!" She tore off her gloves and tossed them on the hall table. When she turned back to me, her eyes were glowing. "Have you any notion, Aunt, what a pleasure it is to be free—and unobserved—and in command of one's own purse, in London?"

It could be nothing like her closely guarded life in Kent, that much was certain. Nothing like the tedium of an unvarying country circle, bound by convention and lashed with gossip.

"I *do* know," I said slowly. "There is a headiness to independence, and the anonymity of a great Metropolis, that is at once invigorating . . . and *dangerous*, my dear."

"It cannot possibly be dangerous to feel so completely myself as I did today," she said in a low voice, her gaze on the floor. "I have stood in the role of *mother* so long . . . to all my beloved sisters and brothers. To move as a young woman alone through a fresh set of rooms, populated by strangers! To consult only one's own interest—to be rid of the stuffiness of convention, and all the expectations of others! To feel the admiration of a gentleman, entirely divorced from the knowledge of one's birth or fortune—"

She looked at me almost wildly. "I intend to return to Somerset House as soon as may be."

"Very well, my dear," I replied. "Let it be Monday. I hope you will not feel it to be *too* lowering, if I elect to go with you."

HENRY HAVING RISEN REFRESHED from his nap, we convened before the parlour fire. Fanny had put off her spencer and bonnet, and was bursting with news. We waited only for the Madeira and cakes that Manon brought round on a tray, before she unburdened her soul.

"There was not the slightest difficulty in breeching the gates of Somerset House," she began. "Mr. West's card provided an instant entrée. I was treated as a favoured visitor, and had a footman to carry my easel, and show me which were the most admired pictures for study. There are so many, Aunt! I declare

I had not expected them to be hung frame to frame, and lining every wall, in such a jumble that one did not know where to train the eye at first. But I elected to devote myself to portraiture, rather than landscape—it being Mr. Isabey's speciality—and professed to admire a picture of a young boy with golden curls, and a cunning pug dog, by Reynolds."

I suppressed a groan. Trust Fanny to spurn the simpler studies in watercolour, that might prove instructive to a beginner, and leap straight for the oils of Joshua Reynolds.

"I was alone in my choice," she went on, "Reynolds being *quite* unfashionable nowadays, and the bulk of the artists present being collected around a Goya lately offered to the Academy, I am told, by the Duke of Wellington. He acquired a number of such things during the Peninsular War—" She shuddered. "*Such* an aspect of terror as the visage held, Aunt! Almost as tho' a sepulchre had opened, and emitted this ghastly witness to the Day of Judgement! I should not have slept a wink tonight, had I spent the past few hours in gazing upon it!"

"Far better to have chosen the cunning pug," I said soothingly, "even if it *did* consign you to a corner of the room."

"Not at all," Fanny earnestly returned, "for it soon became evident that my clumsiness with a brush, and my utter lack of knowledge of such things as how to change my water-cup in all the vastness of the place, brought a constant parade of gentlemen to my side, eager to offer comment and instruction. I was besieged, I assure you, with attention. I cannot tell you how droll some of these artists seem, Aunt, with their disordered locks and their cravats tied carelessly in a bow!"

"Dashed loose screws!" Henry exclaimed testily.

"Possibly," she agreed with a giggle. "I soon had one fellow illustrating the proper method of mixing colours, whilst another explained *perspective,* and a third condescended to guide my hand."

"Impertinent pups. You should not have been allowed to venture out unchaperoned, Fanny. It is one thing to descend upon Canterbury as Miss Knight, the eldest daughter of Mr. Edward Austen Knight of Godmersham Park—but in Town, an unattended female lays herself open to every sort of encroaching freedom." He wheeled upon me. "Jane, you were shockingly beside the road to send her to Somerset House alone. We must hope that Edward does not come to hear of it."

It is this lingering poor-spiritedness on Henry's part that suggests he has not yet conquered his illness.

"Fanny and I have agreed that I shall accompany her on Monday," I said. "But I am glad to know that you were warmly received, Fanny, tho' you *are* clumsy with a brush. Did you learn anything to the purpose?"

She wrinkled her nose. "I am not certain. There were a number of painters working in oils; only three were equipped with watercolours, as I was, and none of them was French. I could not allow either fact to weigh with me, however, as a painter adept in oils may equally have mastered watercolour, and I was not told to search *only* for Frenchmen."

—It being principally Fanny, I thought, who had suggested a Frenchman was behind the present violence.

"I determined to treat each of the strangers around me with equal interest and suspicion."

"And high time, too," Henry said drily. "How many of these shady coves were pretending to study pictures?"

"Seven or eight. The numbers varied with the hours." Fanny shot him a sidelong glance. "After I had accepted the instruction of several, I settled down to paint undisturbed. I made a show of consulting my sketchbook—or rather, Mr. West's. I allowed the copy of the Waterloo Map to slip out of it by chance, and fall to the floor. I continued to work on my painting as tho' unaware the sketch was exposed."

"Very clever," I observed. "The world might pass in review of it, as it lay innocently at your feet, without your appearing to solicit their notice."

"Exactly."

"And did anyone remark upon it?" Henry enquired.

"Several stepped *over* it, in passing," she said. "Until one man, whom everyone called *Bennett*, stooped down to study it. I suspect Bennett is a surname. He is one of the watercolourists—although his speciality appears to be landscape, not portraiture."

I leant forward. "Did he remark upon the sketch?"

"He attempted to steal it! And without a word to me, too!"

"Surely you are mistaken!"

"He studied it narrowly, then rose as if to return to his easel. I hastened after him."

"Brave of you," Henry observed.

"He was most apologetic when I asked for my property back again," she said. "He glanced from the drawing to my face, and said, *You can never have done this. It has the look of Alexandrine.*"

"Alexandrine," I mused. "A surname, again?"

"Christian name of a woman, more like," Henry objected. "Russian, probably—or . . ."

"French," Fanny said. "I particularly enquired. I told him it was a daub done at random by a friend of mine, who has been a great traveller."

"He believed you?"

"Why should he not? He merely smiled, placed it in my outstretched hand, and said he should like to meet my friend."

We were silent an instant, and then I said, "*Alexandrine.* But this is vital, Fanny! He believed he recognised the hand. Is he the sort of man likely to know one painter's stile from another's?"

"I cannot say," she returned thoughtfully. "He was certainly treated with deference by the others, as tho' he belonged to a higher order than they. It was Bennett who instructed me a little in *perspective.* He mentioned at the time that he had once been a student at the Academy. That is why I particularly wished to speak to Mr. West—I thought it possible they were acquainted. Although Mr. Bennett is a good deal younger than he. Much closer to my own age than yours, Aunt."

So it was *Mr.* Bennett, now. I stifled a sigh. "What did he tell you of Alexandrine?"

"Merely that she was a Frenchwoman—a painter of great skill—who often came to work at Somerset House. That is why I believe we should return to the place as soon as may be. If only tomorrow were not Sunday!"

I forgave Fanny this heathen remark, feeling all her frustration with the idle loss of hours that might better have been spent in pursuit of a murderer. Convention forbade me even to use the interval to proof my book—although it might be frittered away in walks to and from the Belgrave Chapel, or in the reading aloud of sermons.

Henry snorted, however. "Neither you nor your aunt ought

to go near the place, my dear! Recollect that Jane has already sustained one crushing blow. We need not send *you* home to Kent, Fanny, with a broken pate! Very fortunate you were, to escape this morning without injury. I may only suppose it was because you encountered this ruffian Bennett in publick, among too many fellows who might name him. Allow West to penetrate the mystery, I beg."

Fanny drew breath to protest, but I forestalled her with a slight shake of my head and a compression of the lips. It would not do to argue with Henry at his most querulous, when what he required was a good dinner and a better night's sleep. Time enough on Monday to overrule him. I rose from my chair by his fire.

"Very well, Henry," I said. "Your caution shall be our guide. I will write to Mr. Raphael West this instant, and beg him to dine with us tomorrow. Fanny may tell him *all*, then."

"Dine with us?" Henry repeated. "On a Sunday, Jane?"

I am afraid I lost patience with his womanish airs. "Our dear Eliza should not have hesitated to invite so valuable a guest, whether the day were sacred or no."

"She was not much for attending church, either, Jane. Her head-ache always seemed to descend at the hour of Divine Service. But with Fanny here—"

"Oh, *pish*, Uncle!" Fanny cried.

I left them to argue the matter between them, and fled to my bedchamber for an interval with pen and paper.

19

THE SPIRIT OF ENQUIRY

Sunday, 19 November 1815
23 Hans Place

My note to Mr. West was sufficiently beforehand to be placed in yesterday's last post; and this morning an answer came, by personal messenger—who proved to be the redoubtable Spence. He was arrayed in a dark blue livery I had last espied at 14 Newman Street, and it became him rather well.

"Does your new position suit?" I asked as I broke open the seal.

"Very well, ma'am," he said, "and very grateful to you I am. You have served me kindly twice over: by securing me a place, tho' I was without a character; and by enlarging my experience, to include Belper stoves. They are extraordinary creatures, to be sure, but that cellar of Mr. West's is the best-heated chamber in London, to my certain knowledge."

"I am glad to know that you are settled." I scanned Raphael West's missive; he had heard nothing from the Duke of Wellington regarding the penetration of our cypher, which was just what I had expected. He agreed to dine with us, however—and I felt that we must come to some sort of conclusion together, whether to continue our interest in the Waterloo Map and Ewan MacFarland's murder, or give it up entirely to others.

"There is no answer," I told Spence, "but pray give Mr. West my compliments."

"Indeed I shall." He bowed and turned to go, then hesitated. "My master was laid to rest yesterday. My *late* master, I should say."

"You have my deepest sympathy." I made no move to quit the doorway, in the event the batman wished to unburden himself further. "Were you able to attend the service?"

"Mr. West gave me leave."

Of course Mr. West did; and probably interrogated you upon your return, I thought.

"I made so bold as to enter the back of the church, tho' seemingly I wasn't wanted. *He'd* have wanted me there."

"I am certain you are right, Spence."

The batman's countenance was set in rigid lines; I detected bitterness in his looks. "Many's the time we've brushed through the worst horrors together, ma'am, and come back to the light o' day, and it didn't seem right to let him go into the earth without a proper farewell."

"I hope the service was well attended?"

"Something beautiful, ma'am. Fifteen carriages followed the coffin, and a mounted group of the Scots Greys—all old friends of ours, what's left of 'em."

"That must have been very gratifying for you."

"It was. One or two of 'em deigned to notice me, and it fair brought the tears to my eyes. If I'd a-been still at Keppel Street, I'd have sent the Colonel's Mephisto after 'em, with his saddle empty, as it should be. But Miss MacFarland didn't chuse to do it. Means to sell the horse, she does; and him the last surviving mount of the Colonel's Waterloo string."

"She was not in attendance, however." Ladies do not go to funerals; we are regarded as too weak to support the grief of the grave.

"No, indeed. But there was one lady standing at the back of the church, alongside o' me, which was a very curious circumstance. Although perhaps I shouldn't call her a lady, saving your presence."

This was a puzzle; did Spence mean that the woman was of the serving-class? Probably not—for then he would never have referred to her as a lady at all. What distinction did he intend?

Comprehension dawned. "Was she familiar to you, Spence?"

"Aye, and would've been to the Colonel."

"His mistress, perhaps?"

"Not his!" The expression of indignation on Spence's countenance was almost laughable. "She was that Lieutenant Dunross's light-o' love, if she were anyone's! But he walked right past her in the churchyard—gave her the Cut Direct, as they say—being too high in the instep to remember his debts, seemingly, now he's to marry Miss MacFarland."

"Ah. Was it to speak to Dunross, perhaps, that she attended the funeral?"

"That was my reckoning, once I'd seen her. Meant to bring him up short, before his old friends—except they don't have nothing to do with Dunross now he's quit the Greys."

"Did she say as much?"

He looked scandalised. "I never spoke to Mam'selle! She's above my touch, besides being a foreigner."

"A French lady, I collect."

"Aye. A number of our lads got friendly with the Enemy."

I wrinkled my brow, attempting to sort it out. Not only the Marquess of Wellesley had a taste for Opera dancers, it seemed. "Is it possible this lady followed Dunross to London, once the battle in Belgium was over, and Napoleon exiled a second time? And the Lieutenant had not expected to meet her here?"

"That'd be the way of it, I reckon."

"I see. And being once more among his own people, the Lieutenant was anxious to cut the acquaintance. Did he speak to you at all, Spence?"

The batman shook his head. "I thought it best to leave before him, ma'am, lest he suspicion I was dogging his footsteps, hat in hand, so to speak. I have my dignity to consider."

And gossiping with a relative stranger about matters of his regiment was probably wounding it even now.

"Of course," I said warmly. "Thank you, Spence, for bringing Mr. West's communication. I shall hope to see more of you, in future."

My brother Henry was not so stout this morning as I should have liked; the exertions of the previous few days had told on his nascent strength; and tho' I was inclined to be amused when he complained of a head-ache, at exactly the hour of Divine Service, and kept to his bed like his late Eliza as a result—I confess that I grew anxious as the day wore on. The recurrence of a slight fever was not propitious. By five o'clock I had given way to trepidation, and called in Mr. Haden.

He bled my brother, and urged a suspension of this evening's dinner, and dosed Henry with a paregoric. As he drew on his coat an hour later, his countenance was exceedingly grave.

"I should not have thought you would strain Mr. Austen's faculties, in a reckless pursuit of pleasure," he told me sternly. "You were an excellent nurse a week since; but something has occurred to unsettle you. I have no business enquiring into your personal affairs, but as those affairs affect my patient . . . Has there been any further intelligence regarding the attack upon yourself, Miss Austen, on this very doorstep?"

"A little," I said. And bit my lip.

He studied me accusingly. "You do not wish to confide in me, I see. I must decline all responsibility, therefore, for Mr. Austen's well-being, as I cannot be certain that I am in possession of all the facts affecting his present situation."

"You are not," I agreed, "but pray do not desert us, Mr. Haden—indeed, indeed, we are in need of your attention, and most grateful for it! We regard you as Mr. Austen's dear friend, not merely his surgeon. And in any case, his other doctor—Matthew Baillie—is in no case to prescribe, being at death's door himself. He was stabbed on Wednesday last, and is at present at St George's Hospital."

"I had not an idea of it!" Haden cried. He appeared thunderstruck. "Who could possibly strike at so eminent a man? How did the attack occur? What are the particulars?"

I imparted them as best I could, making no mention of the Waterloo Map.

"The world is entirely at sixes and sevens! Even Miss Knight—" He broke off, and coloured.

Even Miss Knight is an altered creature.

It was true, of course; Fanny's fever of admiration for *acquarelle* and the intimates of Somerset House had given her a repugnance for the harp. She was disinclined to play, being far too intent upon the mastery of mixed colours. In the interval between our walks to the Belgrave Chapel today, she had brooded over her water-cup and paintbox, insisting that her "work" was intended for the better glorification of God, and thus was as sacred in its intent as any sermon could be. I forbore to argue with her, and indulged in a surreptitious proofing of my *Emma* in the blessed stillness Fanny's absorption allowed.

MR. WEST ARRIVED ON our doorstep in a hackney carriage just as Mr. Haden was taking his leave. The painter offered the surgeon a brisk and cordial hello, which was not so warmly returned. Haden's entire manner today, indeed, was suggestive of a sulky boy; I suspect his present austere looks were due to Miss Knight's appearance at the head of the stairs, and her exuberant cry of: "Is that Mr. West at last? You have been an age, sir—when I have so much to relate to you!"

Haden cast one serious look up the stairs, and turned abruptly aside. It seems clear that he has succumbed to a *tendre* for Fanny and her harp-playing. That he holds as deep an aversion to poor West, is equally probable. I would invite him to dinner, and admit him to the secrets of our little group, but that I am loath to widen the circle of dangerous knowledge and possible harm. That he takes my reticence as a mark of cooling relations between our households is unfortunate; being young and in love, he undoubtedly blames himself—as being unworthy of his object.

There was no time to stammer a useless apology for my callous niece, however, as Manon was already possessed of Mr. West's greatcoat, and scowled at me expressively as she closed the door behind Haden. I was forgetting my duties.

"We are very glad to see you, Mr. West," I said, as I led him up to the parlour.

"The only happy result of this distressing business has been the frequency with which we have met," he murmured. "I would that we might talk of something other than murder."

"Perhaps then we should have nothing to say," I suggested. "Our entire acquaintance has been predicated, after all, on violence."

I felt his fingertips caress the inside of my palm. "Nonsense, Jane. There are a hundred questions I might ask—"

We had achieved the top of the stairs. "Don't, I beg of you," I breathed, and in a more cheerful publick tone: "Here is our dinner guest, Henry!"

My brother had defied poor Haden's attempts to keep him in bed, and on a diet of gruel against the recurrence of his fever; he looked pale and thin this evening, but quite smart in a waistcoat I had never seen, dark green and embroidered with black thread. His coat, too, was black; he wore dove-grey satin knee breeches to dine, a trick borrowed from Pall Mall dandies.

"West," he said with an inclination of the head. "Have you received any word from Wellington?"

How it must delight Henry to utter that name in all carelessness, as tho' he and the Duke have been friends this age!

"I have not, sir," West replied. "Lord FitzRoy Somerset *did* send round a brief message this morning, to the effect that the 'interesting paper' has been delivered to Major Scovell. I must imagine that gentleman is delighted to see it—he has not enjoyed a good bout of cypher-breaking since the end of the Peninsular War."

"Was not the cypher employed at Waterloo?" Fanny enquired, coming forward.

West bowed over her hand. "As I understood it, the French devised the Great Cypher expressly during the latter years of the Spanish campaigns. Indeed, many of the figures correspond to place names and commanders that could have no relevance later in Belgium."

This puzzled me. "Could not they be added, using different figures?"

"If the cypher was composed at random—*yes*," West replied, accepting the chair at Henry's right.

Our conversation was suspended a little, as Manon reappeared with a tray bearing glasses of Madeira.

"I do not understand what you would imply," I persisted as the maid disappeared. "Is not a cypher a direct substitution of letters for numbers? And therefore, could not *any word* desired be so spelled out?"

"Indeed. But the Great Cypher does not follow that plan," West explained as he took an appreciative sip of wine. Henry prides himself on his cellar. "It was apparently a great chart, Miss Austen, of figures assigned to entire words that might be used in military orders. *Cannon* might be the number 70, for instance, or the city of Badajoz number 21. I cannot say, being entirely ignorant of the system. Wellington managed to explain so much; and added that both Paris and the Iberian generals had copies of the chart, which they consulted when in communication."

"So presumably the words *Moscow* and *Smolensk* were not part of the cypher," Fanny observed. "That may be why they were labelled explicitly on the map."

"Indeed," West agreed. "The Duke explained that many of the French orders and reports—which were intercepted by any number of trusty Spanish and Portuguese *guerreros* in the pay of the British—were written in a mixture of clear French and coded words, so that from the context of the sentence it was sometimes possible to guess at the meaning of the cypher figures. Scovell, who proved so adept at the task, spoke French almost as a mother tongue. He devised a system whereby he compared one intercepted message to another, ensuring that his guesses as to the meaning of certain cypher figures were ratified over time. But the work proved labouriously slow."

"I don't suppose we shall ever hear another word about the entire affair—murder, cypher, or map!" Henry set down his glass. "Your Great Men are hardly eager to share their embarrassments with the publick; and MacFarland's poisoning is a grave one. He was buried yesterday, you know, whilst we were calling upon the Duke. Not much of a Hero, if his commanding general did not bother to attend."

"A mounted group of Scots Greys followed the carriages," I said swiftly. "I should judge that the Colonel was loved well enough."

West glanced at me, frowning. "Where did you learn these particulars?"

I related, then, my conversation of the morning with his new manservant, including the unknown Mam'selle who had sought Lieutenant Dunross's attention at the rear of the church.

"Spence said nothing of this to me," West mused.

"Perhaps it is easier to gossip—for that is what it was—with a lady," I suggested. "He met me in the MacFarland household; you, sir, can have no connexion to it in Spence's experience. He is ignorant of our researches. Moreover, you are a new employer. He should not risk his precarious footing by wagging his tongue about the past."

"That is unfortunate—because he knows a good deal, regarding the late Colonel. Spence has told us several valuable things: That his master was careless or ignorant or trusting enough to show him the map; that Dunross knew about its existence, and has looked for it since MacFarland died; and now, that Dunross is being blackmailed by a Frenchwoman."

"Blackmailed!" Henry exclaimed.

"Naturally." West smiled at my brother. "As the batman correctly observed, the lady came to the churchyard not merely to meet with Dunross—who had only to walk away from her—but to parade herself before his acquaintance. She succeeded in showing him that, whether he acknowledge her or no, he was not safe from her reach, even in a place of traditional sanctuary. Her whole appearance at the funeral ought to be read as a warning. Dunross ignores it at his peril."

"You believe—without having seen this woman, knowing nothing of her situation or character—that she is dangerous?" Fanny demanded sceptically.

"If she is indeed a discarded paramour—forgive my frankness,

Miss Knight—then she is quite possibly in want of money," West returned; "and if she is squeezing Dunross with the threat of exposure to Miss MacFarland on the eve of his wedding, then he may be persuaded to turn over any sort of sum she demands. —Provided, of course, that he is as well-circumstanced as his general stile suggests."

"And if not?" I asked drily.

West met my gaze. "Then marriage to Miss MacFarland, who shall certainly inherit all her brother's property, must be essential. All the more reason why Dunross should be anxious to forestall his Mam'selle, by meeting with her as soon as possible. He is unlikely to move on a Sunday, however; he is no doubt dancing attendance on the grieving Miss MacFarland. But tomorrow . . . ? I confess I am curious about the Lieutenant and his French lady; I should like to know more of them."

"Impossible," Henry said. "You might haunt Dunross's club, did you know it; but the lady is obscured to you."

"Dunross shall lead us to her," West said briskly.

"You mean to shadow him?" I asked.

"Or task Spence with the duty."

I shook my head. "Dunross is too well-acquainted with the batman for such a scheme to prosper. He should recognise his shadow, and confront him. But it occurs to me there is one place we might usefully gather information: Gunter's confectionery. Spence tells me Dunross likes to be seen there—and recollect that he stood Colonel MacFarland to coffee at Gunter's, on the very morning of his murder."

"So he did," West agreed, his dark eyes fixed intently on mine. "And the wonder is, I had forgot the fact in all our activity with the map. Never mind Wellington and Apsley House; we ought to have solicited the attention of the principal waiter at Gunter's long since. May I beg the honour of escorting you to Berkeley Square tomorrow, Miss Austen?"

"I fear you must take coffee alone, Mr. West," I replied regretfully, "as I am already pledged to accompany my niece to Somerset House."

"I am perfectly capable of going there by myself, Aunt!" Fanny cried.

"After the impertinent notice your last visit occasioned?" Henry broke in. "Impossible, Fanny. Either accept your aunt's escort or remain at home."

Rebellion seethed in Fanny's looks, and when she might have cried *Pish* at her uncle, Raphael West intervened. "How did you get on at Somerset House yesterday, Miss Knight? I take it you secured a numerous acquaintance?"

"I did," she replied with a quelling look at Henry. "And none of the gentlemen were impertinent, I assure you. They merely seemed accustomed, rather, to a freer degree of Society than is usual in Kent."

"Or Hans Town," Henry muttered under his breath.

"I should be most interested to hear your account," West said.

"Thank you, Mr. West," Fanny replied complacently, and thus encouraged, opened her budget of intelligence.

After she had done, West sank back in his chair and thoughtfully turned the stem of his wineglass.

"The full name of your principal acquaintance is Mr. William James Bennett, and he is an excellent fellow of considerable talent—a student at the Academy some years since. Tho' adept at watercolour landscape, he is particularly inclined towards the perfection of aquatints—which you will know are engravings, supplemented with watercolour for splendid effect. That is probably why he emphasised *perspective* when he instructed you, Miss Knight; for it is vital to the sort of views he engraves—which are often of harbours with ships, and a town disposed in the background. He has learnt much from the Venetians in this regard, tho' they painted in oils. Canaletto, for example—"

"But what of the woman he described?" Fanny interrupted. "What of Alexandrine?"

West shrugged. "I cannot enlighten you, alack. She has not come in my way. I confess I have not frequented the galleries at Somerset House overmuch, in the past twelvemonth; other duties have drawn my attention."

"Then I shall return to the Exhibition Room tomorrow," Fanny said decidedly. "I am anxious to see this paragon of watercolours in the flesh."

"Not without your aunt," Henry insisted.

"Very well." She submitted indifferently. "Aunt Jane may read whilst I paint."

I glanced at West. A ghost of a smile hovered on his lips, but he was studying my face, not Fanny's. A little of my own rebellion must have been visible there. I looked away from him hurriedly. I should have liked to have gone to Gunter's in his company very much.

"Is it decided, then?" I enquired of the table. "Do we mean to persist in our researches—in our hunt for Colonel MacFarland's murderer—tho' the Map is now in Wellington's abler hands?"

There was a diffident silence.

"I feel myself to have been in some wise engaged, by Dr. Matthew Baillie," West admitted. "Were he capable of acting for himself—"

"And I am sure my painting shall benefit from continued study," Fanny said. "There can be no objection in the world to my sitting a few more hours at the Academy—now that you have kindly agreed to lend me countenance, Aunt."

"My health has certainly benefited from the stimulation of enquiry," Henry added.

"That is the *grossest* falsehood." I glared at him. "You know Mr. Haden is distressed. He believes you ought to have kept to your bed another week at least, and have seriously overtaxed your strength."

"Haden is an old woman," my brother said dismissively. "Excellent fellow in his way, and a valuable opponent at chess; but sadly averse to adventure."

I could not suppress a smile; it is for his spirit that I have always admired Henry. "Thank Heaven!" I sighed. "I was afraid that I was going to have to find the murderer myself."

20
ROGUES' GALLERY

Monday, 20 November 1815
23 Hans Place

"Do place your stool and easel before the cunning little pug," I advised my niece in an overly-strident tone that was certain to draw attention, "whilst I place *mine* here in the corner. I do not wish to interfere with your study; indeed, I shall efface myself *entirely,* being present solely in the role of chaperon! I should not wish to disturb you for the world! Or indeed, any of the artists labouring so nobly in this exalted space."

I beamed around the Exhibition Room at the conclusion of this pettifogging speech, and was rewarded with a few curious looks from the men endeavouring to work there. I had arrayed myself assiduously for my role: black silk mittens; a serviceable grey woollen gown; a sober bonnet with a lamentably draggling feather. I looked every inch the maiden aunt I *was.* Fanny, by contrast, was a vision in amber-coloured silk twill, her shining chestnut hair knotted and curled about her face. She drew far more interested looks from her fellow-artists, and presently one approached and said with a bow, "Miss Knight! You are returned to pursue your watercolours, I see, tho' we did our best to bury you under a mountain of advice."

"Mr. Bennett," she replied. "Pray allow me to make you acquainted with my aunt, Miss Austen."

My feather quivered with well-meaning pride as I performed my curtsey. "I was in transports over the work Miss Knight achieved on Saturday, and could not stay away when she declared that she would return this morning. It is a privilege, indeed, to be able to watch her paint; she does it with such a pretty air. I shall be no more trouble than a mouse, I assure you, Mr. Bennett. Do you specialise in charming little doggies, too?"

His lip curled slightly, but he was well-bred enough to contain his contempt. "I do not, madam. I am glad that Miss Knight enjoyed our attempts at instruction; with a little application, she might achieve improvement with time."

"I think her pictures are all that one could desire," I assured him, clapping my mittened hands together, "but then, I am hopeless with charcoal and paints myself. Tatting is more in my line, and constructing a fringe . . . but I perceive that you know nothing of those! Miss Knight's bright eyes are censuring me, to be sure, for I *do* go on in the most foolish manner. I shall just seat myself here in my corner, and promise *not* to say a word!"

Having confirmed my imbecility in the minds of all those present, I drew a black-bound book of Fordyce's Sermons from my reticule and immersed myself. Fanny took her sketchbook from her canvas portmanteau and set yesterday's work on her easel; then stepped back and frowned at Joshua Reynolds's little boy, attempting to apply all she had learnt of perspective.

"That dull blue requires a good deal of white in its mixing," she murmured, "and perhaps a touch of black."

"But not *too much* black," I ejaculated in a tone of horror.

Several heads turned; Fanny stared at me reprovingly.

I held a hand to my lips in exaggerated apology, and returned to Mr. Fordyce.

Perhaps an hour of concentrated effort on both our parts followed. On occasion, one or two of the men would linger in passing behind Fanny's stool, and comment on her stile; but their attentions were subdued as a result of my presence, the spare black crow in the corner. Eventually I rose and strolled about the Exhibition Room, being in want of exercise; and as I did, I glanced with interest at both the paintings on the walls and those on the various easels.

I had been to this place before, of course—most recently two years ago in May, when the Great Exhibition was on view, as it is each spring. It is a lofty, airy chamber with an enormous glass lanthorn atop its roof, which sheds light on the painters below. Perhaps a thousand pictures were hung around the walls, of varying sizes and subjects: portraits, great canvases of sweeping historical or sacred moment, landscapes and small vignettes of bottles or flowers. I loved the historical pictures and portraits best; it was possible to invent rich stories for the faces peering out of the frames. Of brushstrokes and stile I know little; that is more in my sister Cassandra's line—but I experience a deep inner satisfaction when I gaze at a picture I admire, rather like the happiness that comes from writing a perfect line of prose.

I slowed behind Mr. Bennett, as he used the finest of brushes to apply colour to the edge of a wharf, and noted that Raphael

West was correct in his surmise—the artist was studying a painting of Venice. His picture looked nothing like the Waterloo Map; the stile of each could not be more different. I approached another painter whose name I did not know—older than Bennett, with a shocking red beard—and observed much the same thing. West was correct when he detected a singular hand behind the map's painting; and I felt my interest in the subject quicken. That West himself had mastered the unknown's *technique*, as he called it, shewed me how adept an artist he was.

A slight stir at the far end of the room, where Fanny was established, drew my head around. Bennett had risen from his seat and was crossing hurriedly towards a lady who was burdened with a portmanteau and an easel; behind her came a maid carrying a stool and a paintbox. These were set down before a portrait of a young girl, obviously by Lawrence. Bennett arrived at the little group in time to relieve the lady of her burdens; she drew off her pelisse and handed it to the maid, who retired immediately downstairs.

"Madame Gauthier," Bennett said, with an ardent inclination of the head. "It is a pleasure to see you again. I hope you are well?"

"Well enough, my friend," she said, with a charming French accent. "I am always well when I am painting. And you?"

"Much better, now that I have seen you."

I drifted nearer to the pair as tho' absorbed only in the art around me. Madame Gauthier was no older than Fanny, certainly; she was plainly but elegantly dressed in a dark gown; and she was, I suspected, in the family way. Her hair was blond and her features were quite perfect—a subject worthy of Mr. West's namesake, Raphael.

"I was afraid that I had frightened you away," Bennett said in a lowered voice. "I was nearly mad with worry. Say that you forgive me."

"*Mon dieu*, how foolish you are, my friend," the lady returned with a smile. "There is nothing to forgive. I was merely a little unwell, and so stayed in my rooms. But the light there is poor and I could not paint *en plein air*, it has been so wet; *alors*, here I am at last."

She settled herself with grace on her stool and opened her paintbox as tho' the man before her had uttered a commonplace, rather than a cry from the heart. A lady in command of her emotions, therefore; a lady of some experience. Which should not be surprising, as there was undoubtedly a Monsieur Gauthier, given her condition. I drifted closer to Fanny.

"I am out of all patience with this dog," she muttered through clenched teeth. "Indeed, I could happily drown it at the first opportunity."

"You ought to take a turn about the room," I advised. "It is excessively refreshing. Particularly as your Mr. Bennett has discovered a friend."

It is a testament to Fanny's absorption in her painterly pursuit that she had not even remarked the lady's arrival. She lifted her gaze to mine and said, "Where?"

"Behind you," I murmured. "A Madame Gauthier. Decidedly French, tho' I cannot pretend to know her Christian name."

Fanny set down her brush and paintbox. "Thank Heaven. I could not have borne to sit here very much longer, Aunt, and I confess I was dreading a return tomorrow. If you will set this detestable picture of two nameless blue animals in my portmanteau, I shall just offer Mr. Bennett my thanks for his highly beneficial instruction."

She walked sedately in the direction of the two painters whilst I folded her easel with all the busyness of a born chaperon. There was a murmur of conversation behind me, and I judged that Bennett was performing introductions; then all at once, Fanny was returned, and searching through her sketchbook with a pretty air of unconcern.

"Here it is," she cried, and held aloft West's copy of the Waterloo Map. "Mr. Bennett was determined to rob me of it Saturday, Madame, in the conviction that it must be *yours*."

I glanced at the Frenchwoman. She was approaching us slowly, her graceful form rigid with an emotion I could not name. Was it merely surprize? Or something deeper?

She held out her hand wordlessly, and Fanny placed the sketch in it.

"Mr. Bennett says this is very like your manner of painting."

There was a silence. The colour had drained from Madame Gauthier's perfect countenance; her lips were compressed into a line. She turned over the paper, which was blank—and a sigh escaped her. Of relief? —Or disappointment?

"Who made this?" she demanded, darting a glance at Fanny. "Not you."

"Indeed, no. It is a daub done by a friend, to demonstrate what he calls *technique*."

"He is French, this friend?"

"Not at all. Although I believe he lived in Paris for a time."

I wondered if Fanny knew what she was about. It was clear Alexandrine Gauthier was familiar with the original Waterloo Map; her entire being was stiff with knowledge and wariness.

"I, too, lived in Paris," she said carefully. "Perhaps I know this friend. What is his name?"

Fanny lifted her chin. "Mr. Raphael West. His father is president of this Academy."

"Then the son is a cheat, and a liar," Madame Gauthier exclaimed venomously. "This sketch does not belong to him *or* to you, Mademoiselle. It belongs to me. My husband painted it."

And as suddenly as she had arrived in the Exhibition Room, the Frenchwoman clattered impetuously down the stairs, leaving her easel behind—but taking our copy of the Waterloo Map with her.

Fanny grasped my wrist. "We must go after her, Aunt!"

I shook my head. Our acquaintance, Mr. Bennett, had already hastened away, calling out, "*Alexandrine!*" The rest of his fellows were glancing at us curiously.

"We have learnt already all we needed," I muttered for Fanny's ear alone. "Her name is correct; she knew the sketch; she identified the painter—and pursuit can add little."

"But what if her husband is the *murderer*?" Fanny whispered to me.

"He will show his hand in some other fashion, and soon. He has not got what he requires, recollect—only a partial copy. The best course for us, Fanny, is to take ourselves home—and consult with Mr. West as soon as possible."

She opened her mouth as tho' to argue, but I was already retying my bonnet strings and settling my cape. I had just grasped the easel and was moving towards the stairs, when Mr. Bennett reappeared. His countenance was anxious, but his manner towards us far gentler than I expected.

"I must apologise for Madame Gauthier," he said, drawing us to one side of the doorway. "I cannot account for her rudeness. She is generally the soul of decorum, having been used to the first circles in Paris."

"Indeed." I inclined my head. "I must assume she acted under some sort of misapprehension, then. She was most insistent that my niece's sketch—which was given her by Mr. Raphael West—was somehow stolen from Madame Gauthier's husband."

"You are acquainted with Mr. West? But how wonderful!" Bennett returned, momentarily distracted. "He and his venerable father are particular heroes of mine. But I begin to understand. If Alexandrine thought, however wrongly, that her husband's work had been abused, she would betray a natural indignation. She is most jealous in her protection of it."

"Perhaps Monsieur Gauthier may elucidate the mystery." I suppressed my nascent excitement. "Does he also paint here, from time to time?"

"Monsieur Gauthier!" Bennett looked from my face to Fanny's with chagrin. "I am afraid, ma'am, that Monsieur Gauthier is dead."

21

SURPRIZES ARE FOOLISH THINGS

Monday, 20 November 1815
23 Hans Place, cont'd.

We returned to Hans Place in disordered spirits. It was true that we knew a bit more about the Waterloo Map than we did at quitting the house that morning, but our intelligence was sadly incomplete.

On the strength of our friendship with Raphael West—and our unfeigned consternation at the loss of his sketch—Mr. Bennett had told us what he knew of Madame Gauthier, supplementing our conjectures with a few of his own.

"She came to England a month ago," he said, "and has taken lodgings in Cheapside."

"—Her husband's death having urged a removal from Paris?" I enquired. "Was he English, perhaps?"

"I do not think so—tho' Madame has never shared the particulars of her loss," Bennett admitted. "I believe she is very recently widowed. You will have seen that she still goes in mourning."

Her dress had indeed been dark, I thought—but so were many in November. Bennett's discretion prevented him from observing that the lady was a few months pregnant, and thus must be very recently bereaved indeed. It was Fanny who had pounced on the thought hovering in my mind, during our hackney ride to Knightsbridge.

"Is it not probable, Aunt, that Madame Gauthier is the lady to whom that sad final letter was written, on the obverse of the Waterloo Map?"

"The one signed by *Charles*, from La Belle Alliance?" I sighed. "All too probable, if her husband painted that sketch as she claims. She might have seen it an hundred times between the Russian campaign and Waterloo, where he meant to despatch it to her for safekeeping."

And if he had died in June, her *enceinte* state in November required no great explanation.

But Fanny's thoughts were all of romance. "That is why she is determined to retrieve it!" she cried. "It was his dying wish that she safeguard the map!"

"But if it was stolen from the battlefield," I pointed out, "she never read the letter. She ought not even to know that the map survived. Her husband's body cannot have been returned to her, Fanny. Most of the French dead were burnt in great pyres where they lay at Waterloo. If she knew of the sketch's existence, she must have believed it still on her husband's person—and consigned, like him, to the flames."

"She does *not* believe it, however," Fanny said shrewdly. "She looked for writing on the back of our copy, and her whole expression changed when she saw that it was blank. She seemed forlorn suddenly, and lost."

"Did she? I detected an expression of relief."

"Impossible! She has been searching for her husband's farewell ever since she received news of his death! —For of course she expected him to write to her on the eve of battle. True love demands it."

I raised my brows at Fanny's dreamy countenance; she had wandered far from our brutal experience of poison and assault. Alexandrine Gauthier had not come to London by chance; she had been drawn here because someone had come into possession of her husband's map. She had not learnt that fact in a lover's vision from beyond the grave; *someone* had informed her of it. Colonel MacFarland? His batman, Spence? Or Lieutenant Dunross?

Who else had known of the map's existence—and might also have known Alexandrine?

One thing was certain: I must warn Raphael West of the lady. Fanny had very foolishly identified him as the source of our sketch. Our unknown enemy had already attacked Dr. Matthew Baillie at the Newman Street gallery's door. A clever man, in league with Madame Gauthier, might now assume West had the map itself—and make him a target.

I began to be impatient for Hans Place. My note to West could not be written too soon.

HENRY WAS SITTING AT his desk in the parlour, frowning over a letter of business, when I mounted the stairs.

"Are you well enough," I asked, "to look into your accounts already? Can they not wait a few more days?"

"There will be no accounts in Alton," he returned, "if I delay another hour. Matters are very grave there, I am afraid."

"But Mr. Gray and Mr. Vincent are most capable, are they not?" I pursued, naming Henry's banking partners. Alton is a thriving market town perhaps a mile from my own home in Chawton; Gray and Vincent both live there, whilst Henry manages the London branch in Henrietta Street with his principal partner Mr. James Tilson. There are other branches of his bank as well, in various parts of Hampshire and Kent, and the idea of them failing is a puzzle to me. Only a few years ago Henry was so very rich, from being named Receiver-General of the Oxfordshire Militia, that he lent out a great deal of money, with my uncle Leigh-Perrot and my brother Edward as guarantors, to the sum of *thirty thousand pounds.* Neither gentleman has ever had cause for alarm, for Henry appeared to be going on so well. Observing his countenance suffused with care and worry now, however, I felt a flood of uneasiness. If Henry's accounts failed—would Edward and Uncle Leigh-Perrot be obliged to honour them?

"I may have to ride into Hampshire this week, Jane." Henry set down his pen. "You will have Fanny here to comfort you."

"Mr. Haden will not like it," I objected.

"Mr. Haden will like to be paid, however," Henry returned, "and that must satisfy him."

"Are matters so very bad?"

"They could not well be worse. The loss of trade and bustle due to the end of the war has meant a falling off in profits; and the return of so many young men without occupation, from the Army and Navy, has caused a surfeit of labour without wages to be given them. Things are wretched all over the Kingdom, but in places like Hampshire—which depends upon the traffic of war and seaports—they are distressing in the extreme."

"I am sorry," I said. And for once was nothing but thankful that I had concluded my arrangements with Mr. John Murray for the publication of *Emma*. My novels do not earn a fortune, it is true, but they contribute a considerable sum against future want. My mother, Cassandra, and I are sustained by contributions to our household in Chawton from our brothers each year—and if Henry is ruined, and Edward must save him, our economies in the cottage will be further straitened. I did not like to turn Henry's worries into my own—that seemed a selfish act—but his cautionary words about the state of England were impossible to ignore. Not only the returning soldiers were pinched with want, but the orphans and widows of the Waterloo Dead—

"Henry," I said, "only think what Fanny and I have learnt this morning."

I WROTE MY LETTER to Raphael West; all of ten lines, that succeeded, with gratifying concision, in conveying his danger. I undertook to walk in a slight rain to the Watch House in Knightsbridge, and paid for a private messenger—so great was my anxiety.

I said nothing of this to either Fanny or Henry.

The printer's boy came at four o'clock, with a bundle of sheets in brown paper for proofing; and took away with him Volume the First, neatly annotated in my best hand. It was a relief to sit down with my own good prose, beautifully set out in hot-press type, and put matters of maps and violence to the side.

"*Surprizes are foolish things,*" I intoned in Mr. Knightley's voice. "*The pleasure is not enhanced, and the inconvenience is often considerable.*" I have a decided talent for an epigram; I hope it delights my readers as much as myself.

I chose to sit in the dining room, Henry being in possession of the parlour; before me stood Fanny on a stool, whilst Manon pinned a length of muslin around her neat figure. Manon, being French, is a clever and elegant needlewoman; Fanny has wisely engaged her services as a *modiste* whilst in Hans Place, and is having a becoming day-dress made up from one of the lengths we purchased at Grafton House. It was a fine, domestic scene, requiring only lashings of rain against the windowpanes and a merry fire in the hearth to be completely comfortable. I will say *this* for Henry: he may fear penury, but one should never know it from his table or his fires.

A bell rang, signalling the five o'clock post; and Fanny stepped down from her perch as Manon dove below-stairs to fetch it. When she returned, she bore a letter from Mr. West.

"What is it? What does he say, Aunt?" Fanny asked impatiently as I broke the seal. "Did he learn anything to the purpose at Gunter's?"

I scanned the few lines. He had not yet received my missive, clearly, when his own was written.

> *I had hoped to look in on the Artist's Progress at Somerset House, but was tied to Newman Street, by the fact of my father's suffering a slight indisposition. I did succeed in calling at the confectioner's this morning, and have a little to relate. If tomorrow brings improvement in my father's case, as I expect, I shall have the honour of calling upon you at eleven o'clock. Until then, I remain—etc., etc.*

"I hope Mr. Benjamin West is not very unwell," Fanny declared, "but for *my* part, I shall burst! No word of poisoned coffee, or the cypher—and he is unaware of the existence of Madame Gauthier! Every moment that woman may be getting away! Did you communicate to Mr. West all that we learnt this morning, Aunt?"

"I did." So Fanny took it as given that we wrote to each other; and without the least hint of censure. "I only hope he is careful," I muttered under my breath.

Manon was standing once more by her stool, her mouth full of pins. Fanny took up her position with a sigh, and I returned to my wayward Emma. With so much we would have to be content; but the comfort of the room was somehow dimmed.

22

INDECOROUS BEHAVIOUR

Tuesday, 21 November 1815
23 Hans Place

I was awakened a little after six o'clock, tho' the sun had not yet risen and the inducement to sleep ought to have been heavy. Footsteps moved stealthily over the drugget in the passage outside my bedchamber; the faint gleam of a taper glided under the door. *Manon.* She must be tending my brother. Overset by the anxiety attached to his financial prospects, he had sunk once more into a low fever—

I lifted the latch and peered out into the passage.

"Henry!"

He was fully dressed in riding breeches, cape, and curly-brimmed beaver; he clutched a pair of topboots and leather gloves in one hand, a retiring candle in the other, and was creeping towards the stairs in his stocking-feet. He had never been one for riding in the Park at dawn, like so many gentlemen; and so I drew the proper conclusion.

"You leave for Alton? But it still rains!"

"A mizzle, rather. Nothing I regard."

I folded my arms across my chest, having neglected in my haste to put on my dressing gown. "You shall catch your death."

"So be it. At least one cannot dun a dead man."

"Must I send Manon for Mr. Haden?" I demanded severely.

"What—so that he may bleed me into submission?" Henry rolled his eyes and set down his boots. Then he grasped my shoulder and shook me gently. "Jane. *I am quite well.* Or I shall be, once I have met with Vincent and Gray at the Swan this morning. Until then, I am unlikely to gain any benefit from the rest you insist on prescribing, as I cannot sleep a wink, for thinking of the dreadful future I face in debtor's prison. Now for the love of God, allow me to do what I must—or perish in the attempt. Do I make myself clear?"

I lifted his candle and gazed steadily at his countenance. Henry was clear-eyed, if a trifle weary in his looks. His colour was good. And his entire being sported an air of haste. "Perfectly clear," I said.

And let him go.

AFTER THAT, THERE WAS no returning to sleep; I must lie in bed and listen for the closing of the rear door to the mews, and the mare Henry keeps there in a stall for his occasional pleasure. Half an hour later, the sound of Madame Bigeon at her stove fell upon my ears; and then the singing of a kettle. The knife man and the rag-and-bone man came and went; a milk cart rattled near the service area; the smell of fresh bread wafted up the stairs. I was already sitting up in my dressing gown by then, writing in this journal; and by nine o'clock I had breakfasted and was arrayed in what I fancied was a neat day gown of cherry red—quite new, and a gross indulgence as the colour *always* fades abominably with washing. I schooled myself severely to attend to Murray's proofs.

The parlour clock, however, had never moved so slowly. When at last the hands showed eleven, I set aside the printer's sheets and glanced over at Fanny. She was attempting to practise upon her harp, but continually broke off with sighs of frustration. Sheet music was scattered like leaves at her feet. She had abandoned Fashionable airs for those of Haydn.

And still the clock-hands moved.

Half-past eleven.

Twelve.

Fanny set aside her harp and took up a letter she was writing, to her sister Lizzy.

I applied myself to my Berlin-work.* I was fashioning a pair of slippers for Henry, begun when I had thought him likely to be confined to his bedchamber for some time. They now seemed as superfluous as Henry's clock, tiresomely telling the hours.

At half-past twelve, Fanny threw down her pen and searched through the desk for a sealing-wafer. "Are all artists imprecise in their appointments?" she demanded.

"No," I said thoughtfully. "Mr. West is generally not so careless of convention."

"Must we assume that his father has taken a turn for the worse?"

"He ought then to have sent us a line, postponing the engagement. Fanny—"

---

* A form of embroidery similar to today's needlepoint.—*Editor's note.*

She glanced up.

"I believe I shall venture into Newman Street. You may accompany me if you like."

"Of course I will," she said. "What would Uncle Henry say if I let you go without a chaperon?"

AT ANOTHER TIME I might have walked into Town, but the morning was already so advanced that Fanny agreed we ought to make for the hackney stand in the Brompton road, just past Knightsbridge. Tho' the paving was muddy, yesterday's rain had gone off; and in a very little while we were bowling towards Newman Street.

No extraordinary activity was evident when we pulled up before No. 14; no muffled door knocker betrayed a household under siege of illness; and Fanny said hollowly, "What if Mr. West has simply *forgot* our appointment, Aunt? How mortifying to expose ourselves to a gentleman's derision!"

"We shall send in our cards," I replied, "and await the outcome."

But the Wests' porter was inclined to regard us as members of the publick when he found us standing on the threshold, and told us firmly that there were no Special Viewings of Pictures today, before we had a chance to state our names. When he would have shut the door in our faces, I said quickly, "We have come to see Mr. Raphael West."

"Mr. West is not at home." He made to close the door again.

"How vexatious!" I cried. "Has he already left for Hans Place? He had an appointment with us there at eleven o'clock, but failed to appear."

The porter eyed me curiously. I felt my cheeks flush. There can be nothing more unbecoming than a lady's pursuit of a man who has left her in the lurch.

"Pray step inside," the porter said, "and I will enquire."

He took my card and conveyed us to a settee in the ground-floor anteroom. Fanny appeared subdued but glanced interestedly around the high-ceilinged foyer to the sweeping staircase beyond; she had never attended one of Benjamin West's exhibitions during her infrequent visits to London.

Somewhere, a clock chimed the quarter-hour; already fifteen minutes past one. Was Raphael West even now arriving in Hans Place? In my anxiety regarding Madame Gauthier, had I made myself ridiculous? Had the knock on my head induced me to imagine threats where none existed?

The creaking of the staircase drew my attention. Mr. Benjamin West was making his difficult way down the treads.

Fanny and I rose from our settee as he approached. He bowed; we curtseyed. The piercing, birdlike gaze flitted over both our faces; I could not tell if he recollected mine from the picture vault a few days before, or if my countenance had receded into the fog of his years.

"You have called upon my son," he said brusquely. "He ain't here. I don't know why I had to be disturbed about it. Impudence."

I felt Fanny shrink beside me. It is a sad truth that when a girl is gently-raised, she believes that general opinion must guide her private behaviour. I was not so gently-raised.

"Mr. West," I said briskly, "I understand you have been ill. I hope you are much improved."

"Thank'ee," he said. "I had dressed crab for dinner two nights' since, when I should not have. Inflames the gout." He turned back towards the stairs.

"Your son had an appointment with us this morning," I continued in a slightly elevated tone directed at the painter's back, "which he did not keep. We are concerned that some harm may have befallen him."

Benjamin West halted. A high cackle of laughter escaped him, and he slowly wheeled to fix me in his glare. "Rafe ain't answerable to anyone for his time—except me! He went out last night, I'm told, and he hasn't returned. You don't find *me* chasing all over Town to secure him! Might be at his club—might have gone into the country—might be anywhere. If it ain't seemly in a father to ask, it certainly ain't seemly in a dried-up old spinster like yourself! P'raps he's gone to see that mistress of his. Isabella. May he have joy of her, if he has!"

"Come, Aunt," Fanny whispered, her hand at my elbow. "Let us be quit of this place."

Isabella. In my mind I saw again the portrait of the lush woman reclining on a couch in West's draughting room, and felt an oppression I had not lately known.

"In my day, a lady was unworthy of the name if she chose to hunt a man to his very doorstep," Benjamin West persisted. His countenance was suffused with ridicule; he was enjoying this scene enormously. I wondered at what point he had come to resent his son's acquaintance so profoundly. Or perhaps it was his son's place in, and increasing rule over, his own household . . .

"I wish to speak to Spence." My words cut through his, and he stared at me, open-mouthed.

"Who the devil is that?"

I steeled myself and walked right up to the old man. "Your new servant. *Rafe* engaged him a few days ago. Pray ring for someone and enquire. *Spence.*"

He was frowning at me, but the light had shifted from his eyes as I had observed it to do before, leaving them veiled and bewildered.

"The bell," I prompted.

He limped towards the anteroom and pulled it.

"Mr. West told me as how he meant to call in Hans Place this morning."

Spence stood before us in the anteroom, having gently guided the befuddled Benjamin West back to his valet. His hands were locked behind him as tho' awaiting orders from a senior officer; he would not take a seat, being conscious of his place. "He was wishful I should accompany him, having a notion I might come in useful. But he never come home last night. His valet don't know or won't say the truth of it; just looks down his nose like I've no right to arst the question. And the coachman never took him. Went out on foot or in a hackney, Mr. West did. The staff have got the wind up, if you arst me. Hicks, the valet, did say as he's never known Mr. West to be out past noon—when he hasn't been home at night."

So it was a common enough practise for him to sleep elsewhere. *Isabella,* I thought. Perhaps she had made it worth his while to stay long past his expected hour.

"I'd a-told Hicks where Mr. West was, if he'd asked," Spence said diffidently.

I stared at him. "You know?"

"I can guess. He went to see a lady."

Of course he did. I felt suddenly very foolish, and rose from the settee. "Then I have no business enquiring further, Spence, and you have been very obliging to endure this interrogation. Come, Fanny—we have wasted enough time!"

"A French lady," Spence added, "as sent him a letter yesterday evening. I carried it up to him myself."

I stopped still. "Did he tell you her name, Spence?"

"No, ma'am."

And Spence could not read.

"But he said as how he was bound for Gracechurch Street."

Fanny and I looked at each other. "I do not know it, Aunt," she said. "Do you?"

"Yes." My mouth was dry. "It is in Cheapside—where our acquaintance Madame Gauthier is supposed to live."

23

AN INCONVENIENT WOMAN

Tuesday, 21 November 1815
23 Hans Place, cont'd.

She had written out the address on the upper corner of her paper.

Eleven Gracechurch Street.

The leaf was heavy enough to have been torn from a sketch-book, overwritten in dark blue ink, folded in three, and sealed with candlewax. Raphael West's direction in Newman Street was writ large on the exterior.

Spence had found the letter lying on the draughting table in West's room, where I had urged him to look for it, and brought it downstairs to me—accomplishing the whole without disturbing either West's father or his valet.

"I shall read this in the hackney. Thank you, Spence."

"You're afeared the lady may be dangerous?" he said.

"I do not know. But I find it singular that she communicated with Mr. West directly after seizing his drawing from Miss Knight's hands at Somerset House. She was certainly distressed *then*."

"You're never going out to look for him alone," the batman said stoutly.

"I cannot possibly tear you from your station. You might lose your place."

"I'm likely to lose it anyway, if Mr. West learns I sent you into Cheapside without a proper escort."

I could not help smiling at this. Any number of ladies frequent the splendid shops of the district, which run for several miles, and contain the best warehouses in the City; Cheapside was hardly a rookery. If I persisted in my opposition to the batman, however, he was likely to cling to the rear of the hackney when we attempted to leave him.

"Very well," I said. "We shall be glad of your company, Spence—and know how to value loyalty."

The question settled, Fanny and I regained our coach—which had been waiting at my instruction before No. 14's door, the cabman walking his horse against the cold. I told him where to take us; Spence mounted beside the driver on the box; and as the wheels rattled away from Newman Street, I unfolded Madame Gauthier's letter.

The message was entirely in French.

"Pray read it aloud, Aunt," Fanny said.

"I shall have to make it comprehensible in plain English," I told her. "I can never get my tongue around these wretched words.

'My dear M. West—

I imagine myself this note will come to you as a surprize, a voice of the past and one which you will never have heard yet (good Lord, what a complicated verb! I muttered) *from the woman I am now become. There was one time when you liked to play at hoops and battledore with me, over all the lawns at Malmaison, when I was a small girl with curls golden and a dress blue and silk, and my brother was yet alive. My father has told me that you were his dearest friend. My mother—who is dead—has told me you in love with her were once. I hope that the affection you had for my parents will prove strong today and that you will consent to help their poor daughter. I am alone in London without friendship.*

I learnt of you from the conversation of chance with your pretty protected one at Somerset House this morning. Mademoiselle Knight is a girl charming and I hope to know more of her.

With affection,
Alexandrine Isabey Gauthier"

"Isabey!" Fanny cried.

"'Your pretty protected one!'" I added in outrage. "Does she truly imagine you to have accepted *carte blanche* from Mr. West?"*

"I suspect she intended the word in an artistic sense," Fanny replied. "*Protégée* may be understood as referring to a pupil—which I have certainly been, under Mr. West's instruction."

"She lost no time in summoning him to her side," I observed

* This was a term for the protection, financial and otherwise, a man gave to his mistress.—*Editor's note.*

as I refolded the letter and placed it in my reticule for safe-keeping. "If she is truly Isabey's daughter, it explains her desire to see West; but she wrote nothing of having taken his copy of the map. Do you not find that strange, Fanny?"

"Perhaps she repented of her anger yesterday morning, and wished to judge of Mr. West once they met. Having quitted the Exhibition Room in a pet because she believed he had stolen her husband's work, she had time to reflect upon the matter during her journey home—and wished to appear cordial in her communication. He was a good friend to her parents, recollect."

"I told West of her fury in the note I sent round by messenger yesterday. At least he did not go to her unaware." I sighed. "But *why*, Fanny, has he not come back?"

IT WAS ALMOST HALF-PAST three o'clock when we entered the City—that part of London given over to commerce and banking, where the dome of St Paul's hovers above all. Cheapside Street is a lengthy road running roughly parallel to the Thames, lined with every sort of warehouse one may imagine. Tea and snuff are stored here; leather hides ready for fashioning into boots and saddles; every conceivable type of spice, unloaded from the holds of ships at anchor in the river beyond; coffin nails; playing cards; quantities of wax candles and brass knockers for doors. There are also, of course, warehouses full of worsteds and Indian muslins and the finest silks. The ground floors of most of the vast storage-houses were mainly given over to shops, with handsome vitrines full of goods. Fanny's interest was acute as we rolled along towards Gracechurch Street, which cuts through Cheapside at its eastern end; she was nearly hanging out the hackney window.

"I am done with Grafton House forever, Aunt," she said. "Next time we require stuffs for gowns, we are coming directly here."

At that moment our carriage swung left into Gracechurch Street and came to a halt before No. 11. It was a respectable-looking three-storey house of brick, and our arrival *en masse* at the door should no doubt excite comment; too late I thought of stealth. We ought perhaps to have pulled round to the mews. It was done, however; Spence jumped down and opened the hackney door. Fanny was a trifle pale as she stepped out on the paving.

"Be so good as to wait." I pressed a shilling into our driver's palm. He lifted his cap and went to his horse's head. Spence stood protectively between the street and ourselves, surveying the paving pugnaciously, as tho' all manner of enemies might threaten.

I approached the door. There was a large black bell mounted in the frame, and a plump woman with hands reddened from washing answered at my ring.

"Good day," I began.

"I've no rooms free," she said. "Try Mrs. Lemmon, four doors down and across the way."

"I am calling upon one of your lodgers. Madame Gauthier?"

The landlady eyed me up and down. "In demand of late," she said. "Must owe money. Upstairs, at the back. Name's on the door."

She stepped aside, admitting me; but before Fanny had

followed, the woman was gone—returned to her washing with complete indifference. Apparently we were not to be announced, nor were our cards to be sent up to Madame Gauthier; it was to be hoped we should not find her indisposed. But I was oddly relieved. With a landlady in residence, it must be unlikely that any harm had come to Raphael West here last evening.

Spence edged into the house, closing the door behind him.

We mounted the stairs to the first floor. The passage was narrow, with three closed rooms giving off to the right. I progressed to the last of these and rapped on it.

The wood gave way beneath my hand and swung slowly inwards.

I glanced over my shoulder at Fanny, whose brows lifted in surprize.

There was no sound from within; and I recalled the landlady's suggestion that Madame Gauthier was in debt. Had she quitted the place without informing her landlady?

I did not like to cross the threshold uninvited—but there was the question of Raphael West to be answered. I peered around the doorway into the room.

There was no candle lit. No fire in the grate. As she had told Mr. Bennett at Somerset House, the light was very poor. But it was enough for me to discover the figure lying facedown on the floor. From the mass of golden hair I knew immediately it was Madame Gauthier.

I drew a deep breath and went to her. Fanny followed.

"Aunt," she whispered in horror.

I grasped the poor woman's shoulder and turned her over. She was quite dead, already cold and stiff. Her blank blue eyes stared at nothing, and a trail of sickness stained her lips.

"Lord've mercy," Spence said hoarsely behind me. "If it ain't Mam'selle."

"Mam'selle?" I looked up at him. "You mean the lady from the churchyard? The Lieutenant's mistress?"

"Aye. And in the family way. Lord've mercy. No wonder he wouldn't see her. And him about to marry—"

"Spence," I said. "The landlady. *Please.*"

He hastened from the room.

"I need air," Fanny said faintly, and followed him.

Whilst they were absent, I looked about the room. There was a quantity of pictures pinned to the walls, all of them watercolours. There were a few novels in French. A few gowns and shifts in a wardrobe. Her easel, her paintbox, and her sketchbook.

No letters of any kind, tho' I found her pen and inkwell. And no sign of West's copy of the Waterloo Map.

No sign, indeed, that he had ever been here.

But I did discover a teacup with dregs still lingering in the bottom.

Among them were needles of yew.

"AND SO SHE DIED just as poor Colonel MacFarland did?" Fanny asked as our hackney pulled away from Gracechurch Street. We had stayed only long enough to see Mrs. Tuttle—for that proved to be the landlady's name—in command of the body, and declaring grimly that it should have to be buried in a potter's field, for Lord knew where money would be found for a foreigner. I wrote down my direction on a page torn from Madame Gauthier's sketchbook and told Mrs. Tuttle to communicate with me before any disposition of the remains was decided; I thought it probable Raphael West should wish to intervene, from respect for the lady's parents. Indeed, it seemed from Alexandrine's letter that her father Isabey was yet alive, and must be informed of her decease.

If ever we saw West again.

"Perhaps not *quite* as MacFarland died," I said.

Spence—we had ordered him into our hackney the better to discuss the situation—looked at me speculatively.

"But you found yew needles in her cup!" Fanny protested.

"Indeed. Haden—he is our surgeon, Spence—says it is sometimes used to . . . get rid of unwanted babes."

"Meaning Dunross's," Spence said. "That's plain, right enough. Poor lady had no money—Dunross is bound for the altar—won't deign to see her . . . so she decides to be rid of the child and go her way. Only the yew needles did for her like they did for the Colonel."

"That may be what Dunross intends us to think," I said. "It is possible she took her own life, by choice or by accident; it is equally possible that he determined to be rid of an inconvenient woman—and gave her the brew himself."

I had asked only two questions of the harassed Mrs. Tuttle before quitting her house: Had the French lady received any callers last evening, and did one match Raphael West's description?

The landlady had shown several gentlemen upstairs, she replied, which in general she didn't hold with, even if the lady claimed the title of *widow*. Tuttle had known too many grass ones in her time. But these men had looked and behaved so respectable—

By which I assumed they had crossed her palm with gold.

I asked whether any of the gentlemen were particular friends, whom Mrs. Tuttle had admitted before.

"The gentleman in the curricle, what limps with a cane."

Dunross.

I pressed Mrs. Tuttle further on the subject of West. *He* was a man she had never seen before, and she was uncertain how long he stayed, or at what hour he left—"being that plagued with roasting a capon for Tuttle's supper as I was." She was sure the lame man had visited after my gentleman—but then again, it might have been the reverse.

More than this she could not offer, and as the burden of a corpse in her household was clearly a distraction to her, we quitted the place little wiser than when we arrived.

"What if you are wrong?" Fanny said. Her gloved hands were knotted in her lap and her features looked uncharacteristically pinched. It is one thing to lose one's mother when one is fifteen, as Fanny had; it is another to see a young woman no older than yourself staring sightlessly at the ceiling. The wind had whistled over Fanny's grave today. "Her letter to Mr. West did not suggest a woman bent on self-murder. What if we are wrong about everything?"

Spence appeared about to speak, but glanced at me and was silent.

"What if the child was in fact her late husband's?" Fanny persisted. "What if her relations with Dunross were never those of a mistress at all? What if she wanted the sketch because of the letter written on the reverse—her husband's final words—and not for the cypher? She might readily have joined her efforts to Dunross's, simply to secure it."

Romance, again.

"You are suggesting the Lieutenant murdered her to gain sole possession of the map?" I asked.

"It is clear from the scene Spence witnessed in the churchyard that the two had a falling-out."

"Because Dunross is about to be married," I said wryly.

The world deals very roughly with Romantics.

Fanny lifted her shoulders helplessly. "I would only underline, Aunt, that we *cannot know* Madame's motives. We know only that she is dead."

"I'm sure of a bit more than that," Spence said suddenly. "I know my Colonel's dead, and he had the map. I know Dunross was looking for it as soon as the body was cold. Mam'selle found a copy of it yesterday and now *she's* dead, just like the Colonel. My new master made that copy—and now he's missing."

"Yes," I said patiently. "But—"

"'Ere's a story for you," Spence persisted. "Mam'selle summons Dunross to her place and shows him Mr. West's paper. Dunross tumbles to the fact that Mr. West must have seen the real one—which means he has it, or knows where it is! Dunross gets Mam'selle to lure Mr. West to her lodgings with that letter o' hers, and then Dunross kidnaps him. He gives Mam'selle a cup o' tea to settle her nerves—and it does for her, for good. He takes my master away and forces him to say where the *real* map is."

I stared at Spence. There was a terse poetry to his theory that was decidedly persuasive. "If you are correct, then Major Scovell ought to be warned. I must write to Stephen's Hotel."

"Scovell? He's part of the Duke's Family, he is. Came through the Peninsula and Waterloo after. What's Scovell to do with it?"

"He is a master of French cyphers. Wellington gave him the map, in the hope he could make sense of it."

Spence's countenance changed. "I hope West don't tell Dunross that, if indeed he's his prisoner. No reason to keep 'im alive, once the Lieutenant knows Scovell's his man."

A sick horror spread through my heart. "How could a lame man so completely overpower a strong one?" I demanded.

The batman smiled twistedly. "You wouldn't need to ask, ma'am, if you'd handled a pistol as long as Lieutenant Dunross has," he said.

24

THE QUARTERMASTER'S BARGAIN

Wednesday, 22 November 1815
23 Hans Place

There was nothing more to be done last night but deposit Spence in Newman Street. We tarried only long enough to learn whether Raphael West had miraculously returned—a hope Spence negatived—before turning wearily to Hyde Park Gate and the Brompton road.

"I wish Uncle was not gone into Hampshire," Fanny fretted. "Or if my father were with us—being a magistrate—he might know how we ought to proceed."

"We could lay information in Bow Street," I mused. "The magistrate's court is in Covent Garden, just opposite Henry's bank offices. The Runners collect in the Bear, a publick house next door. It is unusual for a lady to venture into either place, I confess; but if there is no word of Mr. West by morning, I shall feel compelled to do it."

"—Inform against Lieutenant Dunross, you would mean? But we have no proofs, Aunt, of his complicity in either murder or kidnapping; it is all speculation."

"—Principally on the part of a servant, whom Dunross angered by discharging," I agreed. "If only a quantity of yew needles might be discovered in the Lieutenant's household!"

Fanny snorted. "They may be found in half the gardens of London."

And a majority of its stables, if I were to credit Spence. The entire matter of *proofs* was vexatious from beginning to end.

Would a magistrate hear my tale without prejudice, or would he dismiss it out of hand? Carlton House had never publicised Colonel MacFarland's murder; only Matthew Baillie knew the man had been poisoned, and he was apparently still recovering in St George's Hospital. Alexandrine Gauthier was a destitute widow who might have taken her own life. Raphael West was a gentleman: he was hardly required to inform the world of his movements, and as his father supposed, might legitimately have gone anywhere under his own power. And of the map—the strange lynchpin of all these accusations—I could not produce so much as a copy. Were I to refer the magistrate to the Duke of Wellington for more information, I should justly be deemed a madwoman and thrown into the street.

As soon as we achieved Hans Place, I required our hackney driver to wait one last time—whilst I wrote a swift note of warning to the unknown Major Scovell. He should be likely to dismiss it as the work of an hysterical female; but I could not rest without making the attempt. I emptied my purse into the hackney coachman's hands, and begged him to deliver the letter to Stephen's Hotel in Bond Street.

Fanny and I spent a subdued evening together before the parlour fire. In Henry's absence, Manon chose to sustain us on pease porridge, which was just as well—my anxiety was severe enough to make a heavier meal unthinkable. Mr. Haden called round at eight o'clock, to be appalled by the news that Henry had ridden into Hampshire in his delicate state of health. I could not explain that only the direst necessity—fear of the Alton bank's failure—had driven my brother thither. Haden was inclined to blame me for want of sense. Fanny was so good as to play her harp, which relieved the scene. It prevented us all from sharing confidences better left unspoken.

MANON BROUGHT MY CHOCOLATE up to my bedchamber on a tray this morning—an unaccustomed indulgence. I understood why when she deposited in my lap a sealed letter, brought round by Special Messenger.

> *Dear Madam:*
>
> *I am in receipt of your communication of yesterday; and tho' its contents surprized me, by their brevity and caution, I was more amazed by the missive I received some hours later, just before retiring. After some thought, I have determined to beg the honour of a meeting with you at Stephen's Hotel this morning. I shall be waiting in the Writing Room any time after ten o'clock.*
>
> *Yours, etc.,*
> *Major George Scovell*

I hastened downstairs to discover the time; it was not yet eight. I stood a moment with the letter in my hand, considering my course, and found Fanny at my elbow. She looked as tho' her night had been as sleepless as mine.

"Is the news very dreadful?" she asked.

"There is no news at all—merely a summons from the man in possession of the Waterloo Map." I passed her Scovell's letter.

She glanced up, her eyes wide in hollow sockets. "But what does it mean?"

"That he was intelligent enough to credit my fears—for reasons he would not disclose in a written communication. Mysterious, to be sure, but admirably cautious. No one will force Major Scovell to drink a cup of poisoned tea."

"Shall I come with you?"

I shook my head. "In the event there *is* some intelligence of Mr. West this morning, I would beg you to remain here, Fanny, to watch for the post."

"I do not like you venturing alone. I could wish you had Spence with you," she said darkly.

"I cannot always be stealing other people's servants." I retrieved the letter and made for the stairs. "I shall not be gone above an hour, I daresay."

MAJOR SCOVELL WAS A slight man with thinning brown hair. His eyes were set deep beneath a high forehead; his manner, more subdued than I was used to expect from men of action. He appeared like a clergyman rather than a soldier, as he sat idle near the Writing Room window. This looked out onto the bustle and colour of Bond Street, but he appeared to take little notice of either.

He rose as I approached. "You are Miss Austen?"

"I am, sir." I curtseyed, aware of his estimating glance.

"And what is your direction here in London?"

"Twenty-three Hans Place, sir," I returned in some surprize.

"Did you receive a communication there this morning?"

"I did—from yourself."

"At what time?"

"I should judge half-past seven—tho' as my brother's housekeeper intercepted the Special Messenger, I cannot be sure."

"What is the name of the Duke of Wellington's personal secretary?" he asked.

"Lord FitzRoy Somerset."

"Exactly."

"He is the last of the Duke of Beaufort's eight sons, I believe," I added for good measure.

Scovell eased back in his chair and permitted himself a small smile. "Now that we have established you are *indeed* Miss Jane Austen, I will say that I am George Scovell, lately of the Department of the Quartermaster-General."

"Are you, sir?" I had not expected him to be attached to the Quartermaster—consumed with obtaining forage for horses and iron wheels for cannonades. It seemed a lowly sort of occupation.

"We may talk freely." He glanced at the open doorway opposite. "I have asked Mr. Stephen to bar all other guests from this room for exactly half an hour."

"You bewilder me, sir. Why am I summoned?"

"Because there is no one else," he replied, and for an instant an expression of anxiety flickered in his eyes, at variance with the containment of his body. "You acknowledged in your letter last night that you were one of the party that brought the Waterloo

Map to the Duke of Wellington. He in turn gave it to me, in the hope I could break the cypher written on its face. I have done so, of course—nothing could be simpler—but the Duke and his household have gone back to Paris. I return there myself tomorrow. In the normal course I should have presented His Grace with both map and cypher translation upon my arrival. But now . . ." He paused. "Now I must wager for a man's life."

I started. "What can you mean?"

"In your note last evening, Miss Austen, you warned me of personal danger. But your concern is ill-placed. It is Mr. Raphael West who is in peril; and like all Quartermasters, I am obliged to barter for him."

He offered me a sheet of paper, penned in West's distinctive hand.

> *Major Scovell,*
>
> *I am compelled to address you by the man who holds me prisoner. You have in your possession a cryptic map, given you by the Duke of Wellington on Saturday last. I must ask that you bring the map—and your translation of the cypher—to the Elephant and Castle in Newington at midnight. There you shall leave them with the publican's wife, Mrs. Hogarth by name, who shall arrange for my release. I am also required to mention that should you fail me, my body will be deposited on the doorstep of No. 14 Newman Street one hour later.*

It was signed simply R. West.

I looked from the letter to Major Scovell. "But this is abominable!"

"Distasteful in the extreme," he agreed. "Have you any notion who holds this West prisoner, and where?"

"There is one man who may be involved—formerly of the Scots Greys. A Lieutenant Dunross."

Scovell's brows lifted. "I have heard the name. He was saved in an act of bravery at the battle of Waterloo."

"—by Colonel Ewan MacFarland. *Yes*. MacFarland was subsequently poisoned—I believe after coming into possession of the Waterloo Map. I discovered the paper near his body in the Library at Carlton House."

"I was not aware of that fact," Scovell said. "Forgive me if I observe, Miss Austen, that you are curiously entangled in this affair from beginning to end. What is your appointed role in life?"

"I write novels, sir."

"Indeed? I regret I have not had the pleasure . . . the classics of antiquity are my preferred selections, when offered time to open a book . . . You are also acquainted with West, I believe?"

"He is a very gentlemanlike man," I said. "I suspect his sense of honour is sorely wrung, at having to plead for his life."

"This is no plea," Scovell countered. "It is the baldest statement of fact. West says only that he *is compelled* and *is required.* I suspect he agreed to pen the letter as a warning—so that I might have time to quit London, with the map in my safekeeping."

I felt my spirits sink and a wild desperation sweep through me. The Major was correct, of course; it was the clear road any member of Wellington's staff should tread; to submit to threats and stratagems, or entertain the notion of trading a military secret for an ordinary life, must be out of the question. Still—*that Raphael West should be sacrificed . . .*

"Is the map so very valuable?" I asked.

Scovell frowned. "I should regard it as nothing compared to the courage and dignity of the man who wrote this letter. Now, how are we to save him?"

25

A SHOCKINGLY BAD WEDDING NIGHT

Wednesday, 22 November 1815
23 Hans Place

I required only a quarter of an hour to explain to Major Scovell the shadowy part Lieutenant Dunross had played in the affair of the Waterloo Map; and he concluded, as I had, that too little proof existed to make a visit to Bow Street useful. We would, he declared, have to catch the fellow in the act.

"Raphael West is the son of the artist, Mr. Benjamin West?" he enquired.

"Yes, but the father is now quite elderly, and can do little for him."

"Pity. Did we inform him of this communication—of his son's plight—"

"He should reply with irritation, doubt, or dismissal," I said.

The Major took a turn before the Writing Room fire, his hands clasped behind his back. "Do you know where this Dunross lives?"

I shook my head. "He only came in my way at Colonel MacFarland's home, in Keppel Street. But there is one person who might tell you—a man called Spence, MacFarland's former batman. He is now employed by the West household, at No. 14 Newman Street."

"Then I shall stop there directly," Scovell said. "Whether I incommode Benjamin West or no, he ought to be told what has occurred. I shall enquire of his servant at the same moment."

"You believe we should descend upon Dunross in his home? Accuse him of murder and kidnapping? —But might that not force his hand to violence?"

"My dear Miss Austen," Scovell said kindly, "I do not propose that *we* do anything. *You* shall go home. *I* intend to follow Dunross in the hours remaining before midnight; he might well betray where West is hidden, so that I may reconnoiter the place with a view to raiding it."

So much for the dull business of Quartermasters.

"Alone?" I asked.

"I shall take this Spence with me. There is nothing like the resourcefulness of a batman who has survived the Peninsula. If we believe we have discovered the hiding place, we shall bring in the Runners."

"And if you cannot discover it?"

"We shall carry the map to the Elephant and Castle as instructed," he replied. "I have no desire to turn it over to a murderer and a scoundrel—but I am incapable of producing a fair copy, and nothing less than a convincing map will do. You tell me that Dunross has seen the thing before. He cannot be tricked."

"But neither can he say whether your translation of the cypher is accurate," I observed.

"No, indeed," Scovell replied. His grave eyes sparked with amusement. "I may certainly confound him *there*. Come, let me escort you to a hackney; I make for Newman Street immediately."

I wished to ask him what the cypher said—what secrets the Waterloo Map held—but now was not the moment. For an indolent-appearing fellow much given over to thought, Scovell proved entirely commanding when moved.

I SPENT SEVERAL WRETCHED hours in Hans Place, tearing out what few stitches I managed to set in my Berlin-work. Proofing my pages of *Emma* was impossible; I could not retain two sentences together. I longed for some word from Major Scovell, and feared what he might relate; and at last Fanny, who had watched me spurn Manon's nuncheon as tho' it were cat's-meat, proposed that we walk out in search of air and refreshment.

I hesitated.

"A watched pot never boils," she said firmly. "We might make for the Belgrave Chapel, and say a prayer for our friend."

I did as she asked.

The day was lowering and filled with November melancholy; the nave was chill. But the stillness and sacred peace calmed my agitated spirit; I bowed in acceptance of what must come.

Upon our return, the hour nearly six o'clock, we found Major Scovell waiting for us in Henry's parlour; and from the gravity of his countenance I knew he had little of good to report.

"What is it?" I demanded.

He rose from his chair by the fire and said simply, "A mare's nest, I'm afraid." His eyes drifted to Fanny, and he pulled himself up as tho' conscious of an indiscretion.

"My niece, Miss Knight," I said. "She is entirely in our confidence. What have you to tell me? What have you discovered, in your observation of Dunross?"

"That the man is married," Scovell said. "I succeeded in witnessing so much; and he appears to have departed for Dover in the last half-hour."

"Pray sit down," I said faintly.

At that moment Manon arrived with her tray of refreshment. The Major tossed back his glass of Henry's sherry in a single draught, and sighed deeply. Manon poured him a second glass without a word of comment, and he inclined his head to her in thanks.

He looked at me steadily. "Immediately after we parted this morning, Miss Austen, I went into Newman Street and suffered a difficult quarter-hour with Mr. Benjamin West. He was inclined to dismiss my report of his son, until I showed him Raphael's letter. At that he was all fire! I succeeded in leaving him behind only with difficulty. I persuaded him that Spence would stand in his stead. Having little knowledge of his servant, West was uncertain; but I impressed upon him all I knew of hard campaigning, as represented by the batman's storied career, conducted like my own in the Peninsula, and Mr. West at length gave way. He consented to remain in Newman Street and await our intelligence.

"I had hired a carriage from Stephen's Hotel, and taken up a Bow Street Runner as security. We went directly to the Albany in Piccadilly—where Spence informed me Dunross had a set of lodgings. It is very fashionable, to be sure, and rather above my touch. But then I am a married man; and you will know that only bachelors are allowed there. I undertook to enquire of the porter whether Lieutenant Dunross was in—and was told that he had vacated his rooms entirely, only this morning."

"Good God!" I cried. "He meant to flee the country, directly he obtained the map!"

"A moment," Major Scovell said, raising his hand. "The porter directed us to a church not far away: St Martins-in-the-Fields. We were arrived in time to discover Lieutenant Dunross, and the lady now his wife, standing in the nave."

"How awkward," I observed. "Did you manage to conceal yourselves?"

"I lurked in the rear of the church, I confess, and endeavoured to appear enraptured by several memorials there. Spence remained outside near the chaise, being too well known to Dunross and his bride. The wedding was attended by no one but two menials in the guise of witnesses. Miss MacFarland—I am told it was she—wore mourning. It was hardly a festive hour. I had stumbled upon the final exchange of vows, and whilst the pair was absent in the sacristy, no doubt signing the parish register along with their witnesses, I hastened to join Spence and the Runner in our hired carriage.

"Not five minutes later, Lieutenant and Mrs. Dunross emerged from the church into a waiting carriage. Our party followed them across the river to Newington—and the Elephant and Castle."

"No!" I cried.

"So he *is* there, waiting for midnight, and the map's delivery!" Fanny seconded.

"He is *not*," Scovell said. "The Elephant and Castle is a modest establishment of considerable age and reputation. Indeed, it has stood on that part of the south bank for centuries, and what it has not seen forms no part of English history. However, it is principally known at present for its stages to Canterbury, and thence to Dover—"

Fanny looked conscious; she ought to have been aware of this, but as a privileged being who travelled from Canterbury only by private coach, she had no notion how mere mortals lived.

"—where the packets depart for Channel crossings to France," Scovell concluded. "I am bound there myself, on the morrow. Lieutenant Dunross and his bride boarded a coach for Dover within an hour of their marriage; and if I do not mistake, Dunross intends to have his honeymoon in Paris."

"I do not understand," I said.

"Nor do I," Fanny interjected.

"That makes three of us," Scovell agreed. "Dunross is fled, and without the map."

"Then he has got away with murder!" I cried. "And for what? He has realised *nothing,* if he is gone without the map. Why poison anybody, or kidnap West, if he meant all along to be content with Miss MacFarland?"

"Your man Spence is convinced that having sown a false trail, in all respectability, the Lieutenant means to return from Canterbury at midnight—and take his plunder from the barmaid as arranged."

"I call that a shockingly bad wedding night," I murmured. "Particularly if Miss MacFarland—Mrs. Dunross—is complicit in her husband's crimes. But where is West hidden? Can Dunross have abandoned him?"

"I have no notion where the poor man may be imprisoned," Scovell returned. "He is certainly not at the Albany—for the porter assured me that Dunross's set is vacant. That is the most confounded part of the whole affair. I have wasted hours, Miss Austen, in chasing a man who appears to have nothing more on his mind than happiness. What if I have been following the wrong hare?"

I had no answer for this. The possibility opened an abyss too wide and deep to contemplate. If all our suppositions were wrong—

West was a dead man.

"Lacking any alternative," Scovell concluded, "I propose to go back to the Elephant and Castle as ordered at midnight, map in hand. I do not know what else to do."

"What will the Duke say, when he learns you have given up the map?" I asked.

"Very little—for I have retained the meaning of the cypher, and that is the paper's true value."

"Not to Madame Gauthier," Fanny said softly. "Her husband's letter was *all* to her."

"You mean to offer a false translation of the figures?" I said.

"Of course. I do not work for Dunross."

"Can you tell us *why* the map provoked murder, Major?"

He hesitated, then lifted his shoulders in resignation. "You have endured a good deal in ignorance; the least I may do is satisfy your interest. It is not my secret in any case, but Buonaparte's."

"Something to do with his Russian campaign, I collect."

"Yes. You know that he fought his way into the heart of Russia in the autumn of 1812, only to be forced to retreat when Moscow burned that October?"

"I did read a few accounts."

"The burning of Moscow was a terrible thing—most of the wealthy nobles had already quitted the place, but common folk remained, and it is rumoured it was they who set the fire, rather than give over the city to the French. As the flames spread, the French troops looted Moscow unmercifully. They stole everything they could carry—priceless paintings still in their frames, sacred icons of considerable age, silver plate, jewels, silk draperies, even Ivan the Great's gold cross from the Kremlin bell tower. The booty was loaded into wagons taken from Moscow liveries and pulled out of the city by the soldiers themselves."

"Such greed!" Fanny exclaimed.

"Such an encumbrance, for a retreating army," I observed more prosaically.

"You are correct, Miss Austen. The Russian snows descended swiftly, and the French Army was without the essentials of survival—fodder for their horses and food for themselves. Moreover, Buonaparte had seized all the Russian cannon abandoned in Moscow. The baggage train included these heavy guns on their supports, to be pulled by mules or horses—which were in very short supply. I may tell you that the numbers of horses throughout Europe have declined in a shocking way, due to the unceasing carnage of battle over the past fifteen years."

"All this plunder, in the midst of an inferno?" I said sceptically.

Scovell smiled. "By some reports, the French baggage train was six miles long when it left Moscow."

"And yet ill-provisioned," Fanny murmured.

"I believe they were reduced to eating what horses remained, before ever they reached the border," the Major said. "It was by all accounts a hellish retreat."

"And the map? The French cypher?" I asked.

"—Is a guide to the place where all the booty was abandoned," Scovell said placidly. "Buonaparte was forced to sink his cannon in a reservoir along the Moscow-Smolensk road, rather than leave them to Kutuzov—that is the Russian general whose forces harried him viciously out of the country. The priceless treasures of Moscow were hidden elsewhere—in a salt mine, of all places. Napoleon enciphered the essentials on this watercolour, believing he should return one day to retrieve his booty. But that will be difficult to achieve from his present distance of St Helena."

"Yet the watercolour was in another's possession, by the eve of Waterloo," Fanny pointed out.

"I suspect it remained in the keeping of the man who painted it." Scovell eyed his empty glass. "He would not have been privy to the workings of the cypher, and must be thought safe. He was probably a military cartographer—Buonaparte carried numerous mapmakers in his train during the years he ran roughshod over Europe."

"Charles Gauthier, a *military cartographer*?" Fanny said in disbelief. This was far less romantic than she hoped.

"Naturally. Napoleon should trust none but an excellent draughtsman and painter to capture his Empire for eternity. It is only in maps, Miss Knight, that the Empire now exists at all."

It was true, I thought. The ambitions of the Conqueror of the World, as he had once been known, were as fragile as paper.

"Now I must take my leave." The Major rose and bowed to us both. "I should like to rest a little before midnight."

"Very wise," I said briskly. "I shall do the same, as I must certainly accompany you."

Scovell looked all his astonishment. "There is not the slightest need, Miss Austen. I shall carry Spence with me as before—"

"There is every need," I said. "I know Dunross by sight. Spence knows him far better, of course—but in this, Spence is a liability. If he appears at your side in the Elephant and Castle, Dunross is certain to smell a rat. He turned Spence out of Miss MacFarland's household, and can have no idea the man is now your informant. Spence must not be seen at all costs."

I observed Scovell to digest this fact. "Then I shall bring my Runner with me," he said.

"Do so by all means, but do not expect him to identify your murderer," I returned. "If you hope to apprehend Dunross, you must have an informed ally at your side."

Scovell said nothing for an instant; then he sighed. "I suppose if I appear in the publick house with a lady, I may be taken for a married man intent upon a Channel crossing. You shall lend me a creditable appearance, Miss Austen."

"Thank you. I shall go veiled, so that Dunross—who only met me once—has no cause to suspect I am not your wife."

"I might pass for your daughter, sir!" Fanny suggested.

He smiled. "Alack, I have none. You must stay safe at home, Miss Knight. As for you, Miss Austen—expect me at eleven o'clock."

26

PROXIES

Thursday, 23 November 1815
23 Hans Place

Newington is a village on the lower border of Southwark, across the River Thames. We travelled east through London and crossed Westminster Bridge; the carters and drays that clogged the Metropolis's streets by day were absent, freeing the roads to an astonishing degree. It wanted only half an hour until midnight, however, by the time we achieved Newington; and our progress was unmarked by any animated conversation. Major Scovell had indeed brought his Bow Street Runner—I discovered the man in possession of the backwards seat when I was handed into the coach. He was perhaps thirty years of age, quite strengthy in his frame, and smelled strongly of pipe tobacco. Major Scovell appeared disinclined to speak of anything of importance in his presence, and so I maintained a subdued composure.

My anxiety, however, was all for Raphael West. Was it possible he was held at the Elephant itself, and that his release should come as soon as the Waterloo Map left Scovell's hands?

What if Dunross did not elect to return from Dover and his wedding-night? Or what if he had employed a proxy—someone I could not possibly recognise? Would the Lieutenant be likely to have made provision for West's release, or . . . was West already dead?

Impossible to know. At least these questions did not torment me in the solitude of my bedchamber; being one of Scovell's party, I might now have the answers within the hour.

The Elephant and Castle sits at the crossing between Newington Butts and the Brighton road. At this hour the village was deserted but for the few coaches depositing travellers bound for the south channel coast, or east to Kent and the French packets. The inn was ancient in appearance, built of wood with a thatch roof.* We pulled into the yard, which was lit with torches and oil lamps in deference to arriving coach traffic; ostlers ran up to Scovell's chaise, and were firmly sent about their business by his coachman—the equipage, as before, having been hired from Stephen's Hotel. The driver was engaged to wait.

"Now, Mr. Ryder," Scovell said to the Runner sitting opposite us, "do you stay near the Elephant's back door, whilst this lady and I enter at front. Our man may show himself within, in which case I shall apprehend him. But if he skulks out of sight and employs the publican's wife as his proxy, he is likely to flee from the rear—particularly if he has kept a conveyance waiting in this yard. That will be your sign to act. Be vigilant, sirrah, and swift."

---

* In 1824 this simpler wood structure was razed and replaced with a much larger brick building in the Regency style.—*Editor's note.*

Ryder grunted, and Scovell thrust open the carriage door. He stepped down and handed me out. Ryder waited until we had moved towards the inn's entrance before quitting the chaise. Glancing back over my shoulder, I saw him dart across the yard and melt into the shadows cast by the flickering torchlight. My sight may have been somewhat dimmed by the net I employed as a veil; but I suspect not even the ostlers espied him.

Major Scovell lent me his arm, and showed the solicitude expected of a fond husband as we entered the Elephant: bespeaking a table in the publick-room near the fire, and requesting two glasses of mulled wine. After half an hour in the coach I confess my toes were numbed with cold, and I enjoyed the prospect of a steaming drink between my hands. I would have to lift my veil to enjoy it, but I intended to keep the bulk of the net firmly over my eyes. This would allow me to survey the company, which was varied and boisterous, without betraying my roving glance.

"It wants but twenty minutes until midnight," Scovell murmured. "Do you see our man?"

I hesitated a little before answering. There were at least two dozen people in the room, many of them local fellows enjoying a tankard of ale. There were no other ladies; these were generally conveyed to an inn's coffee-room in order to refresh themselves in greater privacy, but Scovell had deliberately ignored this convention. Far fewer people would be in the coffee-room. Nobody here, however, resembled Dunross—and I was intently looking for any man who limped, regardless of whether he was dressed with the Lieutenant's usual elegance or no.

"I do not," I said, anxiety for West clutching at my throat.

What if the Lieutenant had sent a confederate? Someone we had never suspected, and never seen?

At that moment a serving-maid placed our mulled wine on the table and asked if the Major required anything further. "I do," he said. "Are you by any chance Mrs. Hogarth?"

"Lord, no," the girl retorted broadly. "Her High-and-Mightiness don't serve in *here.* Never sets foot out of the coffee-room, does Mrs. Hogarth."

"I collect that my wife should be more comfortable there. The crowd in this room is rather . . . loud, and my wife is unwell."

I lifted my gloved hand to my breast in a gesture of faintness. The girl conducted us immediately to the coffee-room, and found us a comfortable place. But unfortunately the chamber was lined with tall oak settles—very private indeed, but difficult to penetrate when one is in search of a particular figure. Dunross might be in any one of them.

We sipped our wine whilst the hands of Scovell's pocket-watch ticked slowly round. Excellent chicken and liver pies were laid before us, and I consumed a little for the sake of verisimilitude. The woman we assumed to be Mrs. Hogarth stood behind a bar counter, carefully surveying her customers and conveying orders to servants and kitchen alike; she was a well-corseted figure in old-fashioned panniers and a mobcap, her visage plain and her eyes shrewd. She gave us only a cursory glance when we took up our table, and never came near us.

"I shall enquire of that woman the way to the privy," I whispered to Major Scovell. "That will allow me to take a turn about the room, and peer into the settles."

"Very well," he said.

I crossed to the bar counter. "Are you Mrs. Hogarth?"

"Yes, ma'am." She bobbed a little on her feet, a half-hearted courtesy. "Have you everything you require?"

"I should like to visit the privy."

"Of course. Through the green baize door at the rear, then cross the hall towards the kitchens. The privy will be at your right hand, before you reach the kitchen threshold."

I thanked her and made my way slowly towards the back of the coffee-room, my veiled gaze roving the various settles. Three were empty. Two held only women, one of them with a pair of children sprawled in slumber on her lap. Mixed parties were in others. Only one had a solitary gentleman—and he was at least twenty years older than James Dunross.

I checked suddenly at the familiarity of his figure: spare frame, dark head, the pert eyes of a monkey fixed on the ale before him. His tall beaver rested on the table by his side; his black frock coat was as neat as ever; his throat was closely bound in a cravat, betraying nothing of the stitched scar and bandages that must lie beneath. Matthew Baillie, the Court Physician! Who only Saturday had been too fatigued to speak much to West . . . but who must immediately have understood, from the tenor of his questions, that West was on the hunt for a murderer.

In an instant, I saw how it was. The doctor had been very clever in affecting ignorance and weakness. He had removed himself from all suspicion, indeed, by placing the Waterloo Map in West's care, and staging the attack upon himself. Had it been his own hand that stabbed his throat, his own lies that implicated an unknown footpad? The map itself was as nothing; it might lie forever in the Newman Street picture vaults, so long as Baillie secured the translation of the cypher it held. He had set about bartering for the cypher's meaning not long after West's visit to St George's Hospital. He had seized West, and used him against Scovell, the only man in England who possessed the cypher's key.

Events, I thought, had fallen out quite neatly for Matthew Baillie. As an intimate of Carlton House, he was in a position to know of Benjamin West's plans for a great canvas, and of the scheduled arrival from Paris of the various Waterloo notables who must sit to the painter's brush. He had probably learnt of the map's existence from Colonel MacFarland himself, who had never seemed alive to the danger of publicity. Baillie had merely to dispose of MacFarland, secure the map, and negotiate with Scovell for the cypher's meaning. The fact that the map was nowhere on MacFarland's person, when the doctor tended him for poison, must have come as a brutal shock.

As, too, had the presence of a meddlesome woman in the Carlton House Library, with her handkerchief stained with yew . . .

And all this time, we had been preoccupied with Dunross. Who intended to observe his wedding night in Dover, after all.

I stood rigid in my spot, my veiled eyes fixed upon the Court Physician. Baillie was but two yards from my hand. I might have reached out and seized him. Instead, I slowly lifted my veil.

Baillie glanced sidelong, disturbed a little by a woman's fixed gaze. But then his countenance altered, and he inclined his head. "Miss Austen," he said. "Do you, too, intend a journey into Kent?"

For the full space of a heartbeat, I could not summon words.

Then I dropped a curtsey, the blood pounding painfully at my temples. "Dr. Baillie," I managed. "I had thought you indisposed. Did I not read that you were lately admitted to St George's Hospital?"

The rogue smiled, tho' he did not accomplish it without obvious pain. "You must congratulate me on my escape, ma'am. I only quitted the horrors of my sickbed four hours ago, and am intent upon the asylum of friends near Canterbury. One always heals better in the country. And you, Miss Austen?"

I doubted very much that he intended to go into Kent—Dover must be his object, and a swift flight to the Continent. I wished to grasp him by his wounded throat and demand the whereabouts of Raphael West—but I mastered my vicious impulse, and thought of Major Scovell behind me, and the force of Bow Street at his command. And so I said with pleasant equanimity: "I, too, make for Canterbury. My brother lives in the village of Godmersham, some eight miles from the cathedral close. Indeed, he is a magistrate of Canterbury Gaol . . . We shall be travelling companions, sir! And now—if you would excuse me . . ."

He inclined his head; not without difficulty, for the swathing of his neck was fearsome. I hurried through the pretence of the privy. I could not now return to Major Scovell—I should immediately betray our association to Baillie, who was undoubtedly acquainted with the Major's object at the Elephant and Castle, having ordered it himself. I stood in trepidation in the coffee-room doorway, my heart thumping painfully. At that moment, an ostler appeared in the stableyard entrance and shouted, "Canterbury coach, loading now!"

Several parties before me exited the settles with bandboxes in hand. Scovell drained the last of his wine and without a glance at me, moved across the room to the woman behind the counter and pulled a sealed packet from his coat. I saw Mrs. Hogarth's eyes widen slightly but otherwise her stout figure betrayed no excitement; she merely bobbed at the Major and disappeared through the door behind her—which must, I reflected, lead to the kitchen. I recollected that the back hall debouched into the stableyard from that passage. It must be an obvious path of escape. Indeed, most of those intent upon boarding the Canterbury stage were heading for that part of the inn now.

Which meant Baillie would lose himself in the crowd.

I glanced about. *Where had the doctor gone?*

"Major," I muttered as he came up with me. "The back door!"

"Ryder is there."

I could not look at Scovell as I eased past. "Your man is of middle-age, spare of frame, with a monstrously high cravat under his beaver. He intends the Canterbury coach. Follow him into the back hall, and he will be trapped between you and Bow Street."

"A flanking manoeuvre," Scovell sighed. "Very well." He surged before me and gained the last of the stage passengers as they achieved the back hall. I looked after him an instant, then turned towards the front entrance. There was always a chance that Baillie had gone that way, and I was not about to lose him now.

I hastened through the publick-room. No simian physician was quitting the Elephant that I could observe. I went out the front door—a few paces ahead of me in the dark was a short, broad figure of a man moving swiftly towards the stableyard. In his right hand was a sealed packet I recognised. *Scovell's packet.* Mrs. Hogarth must have slipped it to him in the kitchen. How had Baillie got there, unobserved?

As I started after the hurrying fellow, he slipped the papers into his coat and lengthened his stride. The distance was not very great—and in all the bustle of the departing stage the sound of my pursuit was lost. As my quarry entered the torch-lit yard, head down and making directly for a hackney, I picked up my skirts and began to run across the cobbles. "Major Scovell!" I shouted. "Ryder!"

Two figures leapt out of the back doorway.

"He is there! Making for the hackney!"

Ryder cried, "Halt! Bow Street!"

The man glanced over his shoulder, then broke into a run.

But in that instant of confrontation, I had seen his face.

Not Baillie—not the duplicitous doctor—but the very last person I expected.

It was the batman, Spence.

"Good God!" I cried out, and at the same moment, Major Scovell shouted, "Spence! Stop where you are!"

He did not. He ignored the waiting hackney—with the Canterbury coach departing, the way out of the yard was blocked to smaller vehicles—and ran instead to a saddled horse whose reins were in the hands of an ostler. Spence levelled the fellow with a blow from his fist, threw himself on the horse's back, and wheeled around. And then, with a kick to his mount's flanks, he sprang past the far side of the coach, obscured momentarily from our view.

Major Scovell clutched my elbow, pulling me up short.

Ryder doubled back and came around the near side of the stage.

Spence had already bolted past.

He was making for the yard's exit. There was just enough room between stage and gate for his mount to shoot the gap; but before he reached it, he twisted in the saddle and levelled a pistol at Ryder. A blue and white flash cut the night.

The shot went wild; Major Scovell pulled me to the ground. I glanced up to see Ryder drawing a gun from his coat.

"Halt! Bow Street!"

Spence rode on.

Ryder fired.

The ball caught Spence in the back. I saw him arch as he passed through the gate, saw his hands clutch tightly at the reins as he fell forward on his horse's neck. Then horse and rider were gone.

Ryder dodged in front of the loading Canterbury stage—its passengers frozen where they stood—and vanished through the gate after his quarry.

"He shall not get far," Scovell said. "Come, Miss Austen—let us return to our carriage."

THE CANTERBURY STAGE SECURED its passengers in haste and departed. Only then could we swing out after it in our hired equipage.

"He will have taken the Brighton road," Scovell said positively. "The rest of the world is gone to Canterbury—and that is what he shall particularly wish to avoid. He can find a boat in Brighton as readily as in Dover."

The Major let down the side window and peered out into the night. The sound of hooves and wheels filled the body of the carriage.

I was silent. My mind was in turmoil—Not James Dunross. Not Matthew Baillie. It was *Spence* who had the map, Spence who had betrayed all of us. We had none of us apprehended that Spence could be his Colonel's murderer.

I had sent him to the employ of Raphael West. And West was missing. If we did not find Spence—

Scovell raised his fist and pounded suddenly on the roof of the carriage. It slowed to a halt.

Ryder, the Bow Street Runner, was standing on the verge. At his feet was a huddled shape. Ryder lifted his head as our carriage pulled up.

"Done for," he called. "Shot through the spine. And the horse is gone."

I thrust open my carriage door and tumbled out, falling on my knees by the batman's head.

"Spence," I said urgently. "*Spence.* Where have you hidden West? *Tell me.* Where is West?"

I shook his inert form.

He groaned, and I thought his eyes opened. He struggled to speak. I held my ear close to his lips.

"Buried alive," he whispered. " . . . never find 'im."

And then the batman expired.

27

THE USES OF BELPER STOVES

Thursday, 23 November 1815
23 Hans Place, cont'd.

We left Bow Street in charge of the body and made our way back to the Elephant and Castle. There we required an ostler and pony cart to fetch Ryder and his burden to the inn—despite the outrage of Mrs. Hogarth, who deigned to set foot outside her coffee-room at last.

"Guns and murder in our yard!" she cried. "We're respectable folk at the Elephant, I'll have you know, and the sooner you take yourselves off, the better I'll be pleased! Disturbing our coach passengers with every kind of violence! No better than highwaymen and thieves, the pair of you! I'll send for the Runners, I will!"

In a few short words, Scovell informed her the call would be wasted, and abjured her to look to her own respectability—as she would likely be taken up for complicity with a murderer. Her amazement was so profound, she actually summoned her husband—Hogarth being the Elephant and Castle's proprietor—who informed us that his helpmeet had no knowledge of

Spence. The two had never met before. The batman was friendly with one of the kitchen maids, and had sat in that part of the inn this evening; he had explained that he was owed wages from his employer, who was quitting the country and intended to leave a packet with the publican's wife. Mrs. Hogarth had not thought it odd that Spence did not wish to meet with his old master; the two had "parted in anger," Spence told her, but he was determined to have his money. He might be able to marry Betsy then, and Lord knows she deserved it. Mrs. Hogarth thought her likely to be in the family way.

We concluded that Betsy was the kitchen maid, and asked to see her.

She appeared with her eyes red from crying. "I've nothing to say to the likes of you," she told us defiantly. "Murderers, you are—and my Bill a hero of Waterloo."

A hero of Waterloo. How many men, little deserving of the phrase, had been called the same since June?

"He has likely murdered two people," Scovell said sternly, "one of them a lady your age. He has died for it, and you might be taken before the Assizes for it—but you might also help us. There is another man, held captive by Spence's design. Did he speak of this to you? Do you know where the man is?"

Betsy denied all knowledge of Raphael West. She had no notion of Bill's plans. He had told her only that he would be rich beyond imagining in a very little while, and should return to make her happy. She was almost as defiant when we left her to Ryder, as she had been at the outset of our interrogation; but I thought it the defiance of despair. Her man was dead; she would never be rich or happy; and she knew in her heart she had been deceived. I did not begrudge her the silence; only the ignorance that prompted it.

AT HALF-PAST ONE O'CLOCK we retraced our journey across the Thames in considerable despair and exhaustion. We were both silent. I no longer asked the hour; we had passed the margin at which West's life must end.

Buried alive. Never find him.

"He might be anywhere," Scovell muttered.

I considered this in silence. It had a decided truth.

But truth was predicated on *facts.* What did I know about West's last movements?

He had been summoned to Madame Gauthier's.

He had certainly gone, for he was admitted by the landlady.

We had not known when we discovered the Frenchwoman's body that Spence was her killer. He must have been one of the men who entered the house on the night of Alexandrine's death—but perhaps he had gone, all along, *with Raphael West.* There should be nothing extraordinary in this. West had admitted Spence to his confidence; and gentlemen often moved with their servants. He might even have ordered that servant to make tea. Spence could have dosed Madame Gauthier's with yew, then quitted the place with his master.

And overpowered West on the way back to Newman Street? In his own coach?

Impossible. The coachman should certainly have noticed.

For similar reasons, Major Scovell—the object of all Spence's calculation—had travelled with him yesterday entirely unmolested. Spence would not be capable of overpowering Scovell, his hired coachman, and a Bow Street Runner; he had been forced to submit to a dumb show of hunting Dunross at the Major's side, when what he desired most was the Major's cypher translation.

So how had he seized Raphael West?

"Spence cannot have dragged West out of the coach insensible," I said aloud, "nor can he have spirited him from Newman Street, even in the middle of the night. West overmatches Spence in both height and weight. To carry him from the house should require accomplices, and Spence does not appear to have had them—other than the maid Betsy."

"And ourselves," Scovell said with a trace of bitterness. "We have indeed been aides to murder, however unwitting. When I think of all I allowed that man to know, and to witness!"

"You did not tell him you intended to hire a Runner," I said comfortingly, "and that certainly saved your life and the key to the cypher. Do not speak of our complicity. I am wretched at the knowledge that it was *I* who helped Spence to a new place. When Dunross had dismissed him without a character! There is a history to be known, there."

Scovell held up his hand. The carriage bumped over the cobbles towards the Brompton road and Hans Place. "You said something just now. *That he could not have carried West from the house.* A criminal servant is limited in his resources. He must *look* and *work* as an ordinary servant to retain proximity to his prize. What were Spence's duties in West's household? He was not his valet, I collect?"

"Not at all! I believe he was being trained in the workings of a Belper stove."

"A what?" Scovell demanded.

"A Belper stove. It is a very recent invention—having been abroad so many years, you will not have heard of it, perhaps. It projects a quantity of air, warmed in an adjacent chamber, through pipes let into several rooms—" I stopped short. "Dear God. The picture vaults."

Scovell stared at me. I clutched his arm.

"*Buried alive!* That is it, Major. West is buried—in the cellars of his own house! *The picture vaults.* He is trussed up in an iron cage, at a level where no one ever goes. And unless I am very much mistaken—there is only one set of keys. Are you willing and able to break a door down?"

Scovell rapped on the carriage ceiling and thrust his head through the window. "Number 14 Newman Street," he shouted. "As quick as may be!"

THE HOUSE WAS SHUTTERED and silent; no light showed. Being that it was nearly two o'clock in the morning, this should not be remarkable. We hammered upon the door, however, and at length the oak was unbolted. The Wests' porter, bleary from his couch, stared at us in confusion.

"I am Major Scovell," my companion told the fellow, "and I spoke with your master only yesterday. I believe I know where Mr. Raphael West may be found. Has anyone keys to the picture vaults?"

We were ushered inside. The porter went to rouse Mr. Benjamin West's valet, so that the valet might rouse his master. But I knew the older man could not help us—it was Raphael who held the keys. If Spence had contrived to overpower him and inter him in the vaults—then we must break down the door. And at this hour of the night, every moment was vital.

"Come," I said urgently, and led Scovell beneath the curve of the staircase. The door to the cellar steps at least was unlatched, tho' we found the oil lamps along the lower staircase extinguished.

"We shall have to feel our way," I said.

"I shall go before." Scovell began to descend, his footsteps unhesitating. Years of night manoeuvres had served him well. I followed less surely, one hand outstretched to the wall. At the bottom of the stairs the Major attempted to unbolt the final door—but it stood firm.

"There is a marked smell of burning," I said apprehensively. "Can it be possible the vaults are on fire?"

"The door is cool, and I do not hear the sound of flames. Step back, Miss Austen."

He dashed his shoulder against the wood. Behind me on the stairs there were footsteps; the porter and the valet. I stood aside to let them pass.

"Here, what do you think you're doing, then?" the valet demanded, clapping his hand on Scovell's shoulder.

"Freeing Mr. Raphael West," he retorted. "Put your backs into it, men!"

The porter immediately complied; the valet hesitated. He wore a dressing-gown of silk, which may perhaps have argued greater care. He removed it and folded it tenderly, placing it without a word in my hands; then he threw himself against the door beside Scovell.

The wood panel shuddered, but held fast.

Again the three men charged it. I heard the sound of splintering wood; the doorframe was giving way.

A final crash of bodies—and the door burst open.

Immediately a haze of smoke poured out.

"Lord love us!" cried the valet, rearing back with his hand to his mouth.

The porter sat down on the lowest step, coughing.

"Fetch some light," Scovell ordered. He pulled a handkerchief from his coat, held it over his mouth, and plunged into the room.

I still wore my veil—it must suffice. I drew breath, put down my head, and followed him.

In the darkness it was difficult to know where one was. Ahead, Scovell was feeling his way, when every second in the smoky atmosphere was perilous.

"There is a central passage," I called out, "lined with barrel vaults. Make for it!"

"Mr. West!" he cried. "Raphael West!"

There was no reply.

The smoke at head-height was overwhelming. *But there was no fire.* I bunched my skirts, fell to my knees, and began to crawl through the clearer air close to the ground, pausing to feel with my hand along the opening beneath the iron gates of each vault. He would not be lying in the first ones; Spence would not want him glimpsed by chance. He was more likely to be at the rear. But could I venture so far? Could Scovell?

"Mr. West! Mr. Raphael West!"

Scovell's voice was rasping in his throat and in another moment I heard him gasp and cough. Fear seized me: I could not hope to drag *two* men from this place if Scovell succumbed.

"Get down, Major!" I cried. "There is air near the floor!"

Then a light sprang up behind me—the porter had brought a candle at last, to fire the oil lamps! The smoke was lessening as well, now that the door was open. I blinked painfully against the smart of it in my eyes, and crawled forward. The porter went past me at a run, pausing to light the final lamp, and there was Scovell—on his knees ten yards ahead. He was struggling to open an iron gate—but as the light reached him, he succeeded.

In another moment he dragged an inert form from the vault.

I hastened forward. It was West—but so deathly pale, so still. A wad of rags was tied round his mouth, and his hands and feet were bound. His eyes were closed.

Either unconscious or—

The porter snuffed out his taper on the stone paving and reached to help Scovell. Between them, they carried West to the stairs.

The valet was waiting with a flask of brandy, but Scovell went past him, mounting the steps in haste, the porter struggling behind. "Quickly," I urged the valet, and he went before me up the stairs.

Scovell was coughing unbearably now, but with the tenor of a man who is grateful for air—no longer stifling. He was working at the binding at West's mouth. As I came up with him he tossed the rags aside and slapped West's cheeks. The valet knelt down with his brandy. Scovell took it without a word, raised West's head on his arm, and tipped the liquor into his mouth.

"Does he live?" I demanded.

West choked on his brandy.

"He does," Scovell said.

My eyes were streaming from the smoke; the porter beside me looked much the same.

"He was lying on the ground," Scovell continued, "which was just as well, for that is where the air was. How did the cellar come to be filled with smoke?"

"Must've been the stove," the porter said. "It's a rare hand at heating a place, provided the vents for air aren't stopped."

"Who is responsible for its maintenance?" Scovell demanded.

It was Raphael West who replied.

"Spence," he said, and his eyes flickered open.

28
A CURIOUS HISTORY

Friday, 24 November 1815
23 Hans Place

"And so the Waterloo Map was never retrieved?" Henry demanded as we sat over glasses of sherry this evening. "Scovell's packet of papers was lost?"

"It disappeared somewhere along the Brighton road," I told him regretfully. "When Spence fell off his horse in the dark, it must have fallen into a field, and Ryder, the Bow Street Runner, was unaware of it. But I believe Major Scovell has a copy of the cypher translation—and he shall give that to the Duke of Wellington. The Major crossed the Channel for Paris today."

I thought of the Ordinance man with esteem and affection; the Crown's soldiers are in excellent hands, if Scovell is to have the management of them.

"I wonder if Old Douro will take up an expedition to Russia," Henry said thoughtfully, "and seize Buonaparte's lost plunder."

"He is more likely to share the intelligence with Czar Alexander," I suggested, "as a demonstration of goodwill between

Allies. The gold cross of Ivan the Great is not an *English* treasure to be recovered."

"I might venture into Russia for the riches myself," Henry said feelingly, "if I knew what that dashed cypher said."

"—Something about salt mines outside of Smolensk. I gather your business in Alton did not prosper?"

He set down his glass deliberately. "It did not. The bank is ruined, Jane. We have called in all our debts, exercised our power over mortgages—made enemies of every farmer in the country, in short—and still we cannot meet our obligations. We shall pay out what monies we have until they are gone; and then we shall close the Alton bank's doors."

I stared at him.

He was very white about the mouth, and his grey eyes—so like my own—were devoid of expression. I had never really believed that Henry's bank would fail. His manner is generally so light, even when talking of grievous things, that it has been impossible to know how deep the trouble ran.

Now I knew.

"And the other branches? London?"

He lifted his shoulders in doubt. "Time will tell. I had hoped to draw funds from Henrietta Street to shore up the Alton accounts, but Tilson will have none of it. He is not a partner in the Alton branch. I cannot blame him. 'Cut off the diseased limb,' he says, 'lest the whole body be poisoned.'"

"And you cannot go to our brothers?"

He laughed abruptly. "What am I to say? —Pray, Edward, throw good money after bad?"

"Oh, Henry." I sighed. "I *am* sorry."

From the front entry below came the sound of greeting and bustle; after a moment, Fanny appeared in her walking dress and bonnet, her cheeks becomingly pink. "Look whom I met with in Hatchard's, Aunt!" she said. "Mr. West has rejoined the living! And he was so obliging as to escort me home!"

He came forward into the parlour and I felt a rush of gladness. I rose and curtseyed; he bowed. His countenance was regaining health and colour, his dark eyes were alight. Only a reddening about the mouth and wrists betrayed where his bonds had hurt him.

"Mr. Austen. Miss Austen. You are both well?"

His voice was still scarred with smoke.

"Very well," I replied.

"Sit down and tell us all we do not yet know, West!" Henry commanded, and West drew forward a chair.

The fire burnt brightly. Manon brought more sherry. Fanny played an air on her harp. In a little while, we repaired to the dining room and enjoyed the latest pheasants sent down from Godmersham. We were able to talk in perfect confidence and laugh with an awareness of our freedom. Even Henry, I hope, forgot his cares for a while.

And this is what West said.

"IT IS NOT ENTIRELY a bad thing to be forced to exist in silence for a while—or to endure hours of darkness. The lack of sound and light, the deprivation of the usual senses, drives one back upon deductive thought. I had learnt much from the simple fact of the batman Spence levelling his Army pistol at me, as I went to retire Monday night. I had just returned from seeing

Alexandrine—Madame Gauthier—in Gracechurch Street, and I had carried Spence with me. As we reentered my father's house, I bade the porter goodnight, and told him he should not be needed again. He had barely taken himself off—I was standing in the anteroom, going through the latest post—when Spence placed the muzzle against my spine.

"He had discovered the keys to the picture vaults in my draughting room before ever we quitted Newman Street. They were in his pocket as we descended the stairs. He had exercised considerable forethought—the rags and ropes that were meant to bind me were already waiting in my cell, and his pistol butt stunned me senseless as soon as I entered it. I awoke with a fearful ache in my skull, my wrists and ankles bound. My mouth was stuffed with rags.

"Spence did not come near me the rest of the night, and I wondered very much what he intended—to rob my father of his valuable pictures, knowing that the old man was indisposed with a gastric complaint and his son was now out of the way. But the utter lack of activity in the vaults belied this suspicion. It was only when another day had passed and Spence freed my hands so that I might write to Scovell, that I understood how deep his crimes had gone."

West furrowed his brow in an effort at calculation. "That was Tuesday, I apprehend, although the passage of time in those circumstances is difficult to measure."

"Did he feed you? Had you water? Weren't you dreadfully cold?" Fanny demanded.

"And why did not Spence kill you once the letter to Scovell was written?" I asked.

"As for that—he did enter the cell some once or twice with water and bread, Miss Knight. Then my mouth was unbound, but my hands were not. Spence fed me like a child. Once I attempted to call for help, but he beat me over the head with his gun a second time, and again I lost consciousness. I was afraid that the next blow might kill me. In any case, it is impossible to discern voices from this cellar in the rooms above. They sound much as cries from the street do—London is a city of noise.

"As for why he kept me alive, Jane—I was to serve as barter for as long as necessary in the game with Major Scovell. Only when he quitted this place for the Elephant and Castle was I consigned to perdition. *Then* he might damage the Belper with abandon; for my witness against him, once the map was in his hands, was a danger he could not afford."

"Dear God," I muttered. The batman had wagered his odds to a hair's breadth.

"Tuesday evening Spence forced me to write the letter to Scovell, and it was then I understood what he was about," West continued. "I had no taste for trading military secrets for my life. I told Spence the map and the broken cypher should be useless to him—he could not, after all, *read.* He assured me that he possessed friends who did. I suppose after they had answered his purpose, he meant to kill them. I determined to write to Scovell in the hope it might serve as a warning—and perhaps buy the Major time."

"He assumed as much," I said. "Did Spence ever tell you *why* he conceived this fantastic idea of finding Buonaparte's treasure—and committed murder to achieve it?"

West looked at me. "It is always the *motivation* of others that compels you, is it not, Miss Austen? You are deeply interested in the minds and hearts of those around you—and the way in which they animate Society. I read it in your work; I see it in your relations; even in the way you listen without uttering a word. Yes, Spence told me why he poisoned his closest friend, and a lovely young Frenchwoman he hardly knew. It was he who found the Waterloo Map in the first place."

MANON APPEARED WITH A syllabub; we waited a little until she had served us all, and quitted the room, before West concluded his tale.

"As Spence told it," he said with his gaze fixed on the wine in his crystal glass, winking in the candlelight, "he was separated from Ewan MacFarland after the Scots Greys' overreaching charge on the French gun batteries at Waterloo. The Colonel made sure that James Dunross reached the British squares, which were re-forming to turn back the French assault; but he himself was taken captive, and sent to the French rear. Spence believed MacFarland was a dead man. He no longer had a master, unless by some miracle MacFarland survived. I believe Spence was sincerely attached to the Colonel at one time—they had come through many dangers together over the years. But the difference in their fortunes had begun to grate upon him. MacFarland had risen in rank and estimation; Spence remained eternally the military servant, a glorified groom-cum-valet, tho' both men were exposed to equal dangers in war. With MacFarland now a prisoner, Spence took good care of Mephisto, the Colonel's last horse. He might need it himself to survive.

"Once the Prussians arrived at dusk, however, and the

French attack turned into a rout, Spence followed in pursuit of the retreating French. He was one of the men who came upon the last guard surrounding Buonaparte's personal carriage, which awaited the Emperor near La Belle Alliance. That was an inn, apparently, at a crossroads of the same name, that served as the French Headquarters the night before the battle.

"Rumours were rife in the Allied ranks regarding Buonaparte's carriage. He was said to move always with a large supply of bullion and jewels—a veritable treasure trove. Spence and a party of Prussians fell upon the guard—perhaps five men—and cut them to pieces. They found no gold or gems in the carriage, of course—but they stole the French soldiers' watches and personal effects.

"Spence stole the map. I suspect, from my conversation with Alexandrine Gauthier, that he stole it from her husband, Charles—a military mapmaker."

"The blackguard killed for it," Henry said.

"Yes," West agreed, "and apparently that fact turned his friends against him, after a time. I do not refer to the Prussians with whom he fell in, during the retreat; but to Colonel MacFarland and James Dunross.

"MacFarland escaped his captors and turned up in Brussels. Dunross was taken back with the wagon trains of wounded. Spence discovered both of them in those first days following the battle, and being unable to read, he showed the map he had stolen to his Colonel. MacFarland in turn consulted Dunross. Both men recognised a French cypher when they saw one—both had served in the Peninsula—but their conclusions differed. You see, Spence had informed the Colonel that the map belonged to one of Napoleon's personal guard. MacFarland could read

French. He understood the letter on the map's obverse—and when Charles Gauthier instructed his wife to keep the paper, because the Emperor would have need of it one day, MacFarland suspected he had stumbled upon a valuable.

"He refused to return the map to Spence."

"His first mistake," I said drily.

West nodded. "His second was informing Dunross that he meant to break the cypher. Dunross insisted the map must be turned over to Wellington's staff. That was the proper procedure for all intercepted enemy communications during the Peninsular War. Dunross thought it treasonous for MacFarland to keep the paper to himself; and hearing the Colonel hailed as a Hero made his resentment worse.

"It was Dunross who made the effort, whilst recovering in Paris, to locate Madame Gauthier. He had merely to look for the widow of a cartographer attached to the Grande Armée, who had seen action in both Moscow and Belgium. There were few enough. Alexandrine's familiarity with the Napoleonic Court—and her father's present intimacy with the Bourbon one—made her an obvious figure."

"So she was *not* the Lieutenant's mistress!" Fanny said triumphantly—and then blushed with embarrassment at her loose tongue.

"No, but she complicated James Dunross's life. Once she knew her husband's sketch from the Moscow campaign had survived—it was an *aquarelle* quite precious to her, as much for its whimsy as its military significance—she could not rest. She crossed the Channel in Dunross's wake and harried him to obtain the sketch for her. The dispute over what should be done with it caused a rift between MacFarland and the Lieutenant—so extreme, that he was forbidden to marry MacFarland's sister."

"Why, then, did the two agree to have coffee on the morning of the Colonel's death?" I asked.

"Spence told me about that," West replied. "Once I had written the letter to Major Scovell on Tuesday, he told me anything I desired to know. He was quite proud of his *manoeuvres,* as he called them, and wished to brag—particularly as his audience was unlikely to survive the week."

Fanny uttered a choking sound, swiftly disguised as a cough.

West glanced at her. "Not all men are evil, Miss Knight," he said gently. "Colonel MacFarland, for instance, had wrestled with his better self, and his better self had won. The Hero of Waterloo was to meet with Wellington at Carlton House, for a celebratory nuncheon at the Regent's request—and his conscience troubled him. He had made no headway in breaking the cypher; he knew nothing of such things. He decided to turn over the Waterloo Map to Wellington himself that day—and he met with Dunross on the strength of it."

"They went off arm-in-arm," I murmured.

"So Spence tells us. He, too, knew that he had lost his prize—for MacFarland was just trusting enough to inform his batman what he meant to do."

"And so Spence killed him?" Henry said. "For a piece of paper he could not read?"

West sighed. "I believe the importance of the map had grown and grown in Spence's mind. He learnt a good deal of the Russian campaign whilst the Scots Greys regrouped in Paris after Waterloo. Many of the French who had survived that day knew of the vast baggage train of plunder—and knew that it never left Russia. Stories of the hidden treasure are everywhere among the defeated French Army. Spence had fed his dreams with hope and exaggeration, and his desire was immense. He felt cheated by the Army, by fate, and by MacFarland—cheated by the master he'd loyally served. His love for the Colonel had turned to hatred over the months following the battle."

"He was not a stupid man," I observed. "Indeed, he was quite clever in most respects. Dunross had an injured hip—and yew needles are often used in a liniment for relief of such pain. Yew, too, can be useful in cases of a pregnancy that is not wanted. In both instances, if murder was suspected—Dunross might be the man. The Lieutenant's coldness to MacFarland in the months leading up to the murder should indict him. So, too, should Spence's report of his search for the map in MacFarland's rooms."

"How Spence must have hated it," Henry said, "when his murder of the Colonel failed to deliver up the map! And then Dunross turned him out of Keppel Street—because he disliked how Spence behaved at Waterloo. The fellow must have been at his wit's end."

"Until he recollected *me*." I met Henry's gaze squarely. "If I had not meddled in Keppel Street, Spence should never have learnt that Baillie suspected poison, or that the map was discovered in Carlton House. I was foolish enough to ask him directly, that first morning, about liniments—and brought round the subject to yew. Neither Baillie nor I should have been attacked if Spence had not feared the circle of suspicion was widening. If I had not meddled, Spence should not have been sent to

Mr. Raphael West—or discovered the inconvenient Madame Gauthier. He should never have met with Major Scovell and been capable of knowing all our movements, up to the very hour of the exchange at the Elephant and Castle."

I paused. "I am to blame. Had I allowed the map to find its way through the proper channels to Wellington in the first instance, a great deal of violence might have been averted."

"But I should be dead," Raphael West said unexpectedly.

I looked at him.

"Only you understood what Spence meant, when he said he had buried me alive," he observed gently. "Only you had the brilliance to trust and act upon it. And I am more grateful to you, Jane, than words may express."

He raised his wineglass. Henry and Fanny lifted theirs.

"To meddlesome women," I said.

29

A MOST UNLEARNED AND UNINFORMED FEMALE

Monday, 11 December 1815
23 Hans Place

To Mr. James Stanier Clarke:

Dear Sir,

My Emma is now so near publication that I feel it right to assure You of my not having forgotten your kind recommendation of an early Copy for Carlton House—& that I have Mr. Murray's promise of its being sent to HRH, under cover to You, three days previous to the Work being really out . . .

I am quite honoured by your thinking me capable of drawing such a Clergyman as you gave the sketch of in your note of Nov. 16. But I assure you I am not. The comic part of the Character I might be equal to, but not the Good, the Enthusiastic, the Literary . . . Such a Man's Conversation must at times be on subjects . . .

of which I know nothing—or at least be occasionally abundant in quotations & allusions which a Woman, who like me, knows only her own Mother-tongue & has read very little in that, would be totally without the power of giving . . . I think I may boast myself to be, with all possible Vanity, the most unlearned & uninformed Female who ever dared to be an Authoress.

Believe me, dear Sir,
Your oblig'd & faithful Servant
J.A.

I posted my prevaricating and pettifogging missive to Mr. Clarke in today's final post, not without a certain pensiveness.* I am to leave London on Saturday, and must spend the intervening few days in securing the last proofs of my dear child from the hands of the typesetters. *Emma* has already been advertized as a pending publication—and yet the text is not complete! Murray has assured me that whenever it is, he will have a complete set of volumes handsomely bound in buff and blue leather, and despatched to His Royal Highness the Prince Regent. He has already earned his ten percent of profits, in my opinion, by correcting the dedication I so airily suggested. I would have put simply *Dedicated by Permission to H.R.H. The Prince Regent.* Murray very kindly set me right, and substituted this fulsome panegyric:

---

* Letter No. 132(D), dated December 11, 1815, in *Jane Austen's Letters* (Oxford: Oxford University Press, 1995), Deirdre Le Faye, editor.—*Editor's note.*

To His Royal Highness
THE PRINCE REGENT
This work is,
By His Royal Highness's Permission,
Most Respectfully
Dedicated,
By His Royal Highness's
Dutiful
And Obedient
Humble Servant,
THE AUTHOR.

Dutiful and obedient indeed, as I never wished for such an honour, and could think of any number of persons who deserve it more.

I am feeling a bit put out as I ready myself for a return to Chawton, and all the festivities of Christmas. Fanny left us three days ago for her home in Kent, tho' not without wishing ardently that I might pass the coming Season there—but it is not to be. Having spent most of the Autumn in London, I am tied to Hampshire for the remainder of Winter—and must trust in the power of composition to solace me. I shall spend my hours in consideration of a young woman long since On the Shelf, the daughter of a foolish but privileged family, whose good sense in chusing a man of action and prowess is rewarded as such wisdom usually is: by being dissuaded from risk, and channelled with the best possible motives into an oppressive and stultifying spinsterhood.

I have not yet decided whether the reappearance of Anne

Elliot's Naval hero is meant to teach her the bitter fruits of Safety, or afford her a second period of Bloom. It will depend, no doubt, upon my spirits as I write—and there can be no predicting their volatility. I fear they turn too much at present upon a particular American painter, whom no self-respecting Englishwoman should ever regard as Safe. He has gone out of my life again—tho' not, I hope, forever. It was only yesterday that we said our goodbyes, in the too-publick entry of this house.

Benjamin West has suffered a renewal of the gastric complaint that demanded his son's attention a few weeks ago; and the anxiety for his health being extreme, all work has been suspended on *Buonaparte Fleeing the Field of Waterloo.** Indeed, Raphael West has been obliged to take his father to Bath for a trial of the waters, on the recommendation of his personal physician.

"My daughter, Charlotte, shall join us there for the Christmas Season, with her husband, Mr. Benedick. I could wish you might visit the city as well, Jane," he said as we stood before Henry's front door last evening. "Nothing should give me greater pleasure than to present my daughter to your acquaintance."

"Why? Is Mrs. Benedick a reader of novels?" I asked artlessly. Introduce me to his daughter, indeed! Why should Raphael West desire a further connexion between his family and mine, unless it be to deepen that between *ourselves*? And yet not one word of the future has he spoken; no personal assurance has he made.

"She has certainly read yours," he said gently, and reached

* No great historical painting of Benjamin West's on the subject of Waterloo survives.—*Editor's note.*

for my shoulders. "I have no right to ask anything of you, Jane. At such a time, much might be said—but the uncertainty of my father's condition makes me anything but my own master. I may not even command my own home, or the conduct of my days; all rests upon the decision of his doctors and his Fate. But I hope you know the depth of my regard."

I should have spoken.

I should have said, loudly or softly, *You know that you may command me in anything, Raphael West.*

But there is no fool like an old fool. The haunting image of a creature named Isabella rose before my eyes. It must be impossible to ask him directly about her importance in his life. He is a man of the World, after all, as his father is forever telling me. He owes no explanation of his habits or arrangements. Once, I was a green girl enough to dream of happiness with an improbable suitor, from an utterly different world—but the sudden taking of Lord Harold Trowbridge exposed me to a pain from which I was long in recovering. Nay, I have not recovered from it yet.

I will turn forty on Saturday, the morning I leave London. Raphael West will be long since established in Bath, enjoying the gaieties of Christmas, attending the concerts and the Assemblies with his lovely daughter. I refuse to pine, alone and forgotten, in the dreary greyness of the countryside, wishing for his return. I refuse to disrupt so completely the tenuous peace of my life. I am done with longing for a gentleman to save me.

And so I said merely, "You honour me, sir. I hope I shall always know how to value my friends. Perhaps we may meet again, when I am returned to London."

He dropped his hands to his sides, and left my arms the

colder; but his gaze did not waver. "Impossible that we should not, my dear. So long as there is breath in my body, my soul shall seek yours, wherever it wanders."

Shall I be forced to regret my policy of Safety, indeed? Or enjoy a renewed season of hope and Bloom?

With Anne Elliot, I cannot say.

But as I watched West's equipage pull away from Hans Place, I felt a blank pit of loneliness just below my heart. And hoped, for all of us, in the promise of Spring.

AFTERWORD

The letters Jane Austen sent from London to Chawton Cottage during the roughly six weeks she stayed with her brother Henry in the autumn of 1815 are wonderfully detailed accounts of numerous events: Henry's illness and treatment at the hands of Charles Haden and Matthew Baillie, the Court Physician; his anxiety over his failing bank fortunes, as the British economy sagged in the months after Waterloo; Jane's visit to Carlton House and her correspondence with James Stanier Clarke; and her niece Fanny's harp-playing for their Hans Place neighbor, who was clearly half in love with the elegant young lady from Kent.

Although Jane writes with vigor of her treks to Grafton House in search of purple stuff for a gown, and deplores the slowness of *Emma's* printing—not to mention the necessity of dedicating her latest novel to the Prince Regent—she never offers her family the slightest hint of the deadly investigation she had undertaken into Ewan MacFarland's death, as recounted in these journal pages.

We must assume that following the attack that struck her down on Henry's doorstep, Jane was too aware of the threat to her life to alarm her mother, Cassandra, or Mary Lloyd with the compelling history of the Waterloo Map. Henry's reluctance to allow either Jane or Fanny to remain in Hans Place is evidence of the protests that would have greeted Jane's latest embroilment in murder. A second, more delicate reason for her silence may be due to the presence of Raphael West. Jane would not wish to expose herself to speculation, or show Cassandra how much she was missing.

There are few episodes in history more stirring, heroic, or tragic than the Battle of Waterloo on June 18, 1815. I was aided in my understanding of Jane's account of the Scots Greys by two volumes: *The Battle*, by Alessandro Barbero (New York: Walker, 2003), and *Waterloo: The History of Four Days, Three Armies and Three Battles*, by Bernard Cornwell (New York: Harper, 2015). Barbero's is a book I return to repeatedly for its excellent military analysis; Cornwell's is a highly accessible narrative. My inability to grasp the essentials of the Great Paris Cypher was relieved by Mark Urban's excellent history of George Scovell, *The Man Who Broke Napoleon's Codes* (New York: HarperCollins, 2002). A revelatory journal of sketches and personal observations, *The Wheatley Diary*, by Edmund Wheatley, a soldier in Wellington's army, brings period eye-witness authority to what historians can only imagine. (London: Longmans, Green and Co. Ltd., 1964, Christopher Hibbert, editor.)

Carlton House, The Prince Regent's London residence from 1793 to 1820, was torn down in 1825 and replaced by two terraces of white, stuccoed houses known as Carlton House Terrace.

The rooms Jane toured with James Stanier Clarke are thus lost to history; but detailed aquatints of the interior rooms remain, engraved by Charles Wild and William H. Pyne, in the collections of the Museum of London and the New York Public Library. Those who would like to learn more about the Regent cannot do better than Saul David's *Prince of Pleasure* (Atlantic Monthly Press, 1999).

Apsley House, where Jane called upon the Duke of Wellington, was later renovated and redecorated when he took over his brother Wellesley's lease; it may be toured through English Heritage. Richard Holmes's *Wellington: The Iron Duke* (London: HarperCollins, 2003) gives a concise account of a lengthy and storied life. Fanny Wedderburn-Webster wrote her own history in *The Diary of Lady Frances Shelley*, edited by her grandson, Richard Edgcumbe (New York: Scribner's, 1912), and it offers a fascinating and vivid account of the *haute ton* of Austen's era. Chris Viveash's privately printed biography, *James Stanier Clarke: Librarian to the Prince Regent, Naval Author, Friend of Jane Austen* (Winchester: Sarsen Press, 2006), gives color and background to the glimpse Austen gives us of the clergyman in their correspondence.

West's New Gallery at No. 14 Newman Street, as it was simply called in the 1826 guide book by John Britton, *The Picture of London,* is no longer the repository of Benjamin West's paintings. That part of London, however—known as Fitzrovia—has long been associated with cutting-edge lifestyles: Oscar Wilde favored it, and these days Madonna has located her Kabbalah center there. Hip restaurants, boutique hotels, and yes, even art galleries, can be found in Raphael West's neighborhood.

Hatchard's Books, at 187 Piccadilly, is still serving readers two hundred years after Jane walked through its doors. Founded in 1797, it is the oldest bookshop in England.

Stephanie Barron
Denver, CO
September 11, 2015